Guilt

and

Ginataan

Mia P. Manansala

BERKLEY PRIME CRIME
NEW YORK

BERKLEY PRIME CRIME
Published by Berkley
An imprint of Penguin Random House LLC
penguinrandomhouse.com

Book design by Kristin del Rosario

Library of Congress Cataloging-in-Publication Data

Names: Manansala, Mia P., author.
Title: Guilt and ginataan / Mia P. Manansala.
Description: First edition. | New York: Berkley Prime Crime, 2024. |
Series: Tita Rosie's Kitchen Mystery
Identifiers: LCCN 2024008552 (print) | LCCN 2024008553 (ebook) |
ISBN 9780593549186 (trade paperback) | ISBN 9780593549193 (ebook)
Subjects: LCGFT: Detective and mystery fiction. | Novels.
Classification: LCC PS3613.A5268 G85 2024 (print) |
LCC PS3613.A5268 (ebook) | DDC 813/.6—dc23/eng/20240226
LC record available at https://lccn.loc.gov/2024008552
LC ebook record available at https://lccn.loc.gov/2024008553

First Edition: November 2024

Printed in the United States of America
1st Printing

To the Winners Circle, my very own Brew-ha crew.
May we continue bonding over fandom and
eating until we hate ourselves, forever and ever.
Love you all!

Author's Note

Thanks so much for picking up *Guilt and Ginataan*! This book focuses on one of my absolute favorite characters in the series, Lila's best friend, Adeena. She's gotten into a nasty situation, but with the Brew-ha crew on the case, you can rest assured that the power of friendship will once again save the day. As this is a murder mystery, the story will touch on some heavy topics. If you'd like to avoid spoilers, skip this section. If you'd like to know the content warnings for this book, read below.

This book deals with emotionally difficult topics, including physical violence, anti-fat comments, possible stalking, political corruption, and mentions of past sexual harassment. Any readers who believe that such content may upset them or trigger traumatic memories are encouraged to consider their emotional well-being when deciding whether to continue reading this book.

Glossary and Pronunciation Guide

HONORIFICS/FAMILY
(THE "O" USUALLY HAS A SHORT, SOFT SOUND)

Anak (ah-nahk)—Offspring/son/daughter

Ate (ah-teh)—Older sister/female cousin/girl of the same generation as you

Kuya (koo-yah)—Older brother/male cousin/boy of the same generation as you

Lola (loh-lah)/Lolo (loh-loh)—Grandmother/Grandfather

Ninang (nee-nahng)/Ninong (nee-nohng)—Godmother/Godfather

Tita (tee-tah)/Tito (tee-toh)—Aunt/Uncle

FOOD

Adobo (uh-doh-boh)—Considered the Philippines's national dish, it's any food cooked with soy sauce, vinegar, garlic, and black peppercorns (though there are many regional and personal variations)

Arroz caldo (ah-rohz cahl-doh)—A savory rice porridge made with chicken, ginger, and other aromatics

Champorado (chahm-puh-rah-doh)—Sweet chocolate rice porridge

Escabeche (es-cah-beh-che)—A dish that exists in many countries, but in the Philippines is specifically a sweet and sour fish dish consisting of fried fish covered or marinated in a sauce of vinegar, garlic, sugar, bell peppers, and other aromatics

Ginataan (gih-nah-tah-ahn)—Any dish cooked with coconut milk; can be sweet or savory

Ginataang mais (gih-nah-tah-ahng mah-ees)—A sweet porridge consisting of glutinous rice and corn cooked in sweetened coconut milk

Keso (keh-so)—Cheese (same pronunciation as the Spanish "queso")

Lugaw (loo-gow)—Savory rice porridge, similar to Chinese congee or Korean jook

Lumpia (loom-pyah)—Filipino spring rolls (many variations)

Mais (mah-ees)—Corn (same pronunciation as the Spanish "maíz")

Mamon (mah-mohn)—A Filipino chiffon cake, made in individual molds as opposed to a large, shared cake

Matamis na bao (mah-tah-mees nah bah-oh)—Coconut jam (also known as minatamis na bao)

Pandan (pahn-dahn)—Tropical plant whose fragrant leaves are commonly used as a flavoring in Southeast Asia; often described as a grassy vanilla flavor with a hint of coconut

Patis (pah-tees)—Fish sauce

Salabat (sah-lah-baht)—Filipino ginger tea

Tokwa't baboy (toh-kwat bah-boy)—Filipino side dish consisting of fried tofu and boiled pork cooked in soy sauce, vinegar, and chili, and usually topped with green onions

Ube (oo-beh)—Purple yam

Yelo (yeh-loh)—Ice (same pronunciation as the Spanish "hielo")

OTHER

Bruha (broo-ha)—Witch (from the Spanish "bruja")

Diba (dih-bah)—Isn't it?; Right?; short for "hindi ba" (also written as "di ba")

Langis (lahng-ees)—Oil

Macapagal (Mah-cah-pah-gahl)—A Filipino surname

Oh my gulay—This is Taglish (Tagalog-English) slang, used when people don't want to say the "God" part of OMG. "Gulay" (goo-lie) literally means "vegetable," so this phrase shouldn't be translated.

Susmaryosep (soos-mah-ree-yo-sehp)—A portmanteau of Jesus, Mary, and Joseph. Used as an exclamation of surprise, disappointment, shock, etc.

Tsismis (chees-mees)—Gossip

Tubig (too-big)—Water

Guilt and Ginataan

Chapter One

W elcome to the thirty-fifth annual Shady Palms Corn Festival!"

Mayor Gunderson raised the corn cob scepter in his right hand as he looked over the crowd at the opening ceremony of the town's beloved Corn Festival. His wife stood to the side and slightly behind him, dressed in a complementary costume as the town's reigning Corn Queen: a long yellow dress with a lavish green cape about her shoulders and a crown whose points resembled ears of corn atop her head.

I enjoyed a good spectacle as much as the next person, but considering how much the mayor loved the sound of his own voice, I tuned out the rest of his speech as I finished preparing the Brew-ha Cafe booth. My best friend and business partner, Adeena Awan, was still setting up the drinks station where she'd be serving her usual house blend coffee, as well as the atole, ginataang mais latte, and oksusu cha that she'd added to the special festival menu. Elena Torres, our other business partner and Adeena's girlfriend, was filling the compostable tea bags with the roasted corn we used for the oksusu cha and arranging the corn husk crafts that she and her mother had prepared.

My boyfriend, Dr. Jae Park, was joining the Brew-ha crew that weekend as our resident grill master. Elena came up with the idea of a fusion elote, taking her beloved Mexican street corn and adding Pakistani and Filipino twists to match with Adeena's and my respective backgrounds. Not only did Jae give us his mother's recipe for the oksusu cha, or Korean corn tea, but he'd also volunteered to handle all elote duties: slathering the corn with thick, creamy coconut milk before rolling it in a fragrant spice mix that included amchur powder and red chili powder, grilling it, then squeezing calamansi over the corn before sprinkling it with your choice of kesong puti or cotija cheese. It was a simple yet laborious task, but he seemed to enjoy himself (I wasn't one for gender stereotypes, but what was with guys and grills?) and I'd caught him sneaking more than one smoky, salty treat as he worked. The benefit of being the cook.

Meanwhile, I arranged the sweet offerings I'd prepared: mais ube sandwich cookies, mais kon keso bars, and two types of ice candy— mais kon yelo and ginataang mais. Corn as a dessert ingredient may seem strange to some people, but Filipinos absolutely love and embrace corn in all its salty-sweet possibilities. My first offering sandwiched ube buttercream between corn cookies, the purple yam's subtle vanilla-like sweetness pairing well with the salty-sweet corn. Cheese and corn are a popular savory pairing, but guess what? It makes one of my absolute favorite Filipino ice cream flavors as well, and I channeled that classic combo into a cheesecake bar with a corn cookie crust.

Mais kon yelo, literally corn with ice, is a Filipino dessert consisting of shaved ice with corn, sugar, and milk, while ginataang mais, a simple porridge made with coconut milk, glutinous rice, and sweet corn, is usually served warm for breakfast or meryenda. My take on these simple, refreshing snacks utilized those same flavors in a portable, easy-to-eat ice pop bag. However, if you wanted to try the traditional versions, you could just pop down a few booths over to Tita Rosie's Kitchen, the restaurant run by my paternal aunt and grandmother. While my aunt, Tita Rosie, handled the savory side of the menu, offering small cups of corn soup and paper cones full of cornick, or corn nuts flavored with salt and garlic, my grandmother, Lola Flor, reigned over the sweets. The aforementioned mais kon yelo and ginataang mais were the desserts on offer, in addition to maja blanca, a simple corn and coconut pudding. Truly a gluten-free sweet tooth's paradise.

They also had an extra helper at their booth, Jae's older brother, Jonathan (or Detective Park as I still called him, despite him no longer being with the Shady Palms Police Department), who happened to be my aunt's boyfriend. He was handling all the customer-facing tasks since Tita Rosie's love of cooking and feeding people did not extend to the more business side of the industry, a fact that nearly cost her the restaurant last year. Luckily, my quarter-life crisis happened to coincide with this family emergency, and I had stepped in and set up a simple system for her and my grandmother to follow. It took some time and a couple of tweaks, but now business was booming.

I put the finishing touches on the Brew-ha Cafe booth just as Mayor Gunderson's speech drew to a close with "And please join me in a warm Shady Palms welcome as Shelbyville's Mayor Reyes says a few words to kick off the celebration!"

There was a bit of rustling in the crowd as Mayor Judy Reyes stepped up to the mic. This year, in an absolutely brilliant move by

Beth Thompson and her former sister-in-law, Valerie Thompson (both heads of the town's most successful company and illustrious family, and now the chamber of commerce), the Corn Festival was put on in partnership with the neighboring town of Shelbyville. Not only would this expand the reach of our festival, but our town wouldn't have to bear the brunt of the expenses. There was a catch, though.

Shelbyville was bigger, had way more money, and was home to the only community college in the area (you had to travel about forty miles before you got anywhere near a university, so higher-learning opportunities were few and far between). As such, there was a fierce rivalry between the towns since the people of Shelbyville tended to look down on us and most Shady Palms citizens felt we had something to prove. Our town's chamber of commerce had been hard at work trying to increase tourism and commerce in the area, so they decided to take advantage of Shady Palms's natural resources and charm as well as Shelbyville's larger size and greater access to hotels and B&Bs.

Mayor Reyes had readily agreed, but left all the details to her assistant, who used the opportunity to go on a bit of a power trip. According to Beth, who loved dropping hot goss in our WOC entrepreneur group chat, the assistant provided a ridiculous list of demands that rivaled any celebrity greenroom horror story, including a stipulation that Mayor Reyes officially opened and closed the festival during the ceremonies on the first and last weekends of the month. That last bit was almost the dealbreaker for the self-important Mayor Gunderson, and it took weeks of negotiating and soothing to get him to agree.

Mayor Gunderson stood onstage, glaring daggers at Mayor Reyes, who blithely continued with her warm, funny, and, most importantly, concise welcome speech. "I hope you all take advantage of the many wonderful things that Shady Palms and Shelbyville have to offer.

Now if you'll excuse me, I saw a booth selling corn cookies that I'm dying to try. Remember to have fun, be kind, and support local businesses!"

With that, Mayor Reyes exited the stage with her wife and headed straight for the Brew-ha Cafe booth, followed closely by her assistant. As they drew closer, Elena, our secret weapon when it came to sales (and just about everything else), greeted them cheerfully.

"Well, hello there, Mayor Reyes! Welcome to the Brew-ha Cafe. I'm guessing it was our corn cookies that you just referenced onstage? Thanks for that, by the way."

Mayor Reyes smiled. "Yes, I noticed your booth when you were setting up earlier. Your menu sounded so delicious and different from what most of the booths here are doing, so I knew you had to be my first stop."

The mayor's wife sniffed. "You are far too gracious, Judy. Though I suppose you're right that this booth is the only interesting one I've seen so far."

The mayor's smile grew strained, and her assistant, likely noticing this, stepped in. "Yvonne, didn't you say you were dying for a cup of coffee? I've heard it on good authority that this cafe has the best coffee in the entire county."

Yvonne gave me and my fellow Brew-has the once-over and smirked. "I hope your coffee is as bold as that statement."

Elena met her eyes in a challenge. "I guarantee that my girlfriend's drinks are the best in the county. And when you agree, I hope the good mayor uses us to cater some of her events."

Mayor Reyes laughed. "Considering you're brave enough to take on my wife, I'd be delighted to. She'll take the biggest coffee you've got and I'd love some of your atole. It's been forever since I've had any!"

Adeena got to work preparing the drinks while the mayor's assistant studied our menu. "So oksusu cha is Korean corn tea? What does that taste like?"

"It's a bit of an acquired taste," I said. "It has a toasted nutty flavor, similar to barley tea or genmaicha green tea. A little bit savory, a little bit sweet. I'd be happy to give you a sample if you'd like."

He accepted the sample cup and took a few sips. He tried to hide his grimace, but failed, and Jae and I both burst out laughing.

"Don't force yourself if you don't like it," Jae said, holding his hand out for the cup to throw in the trash. "Like Lila said, it's an acquired taste. I used to hate it as a kid, but eventually became addicted to the iced version my mom makes. It's really refreshing in the summer."

The mayor's assistant handed it over. "Sorry! I try not to be picky, but you're right. I usually like savory drinks, but something about it is throwing me off. It's like my brain and tongue don't know how to react."

Mayor Reyes handed a steaming cup of atole to her assistant. "Here you go, Zack. Atole is a corn drink you'll love, I'm sure of it. This is even better than my mom's, though don't let me catch you saying that to her."

"The coffee's really good, too," her wife muttered. "I think it might be even better than that new cafe that opened up near the boutique."

"Didn't I tell you that Shady Palms had the best coffee in the county?" Mayor Gunderson said, strolling up to join us. He was still wearing his Corn King costume and used his ridiculous scepter to point at Adeena. "Adeena! Coffee for both me and the missus. You know how I like it."

I hadn't even noticed his wife joining us, but there she was, looking over our offerings while checking out Jae from the corner of her eye. She flushed when she saw that I noticed and tried to cover it up by ordering one of everything.

"Oh, and Dr. Jae, would it be possible to have the corn in a cup so I can eat it with a spoon? It's just so messy on the cob."

Jae smiled at her. "The mess is part of the fun! But sure, Mrs. Gunderson. Happy to accommodate you."

"Thanks for the recommendation, Mayor Gunderson," Mayor Reyes said, smiling over her cup of atole. "I'll have to stop by Shady Palms more often. You're so lucky to have such a wonderful business nearby. Maybe you can open a branch in Shelbyville."

She winked at us, clearly joking, but Mayor Gunderson's response was a little too strained to match the playful tone he was going for.

"Now now, Judy, are you trying to poach businesses from my town? That's not really in the spirit of our collaboration, is it?"

Yvonne rolled her eyes. "She was just joking, you humorless—"

"Yvonne," Mayor Reyes said sharply.

"You don't have to kowtow to him, you know. You're supposed to be equals in this collaboration. But whatever. Just continue grinning and bearing it, as always." Yvonne finished her coffee and tossed the empty cup in the trash. "I'm going to look around. Catch up with me when you're ready."

Mrs. Gunderson reached out to Yvonne as she passed, perhaps to play nice and convince her to stay, but a cutting glance from Yvonne was enough for her to snatch her hand back as if she'd been burned.

Mayor Reyes's assistant, Zack, rushed forward. "Mrs. Gunderson, you've lived in Shady Palms your whole life, right? Would you mind keeping me company as I wander around the festival? I'd love to learn more about the town from someone who's such a valued member of the community."

Mrs. Gunderson was a bit of a wallflower, always keeping to the background and letting her husband take the lead. But under Zack's attention and kind words, a smile unfurled across her face, and she seemed to blossom.

"I'd love to! I'm on the historical committee, you know, so if you have any questions about our town's history, feel free to ask."

She fell in step beside Zack and started chattering away, and Mayor Reyes joined them, saying she'd love a guided tour of the festival from Mrs. Gunderson.

Mayor Gunderson glared at the trio as they moved away from him, but instead of following, he turned on his heel and headed in the opposite direction.

Once they were all finally gone, I turned around and noticed Adeena and Elena looking like the "Jessica Fletcher eating popcorn" gif as they shared a bucket of popcorn while enjoying the drama.

"OK, I get that we're at a corn festival, but how did you get the popcorn so fast? Do you travel with props for moments like this?"

Adeena winked. "You know how dedicated I am when it comes to a bit. But no, your sweet boyfriend left when things started getting heated and returned with snacks for us."

Jae turned red as he held out a cone full of cornick from my aunt, a disk of corn tempura from our friend Yuki's booth, and other yummy corn-related snacks. "It was getting uncomfortable, and I figured I might as well make myself useful. I know what happens when you all get hungry, so I figured I'd grab food for you before it gets too crowded."

"He's a keeper all right," Elena said, grinning at him as she dipped the corn tempura disk into the accompanying sauce.

I helped myself to some tempura as well, and as I enjoyed my deliciously crisp, salty-sweet treat, I prayed that the argument we'd just witnessed would be the worst thing to happen at the festival and that it'd be smooth sailing from here on out.

I raised my ginataang mais latte in a toast. "Here's to a successful, drama-free festival!"

Adeena, Elena, Jae, and I all clinked cups, though I was sure they were thinking the same thing I was:

When has Shady Palms ever been drama free?

Chapter Two

"Thank you so much! If you stop by early tomorrow, we'll have plenty more stock available. And I'll make sure to plan better for next weekend."

I handed the takeout bag and drink holder to our final customer, who'd cleaned us out of what little we still had at our booth. It was early afternoon and we'd run out of stock much earlier than planned. I didn't know if it was Mayor Reyes's endorsement or just general word of mouth, but we'd had an endless stream of customers pretty much since we'd opened.

"You're closing already? Now where am I supposed to get a decent cup of coffee?" Yvonne, the Shelbyville mayor's wife, had stopped by several times that morning to grab more cookies and caffeine and verbally spar with Elena. She strolled up with our reusable travel cup in hand and a cutesy pout on her face.

"Sorry, but we're out. We'll make sure to stock up extra for tomorrow. Let us know if there's anything you'd like us to set aside for you," Elena said, pulling off her Brew-ha Cafe apron and folding it neatly before stretching. "Mmm, Adeena, Lila, remind me to fit in stretching breaks tomorrow. We've been too busy getting ready for the festival to go to Sana's yoga classes lately."

She stretched again, her crochet crop top rising with her languid movements, a strip of smooth brown skin and her belly button ring now visible without the apron covering her.

Yvonne studied her. "Will you be working the booth tomorrow as well?"

After Elena replied in the affirmative, Yvonne said, "Good. I trust you to surprise me then. See you all tomorrow."

"What is her deal?" I asked, watching her walk away.

Adeena gave me a look. "She's clearly flirting with Elena."

"That's flirting?" Jae asked.

Elena shrugged. "The combative types really seem to like me. Arguing with me is like their version of courtship."

She rolled her neck and moved her arms into the Cow Face yoga position (a stretch so deep, I couldn't do it without a strap between my hands) for thirty seconds before sighing and lowering her arms. You could almost feel the contentment beaming out of her like the sun.

"It's because you're so chill," Adeena pointed out. "They think it's a fun challenge to get you to break. They don't know that your weak point is—"

"You better watch yourself, love," Elena said, her tone playful but her eyes carrying a warning. "I know your weakness as well."

"And that's why we work so well together. The threat of mutual destruction powers our relationship." Adeena slung her arm around her girlfriend's shoulders and gave her a firm kiss on the cheek. "So, what do we do now with all this unplanned free time?"

"I wanted to check out the arts and crafts area," Elena said.

"And I've been wanting to hit up all the food booths since I haven't had a proper meal yet," I said.

"Ugh, typical. I really wanted to play some games." Adeena frowned at the two of us before turning to Jae. "How about you?"

Jae's eyes wandered around the large space, likely trying to find a compromise for all of us. "How about a round of Bags? Loser buys us all lunch and then we can check out the arts and crafts area together."

We agreed that was a great plan and headed to the area where various boards with holes were set up alongside containers of bean bags. Because this was the Corn Festival, the staffers were calling the game Cornhole, but we all knew it was really Bags. To save time, we decided to play in teams, so Jae and Adeena lined up at one board, Elena and I at the other. Jae used to play basketball and I played Bags all the time in college, so you'd think it'd be a quick game, but Adeena was the most competitive person in the world and Elena was somehow good at everything, so it was a fairly close match.

In the end, Jae and I prevailed, and Adeena and Elena bought us all hush puppies, fried corn, and cornmeal-crusted catfish from our friends George and Nettie Bishop at Big Bishop's BBQ. After our feast, we followed Elena to the arts and crafts section where we got our faces painted, and Adeena, Elena, and I all splurged on some gorgeous beaded jewelry from a local Potawatomi artist. The sun was starting to dip by the time we were done with everything, but it was still too early to call it a day.

"How about one more competition?" Adeena asked. "Let's see who can get through the corn maze the fastest. Winner gets to choose all the activities for tomorrow and doesn't have to pay for any of them."

The Shady Palms Corn Festival boasted the second-largest corn maze in the state. It was actually four separate mazes that could be completed individually, though if you wanted a challenge, there were checkpoints that connected the labyrinth so you could experience the full eight-mile mega maze. The Corn Festival was held over the entire month of September, with the first weekend celebrating the opening of the corn maze and more family-friendly activities, and the fifth/closing weekend focusing on musical acts and local performers. The beer garden run by Shady Palms Winery (which my cousin Ronnie co-owned) was open every weekend during the festival and one of the most popular destinations since they served alcoholic beverages of all kinds. The festival grounds would still be open during the week, but on a lesser scale and with fewer booths and events and prizes. While you could technically enjoy it at any time during the festival, the corn maze on opening day was something special.

Jae groaned. "That sounds like so much fun, but I promised my dad I'd hang out with him at home while Jonathan shows my mom around the festival. His health hasn't been great lately, so it's up to me to make sure he doesn't sneak any junk food while Mom's out."

"Oh, I think Jonathan mentioned that earlier. Make sure to stop by Tita Rosie's booth. I think she prepared something for you and your dad. Something healthy and delicious," I said, grinning. I knew his dad didn't think those two words went together, but I trusted Tita Rosie to prove him wrong.

"Will do." With a quick kiss for me and a wave at the other two, he started walking off. "Enjoy your girls' night! And stay out of trouble!"

Adeena, Elena, and I headed in the other direction, the two women holding hands as I trailed closely behind them.

"Why does he say that every time he leaves the three of us alone? What does he think we get up to?" Adeena asked.

Elena and I both looked at her, eyebrows raised, and she laughed and lifted her hands. "OK, fair. But we're just doing a corn maze at a Midwestern corn festival. Doesn't get much more wholesome than that, does it?"

Exactly. How much trouble could we get into in a corn maze?

Chapter Three

The closer we got to the maze, the more the cornstalks towered over our short frames, Elena the tallest of our group at an impressive five feet four, though at least an inch or so was due to her big, curly hair. Combine that with the rapidly setting sun dyeing the sky orange and red, and the image was both beautiful and ominous.

"How are we doing this? We can't all go in the same entrance. I don't want anyone accusing me of following them or cheating."

I said "anyone" but really meant Adeena and she knew it.

"There are four different mazes, so we'll start at different entrances. Once we're all in position, I'll do a group video call so we can see that we're all ready and there are no shenanigans going on." Adeena hated cheating so much, she was reduced to using words like "shenanigans" to refer to it. She continued, "First person to reach the end of their maze will take a picture with the staff member at their exit and text it as proof. Does that sound fair?"

She'd clearly put a lot of thought into this, which wasn't

surprising. Adeena was the person who always did THE MOST when it came to competitions, the absolute scourge of Shady Palms game nights. But something like this, where we were all separated and I could work on my own without her screaming in my ear about how I was doing it wrong? This I could do.

The three of us split up and I made my way to the entrance staffed by one of the teens I remembered from the Miss Teen Shady Palms pageant last summer. We smiled at each other and exchanged brief hellos before I video called Adeena to let her know I was ready. Adeena's big head filled the screen and in a separate box I saw that Elena was ready as well.

"All right, ladies, may the best Brew-ha, aka me, win! Game starts now!"

The screen went black as soon as Adeena finished her announcement, and I knew she had already barreled ahead thinking she had this win in the bag. I might not have played all the video games and puzzle games that Adeena did, but that didn't mean I couldn't find my way through a maze. It had been a few years since I'd done one of these, but you just had to put your hand along one wall and follow it all the way through, right?

Thirty minutes later, my wall-following method failed me as I came across an island of corn that had me looping around it twice before I realized what I was doing. I took a deep breath and tried to form an alternate plan, but the maze was eerily quiet other than the rustling sound the gently waving stalks made, and the isolation and darkening sky were playing tricks with my mind. More than anything, it was the silence that got to me. We weren't that far out from the rest of the festival, were we? There had to be other people doing the same maze as me, right? It was opening weekend, after all. Shouldn't this place be packed?

I was going in circles (literally and figuratively) when I finally came across a little kid who couldn't be older than six or seven huddled near an island of corn. There's no way the staff would let in a kid this young by themselves, so I assumed they got separated from their adult. I didn't want to spook them by getting too close (last thing I needed was a kid freaking out from a Stranger Danger moment), so I tried to keep my voice soft as I called out, "Hey! Are you OK?"

The kid stiffened at my voice and then slowly stood and turned to look at me. I couldn't help but notice it was a young white girl with very pale blond hair and ohmigod why did I let Adeena talk me into watching *Children of the Corn* last week? Why did I let Adeena goad me into another competition? And most of all, why was this little girl silently advancing on me? I noticed her clutching a corn husk doll and resigned myself to my fate. Of all the terrible things that have happened in this town, me meeting my end at the hands of a child cult member was not on my Shady Palms Bingo card.

"Sarah! There you are!" A woman ran past me, sweeping up the demon (?) child in her arms, who suddenly started crying and clinging to the adult. "Security had to come find me. Why didn't you follow the nice man who tried to help you?"

"I was so scared!" the little girl wailed. "You told me never to follow a stranger anywhere!"

I hid a smile and moved down a different corridor to continue the challenge now that I knew the kid was safe (and so was I). With the creepy moment over, I realized that the kid hadn't said anything because they weren't supposed to speak to strangers, and I rolled my eyes at my overactive imagination, swearing that I would never, ever let Adeena talk me into watching a scary movie ever again.

I passed several other groups making their way through the maze and had reached another dead end when the quiet was shattered by a loud, sharp scream that suddenly cut off. Someone was in trouble! I ran toward the sound of the scream, hoping I'd come across a staff member along the way. Enough people had gotten lost and scared in the maze that the festival employed security and volunteer staff members to patrol the maze in case of emergency.

I ran through the maze, taking twists and turns without noting where I was going or which direction I'd come from. I soon regretted that since the scream had cut off too soon for me to get a good idea of where the person was, and the only thing I'd managed to do was get myself even more lost. I briefly wondered how embarrassing it would be if I just stood in place and cried until someone found me, when the wavering light of a flashlight caught my eye. I sprinted toward it and nearly collided with Marcus Martinez, my Ninang Mae's younger son.

"Marcus! What are you doing here?"

A ridiculous question considering he was wearing the bright orange logo shirt that all Shady Palms Corn Festival staff wore. I felt even sillier when he just pointed to the word "SECURITY" (in all caps, no less) on his shirt.

"I heard screaming and already radioed for help, but I'm having trouble locating the person. Have you seen or heard anything suspicious?"

"No, I heard the scream and tried to follow it too, but it stopped before I could find them. I got lost and—"

Before I could recount my failed rescue mission, screams once again ripped through the air. Marcus and I glanced at each other for a split second before hurrying toward the terrified sounds. This time, I could make out more than one person screaming and there was definitely someone calling for help.

We crossed quickly into an adjoining maze and followed the sounds toward a small crowd staring at something in the recesses of a corn island.

"Excuse me, security coming through! Excuse me!"

The buzzing crowd parted to let me and Marcus through so we could see what had everyone so scared.

The first thing I saw was Yvonne, Mayor Reyes's wife, lying on the ground. The back of her sweater was covered in blood, and she wasn't moving.

The next thing I saw was Adeena, unconscious next to her.

The last thing I saw was the bloody knife clutched in Adeena's hand.

This time, the screams came from me.

Chapter Four

"Where's my sister?"

Amir Awan, Adeena's older brother and the best lawyer in Shady Palms, hurtled through the Shady Palms Police Department's doors. Elena and I had given our statements at the scene and headed straight to the police station to wait for Amir and fill him in on what had happened.

Adeena had gained consciousness shortly after Marcus and I found her, and the EMTs on the scene looked her over and declared her fit. Despite her insistence that she was innocent, the cops arrested her and took her to the station for questioning. We weren't allowed to see her yet, but considering both her father and brother were lawyers (though only Amir handled criminal law), I bet she was giving the interrogator hell until Amir arrived.

I brought him up to date on the situation and he squeezed my shoulder as thanks, hand gently brushing down my arm, before striding away to be with his sister. The feel of his large hand spread a warmth and comfort throughout my body, and I stared after him a moment before shaking myself and sitting back down between Jae, who'd rushed over when I called to tell him what had happened, and Elena. That moment of weakness had nothing to do with Amir and everything to do with what he represented—a way to save Adeena.

I had no idea how much time passed as we sat in that hideous waiting area, but the moment Adeena and Amir emerged from the back rooms, Elena leapt up and ran to hug Adeena, her frantic momentum nearly knocking them both to the ground.

Adeena laughed and wrapped her arms around her girlfriend, squeezing her tight. "Hon, it's only been a couple of hours. You're acting like I've been locked up for years and this is my first time on the outside."

I hadn't realized Elena was crying until I saw Adeena tenderly wiping the tears from her face. It was a moment that should've been sweet, but I found terrifying.

Elena was our calm, rational member, the one we relied on when Adeena and I were running hot and needed someone to step in and step up. So seeing her lose control like this was both gratifying (she wasn't perfect after all!) and horrifying. If the SPPD decided to be ridiculous (and they almost always did) and pursue Adeena as Yvonne's killer, we would need everyone on board and at their best. We couldn't afford to have Elena fall apart if we wanted to keep our business running and clear Adeena's name.

Jae put his arm around me, and as I glanced up at him, his kind, empathetic face as he watched my best friends comforting each other shamed me. Elena loved Adeena. Of course she would freak out if she thought her life partner was going to be arrested for murder. Like I'd be any different if something similar happened to Jae. Time to be a good friend.

I stood up to join them and was surprised when my legs suddenly gave out and I plopped back down on the seat. Now that I knew Adeena was OK, I guess the shock of finding my best friend with a dead body was wearing off and the haze I'd been in was slowly lifting, allowing me to fully absorb the situation. You'd think I'd be used to this by now, but I was glad I wasn't. Glad I hadn't become so hardened that a life lost was just another puzzle for me to solve. Yes, I was glad, but it also really sucked being forced to feel feelings.

I took a deep breath and Jae murmured in my ear, "That's right, deep breaths, sweetheart. I've got you. It'll be OK."

I shot him a grateful look before I got unsteadily to my feet and headed over to Adeena and Elena. They were still so wrapped up in each other, they hadn't noticed my embarrassing stumble, but they both turned to look at me when I put my hand on Adeena's shoulder.

"Are you hungry? I told Tita Rosie what happened, and she said we could head to the restaurant whenever we were ready. She has a pescatarian feast waiting for you."

"That would be great," Adeena said before turning to her brother. "Do you have time, Amir Bhai? I think it'd be best to go over everything together. That way we don't have to repeat ourselves and you can ask us all questions."

Amir glanced at his watch. "I'd love some of Auntie's cooking. It's been a while. But we can't stay long. You do realize the only reason Amma and Abbu haven't stormed the place is because I talked them down, right?"

Adeena groaned, but he was right. It's not like we could keep what happened a secret. The *Shady Palms News* team had made it to the scene just as the ambulance Adeena was in pulled away, and the incident would obviously be front-page news. Honestly, her parents were showing incredible restraint in waiting for Amir to take her home. Either that or they just trusted him that much. Considering "restraint" was not a word I imagined being in their vocabulary, my money was on Amir.

"All right, everyone, see you at Tita Rosie's Kitchen for the usual: yummy food and investigation talk."

A deena, eat, eat! You need your strength after that terrible ordeal."

Tita Rosie ladled out another bowl of crab and corn soup for Adeena and began heaping more vegan sisig and rice on her plate. If it were anyone else, I would've stepped in, but I knew Adeena enjoyed the attention, so I just helped myself to more vegan sisig as well.

Around the table at my family's restaurant were the usual suspects: Tita Rosie and Lola Flor, Detective Park and Jae, Adeena and Elena, Amir, and, of course, the Calendar Crew (my godmothers Ninang April, Ninang Mae, and Ninang June). I wasn't quite sure what the aunties were doing there considering I hadn't seen them at the festival, but knowing them, they had all the good gossip about everyone involved and would've been pissed if we'd left them out.

Sure enough, as soon as everyone had been served, Ninang Mae leaned close to Adeena. "I heard Mayor Reyes's wife is dead and you were found with the body in the maze. Is that true?"

"Mae!" Lola Flor snapped. "Absolutely no tact . . ." and here she muttered something in Tagalog that I thought best not to translate in front of company.

"Honestly, Mae. Have you learned nothing?" Ninang June said, glancing at Ninang April. Earlier this year, Ninang April had lost her niece, and while my gossipy godmothers weren't responsible for her death, Ninang Mae running her mouth had caused more than enough problems during that time.

Ninang April helped herself to more soup and continued on as if she hadn't heard the exchange. "I'm assuming Rosie invited us here because she thought we could help in some way. Adeena, Amir, care to fill us in?"

Adeena glanced at her brother, who nodded his assent and ladled more escabeche sauce over his fried fish. At his OK, Adeena recounted everything she'd told the police.

"I was making my way through the maze and hit a dead end. I must've made a wrong turn or something because the area was totally empty. And even though I'd mostly been alone while going through the maze, something about this section was, like, creepy quiet. Almost unnatural, you know? And then I heard a noise, like the wall of corn near me rustling. I couldn't tell if it was a strong wind or if a person was trying to hide or break through or something, and I was trying to calm myself down, like, it's all in your head, Adeena, when suddenly someone screamed." She closed her eyes and took a deep breath before continuing. "I booked it out of there. I was in such a hurry, I didn't see the body on the ground and I tripped over it. When I realized what I was looking at, I just started screaming and screaming. The EMTs said I must've hyperventilated 'cause next thing I know, my head was all fuzzy and then I passed out. When I woke up, there was a whole crowd around me and an EMT trying to talk to me. And then I got arrested. And . . . yeah. Here I am."

Adeena recounted this story in a weird, detached way, her eyes focused on the distance and not on any of us, her recital of the events of the day almost robotic, as if she was just repeating what she told the police verbatim. If it wasn't for the occasional quiver in her voice and the fear she hid behind the blankness of her expression, I would've thought the full impact of the murder hadn't hit her yet. But I knew her well enough to look for the signs.

I put my hand on hers. "What did the police say?"

She met my eyes. "You were in that crowd when I woke up. You know how it looked. What do you think they said?"

"Do you remember picking up that knife?" I asked.

Adeena shook her head. "There are some details I'm hazy on, but that I'm sure about. I don't even remember seeing a knife, just a person facedown and their back all bloody. I think it's when I moved closer to check if they were breathing and saw that it was the Shelbyville mayor's wife that I started freaking out."

"Which means that someone could've planted that knife on you," Amir said. He pushed his plate away. "And if that's the case, the killer must've still been nearby."

"How long does it take to die from a stab wound? I mean, it's not like the movies where the person stabbed either dies instantly or carries on a long, dramatic speech before passing away, right?" I asked, looking at Ninang June, who used to be the head nurse at Shady Palms Hospital.

Ninang June wiped her mouth. "It depends on the location and depth, but it can be anywhere from a few minutes to days. If she was already dead when Adeena found her, and you saw her that afternoon before closing your booth, there is quite a range for the time of death."

Amir grimaced. "Guess we'll have to wait for the autopsy report. We can still try and narrow it down by talking to the people who knew her and build an order of events."

"What was she doing in the maze alone? Most people would go in groups, or at least with a partner," Ninang Mae asked.

Adeena, Elena, and I all looked at one another. She was right. Had she been doing a similar competition to ours and that's why she was alone? Had she gone in the maze with someone, her wife perhaps, and they got separated? Or . . . had she gone in the maze with her killer?

"As far as I know, the only people she knew at the festival were her wife and her wife's assistant," I said. "Of course, we only met her briefly and the event is meant to be a collaboration with Shelbyville, so there's a possibility she met up with some friends after visiting our booth."

"You need to talk to the people who were close to her, but that might be difficult," Detective Park said. "We have no idea what the motive is, and considering the victim was married to a political figure . . . the *Shady Palms News* is probably having a field day with that."

Amir and I groaned. I'd been the subject of more than a few sensationalized stories thanks to my involvement in several murder cases, and it was only through Amir's help that I'd become less of a target. To paraphrase the inimitable Sharon Cuneta, the *Shady Palms News* team and ethics were tubig at langis—water and oil.

It wasn't that they published completely fake news (not usually, anyway). They just preferred to think up the most outrageous, scandalous angle on a story (they even attempted to sexy up their story on the downtown area implementing parking permits) and tried to push the narrative to fit their clickbait headlines. I got that journalism was a dying industry and they needed to draw in more readers, but their methods had made my family's life hell way too many times.

"Don't worry, I'll handle the press," Detective Park said.

"You're not a cop anymore. Will they still cooperate with you?" Jae asked.

"I may not be part of the force anymore, but Wilson Philipps knows not to mess with me. And now that I'm a PI, we've got an understanding." Detective Park added more sisig to his plate. "Their journalistic integrity may not exist, but they're great at ferreting out sources and they have the archives at their disposal. The *Shady Palms News* team and I have become reliable resources for each other."

"That's a relief. Not that I trust Mr. Philipps to hold off on anything too juicy, but at least we have some options with them," Amir noted.

"So Amir is in charge of the autopsy report and other official documents and Detective Park is handling the *Shady Palms News* angle. How about you, ninangs? Do you know anything about Yvonne Reyes?"

Ninang April shook her head. "We don't really concern ourselves with people from out of town, diba?"

"But St. Gen's has done some work with St. Francis Xavier's in Shelbyville, so we can talk to the people we know there. Even if that woman wasn't part of the church, she was married to the mayor. Somebody there will have the information we need," Ninang Mae said.

"That leaves us," I said, looking at Adeena and Elena. "Do we want to split up and investigate different people, or are we sticking together for this?"

"I'd prefer doing it as a group. At least for now," Adeena said. "If people think I'm a murderer, there's not a whole lot I can get done on my own, you know?"

Elena and I glanced at each other. She bit her lip, as if holding back false words of encouragement. We both knew how these investigations went, how this town could be. The only thing we could do now was try to wrap up the case as quickly as possible. That was the best way to support Adeena.

"All right, everyone! You've all got your missions. Now let's enjoy Tita Rosie and Lola Flor's food before it gets cold." I smiled at Adeena, trying to lighten the atmosphere.

I had no idea if it worked, but as the meal drew to a close and we were boxing up leftovers to take home, Adeena addressed the people at the table. "Hey, everyone. I just wanted to say thanks. Thanks for believing in me. And for all your help. You have no idea what it means to me that you never questioned my innocence."

"Of course not! You're a good girl and a wonderful friend to Lila.

We will always be there for you," Tita Rosie said. "You're family too, diba?"

Adeena got so choked up, she couldn't even crack a joke like she usually would. But my aunt was right. Adeena was my ride or die, the person who'd always been there for me even when I was being a crappy friend. This was my chance to finally return the favor for all her years of support.

"We got you, girl. Someone's about to find out what happens when you mess with a Brew-ha."

Chapter Five

I appreciate your devotion to the hustle, but you know you could take the day off, right?"

I'd told Adeena last night to stay at home to recover and had called in Leslie, our new full-time employee (a recent high school graduate I'd met when judging the town's beauty pageant last summer), to help us open.

Adeena stood next to Leslie, instructing them on how to prepare our new seasonal drinks. "What, so I could sit around and be grilled by my mom and aunties about what happened and then listen to them lamenting all the ways I've ruined my life?" She watched Leslie measure out the sweet corn–coconut milk mixture for the ginataang mais latte before continuing. "Yeah, no thanks. At least here I can make money and eat my feelings while people talk about me as if I'm not there."

Fair enough.

"I'm going to get started on my baking. Let me know if either of you need anything." I was halfway to the kitchen before I realized what was amiss. "Where's Elena?"

The Brew-ha Cafe was doing well, but we weren't at a point where we could take on lots of staff yet, so every day was all-hands-on-deck for opening unless there were special circumstances.

Adeena tilted her head. "I was waiting for her to pick me up and when she didn't, I called her and she said she was running errands since she didn't think I'd be coming in to work. I thought she would've told you since she knew you were expecting her to help you open."

Weird. It wasn't like Elena to flake like this. That was usually my thing (though to be fair, I only ever failed to show up when I was investigating. I was always super professional unless murder was involved), but I guess we were all allowed off days.

"It's Elena, so I'm sure she had a good reason. And since both you and Leslie are here, we should be fine. I'll get our bakes ready first, then I'll need to drop off the usual for Sushi-ya."

I was in charge of the dessert menu at my friend Yuki's restaurant, and while some things could be made in bulk ahead of time (like my matcha white chocolate chip cookies) other dishes were best prepared in small quantities and served fresh. Usually Helen Kowalski, Leslie's mother and our part-time delivery person, would be the one doing the drop-off, but she had a catering order to handle. Besides, I wanted to check in with Yuki and see if she'd heard anything about the murder.

I washed my hands and got to work, losing myself in my baking as I prepared staples like ube scones and calamansi chia seed muffins as well as our seasonal offerings. I'd just filled our pastry cases with the still-warm goods when the Calendar Crew piled into the cafe, way too loud and flashy for seven in the morning.

"Good morning, Aunties! What can I get you?" Adeena asked.

"Are you not going to the Corn Festival today?"

"I'll have the ginataang mais latte."

"You don't have those peach mango cookies yet?"

My godmothers, as usual, all spoke at once, their voices overlapping with one another. Leslie looked overwhelmed, but Adeena and I were used to it. The Calendar Crew were like a Greek chorus—always together as one, no real need to distinguish one from the other, though they each had their own distinct personality.

"Leslie, get started on the ginataang mais latte, please. Actually, make it three lattes since they'll all want one. Ninang April, we don't have the peach mango crumble cookies right now, but I think you'll really like these mais kon keso cookies. And Ninang Mae, I don't think we can make it to the festival today." I rattled off these orders and responses while also packing up sweets I knew my godmothers would love. "Shouldn't you all be at church?"

"We thought we'd come by to see if you needed help first. We can always catch a later Mass," Ninang April said. "God will understand."

"And it's a good thing we came!" Ninang Mae added. "You paid good money for that booth and you're not going to use it? What a waste."

"I don't think we're ready for that right now," I said, enunciating my words carefully while my eyes warned them to be more sensitive about the subject in front of Adeena.

Adeena forced a smile as she helped Leslie hand out my godmothers' drinks. "It's fine, Lila. I mean, I don't think I can handle being there, but there's no reason for you to be stuck here."

"I'm not 'stuck' anywhere, I'm choosing to be here. Besides, I can't handle the booth alone and Jae already promised his parents he'd spend the day with them."

"We'll work the booth with you."

"Oh Ninang June, I couldn't . . ."

"Don't worry, you don't have to pay us. Just let us eat and drink as much as we want and we'll call it even," Ninang Mae said with a wink.

"But who'll run the laundromat while you're out?" My godmothers had opened a business together this past spring, and it had a rough beginning, to put it mildly. They were doing better now, but it's not like they were in a position to slow down just yet.

"Marcus is handling the deliveries as usual, and we didn't have any bookings for our other amenities. The machines are self-service, so unless there's a problem, we don't have to be there, especially now that we're open twenty-four seven," Ninang June said.

I understood what they were saying, but I didn't want to leave Adeena alone, not when she needed me most. And not going to lie, the idea of working for hours alongside my godmothers sounded more like a punishment than a favor. Then again, we'd paid a pretty penny for that festival booth, and now that we'd taken on additional staff, it's not like we had money to burn (not that we'd been super flush to begin with).

Sensing me wavering, Ninang April added, "People are nosy, and I bet plenty will stop by to talk about the murder. You can make money off all the gossips while also gathering clues for the investigation. Two birds, one stone, diba?"

I really hated it when they made sense. "I guess that could work."

"Thank you, Aunties, that's a great idea," Adeena said way more graciously than my grudging reply. "If you don't mind waiting for a bit, I'll prepare the carafes. Lila, do you have enough time and supplies?"

I did some quick calculations. "Ninangs, could you do me a huge favor?"

"You mean in addition to working at your booth for free?"

I closed my eyes and took a deep breath, in through my nose, out through my mouth, like my friend Sana taught me. "Yes, in addition to that. Could you drop something off at Sushi-ya while I work on the desserts for the booth? Most of the prep is done, so I'll only need an hour or so."

Talking to Yuki could wait since my godmothers were sure to gather more info than I could on my own. The aunties agreed, with only a minimum of guilt-inducing commentary on their part, so I handed them the order and headed to the kitchen to finish festival prep.

Someone was sure to give us our next lead. I just had to put up with my pushy aunties long enough to get it.

Sorry, I can't really tell you anything about what happened yesterday. Hope you enjoy your cookies!"

I forced a smile and waved goodbye to the latest set of customers whose disappointment over my lack of gossip was tempered by the deliciousness of my baking. I kept striking out when it came to finding clues about yesterday; most people wanted to get info from me rather than provide it. However, despite my earlier hesitance, my godmothers were proving effective with their odd mix of extremely hardworking and gossipy AF.

"She ran a boutique? Oh, that's surprising! I would've thought she was a homemaker, being the mayor's wife and all. Good for her, having a career of her own," Ninang Mae said as she handed a customer her order. "Though with her gone, I suppose it's going to shut down? I feel bad for her employees."

"Oh, she was almost never there. She left everything to Quinn to handle. Her best friend and business partner," the customer explained, taking a sip of her coffee. "Yvonne was more the face of the store. And probably the money too since the mayor's family is loaded. Quinn, she . . . well, she's a hard worker. I'm sure the shop will be fine."

I stored that interesting tidbit to explore later while I took care of another customer. I nudged Ninang Mae, who was standing next to me, to continue the conversation with the chatty customer to see if she'd share anything else.

"What was the name of the boutique again? We should probably visit and give our condolences. I'm sure it must be a difficult time for her," Ninang Mae said, playing her part perfectly.

"From what I've heard, the mayor's wife was a very fashionable woman, so a shopping trip is a must," Ninang June added. "It's important to provide financial support during times like this."

"Oh, it's called Blue Violet Boutique. But I tried stopping by earlier and there's a sign saying they're closed for the rest of the week. So you'll have to wait awhile," the customer said.

The customer chatted with the aunties for a few more minutes before moving on, but she didn't have any other useful information for us.

"Lila, you need to find a way to talk to that best friend. She'll know the victim better than anyone else," Ninang April said.

She was right. I still needed to talk to Mayor Reyes, but considering her position, it probably wouldn't be easy to just waltz up to her and start asking questions. But Yvonne's best friend? If she was anything like me and Adeena, Yvonne had told her things she'd never bring up around her wife. But how to find her if she wasn't going in to work anytime soon?

I let my godmothers handle the line while I googled Yvonne's boutique. I had to modify the search a few times, but I eventually found various social media pages for the shop, along with Yvonne's personal profiles and the profiles for a Quinn Taylor linked to ones for the boutique. The woman in Quinn's profile picture looked fairly average: white, possibly mixed, with straight, light brown hair and freckles. She was posing with Yvonne in the photo, which showed her to be about average height with an average figure. Everything about her screamed "Basic!" except for her outfit. Blue Violet Boutique's social media pages described the shop as "a haven for those seeking unique boho chic clothes and accessories," and, based on their styles, Yvonne was the chic one while Quinn brought the boho vibes.

I was about to text this info to the Brew-ha group chat when I got a call from Leslie.

"Lila? Sorry to bother you, but Adeena got called into the police station and Elena went with her. I'm all by myself at the cafe. What should I do?"

I was silent for so long that Leslie asked, "Lila? Are you there?"

"Sorry, that was a bit of a shock. Let me think for a minute."

The booth was good advertisement, but on my list of priorities, it was definitely last. I was totally fine just leaving behind business cards and coupons and calling it a day. I knew I should head straight to the cafe since there was nothing I could do for Adeena at the station, yet I couldn't help feeling like I needed to be waiting there for her anyway. But Leslie couldn't work the cafe alone . . .

I glanced over at the Calendar Crew, who weren't even trying to hide the fact they were listening in on my conversation, and I knew what to do.

"Don't worry, Leslie. Help is on the way."

Chapter Six

"Hey, where were you this morning?"

The first person I saw after entering the Shady Palms Police Department, a place that had become all too familiar to me over the past year and a half, was Elena, pacing back and forth in front of the crusty plastic chairs they provided in the lobby. She stopped so suddenly when hearing my voice, I worried she would twist an ankle.

"Adeena was taken in for questioning by the police and that's what you want to ask me?" she said.

Well, dang.

I knew she was upset and had every right to be, so instead of snapping back, I just raised an eyebrow.

"Sorry," she said and started pacing again. "It's just, the cops showed up at the cafe saying they needed her to come in for more questions. And they made a big deal about it, saying she wasn't under arrest, so she didn't have to call her lawyer, but of course we did. Amir's with her now."

"Any idea what they wanted to ask her about?"

"Not a clue."

I texted Jae to let him know what was going on and was in the middle of texting Detective Park to see if he knew anything when he walked in the door. To add to the moment of kismet, I recognized the woman with him from her profile picture: Quinn Taylor.

"Detective Park! I was just messaging you," I said, holding up my phone. "What are you doing here?"

"Mayor Reyes hired me to assist with the investigation. This is Quinn Taylor, Yvonne Reyes's best friend and business partner," Detective Park said. "Ms. Taylor, this is Lila Macapagal and Elena Torres. They're residents of Shady Palms and have helped in several cases."

"I'm so sorry for your loss," I said, and Elena echoed my sentiments.

Quinn gave a halfhearted attempt at a smile. "Thanks. Do you . . . did either of you know Yvonne? Is that why you're here?"

Elena and I glanced at each other. Should I let her know that my best friend was the main suspect in her best friend's murder?

"We just met her the other day," Elena said finally. "We own the Brew-ha Cafe and were working at the Corn Festival opening day. She stopped by with Mayor Reyes, and we chatted for a while."

"Oh, she told me about your cafe! Said the owners had a lot of attitude but the skills to back it up. She meant it as a compliment," Quinn added.

"You were at the festival?" I asked.

"Briefly. I thought I could leave one of our part-timers in charge while I spent some time networking with Yvonne, but I was needed back at the shop." A look of heartbreaking sadness swept over her face. "I still can't believe she's gone. I—"

"Quinn Taylor? We're ready for you." A cop emerged from the back and beckoned for Quinn.

Quinn nodded at the cop in acknowledgment before turning back to us. "I've got to go. It was nice meeting you two. Hopefully I'll get a chance to stop by your cafe sometime."

Elena stepped forward and handed her our business card. "Your first order is on the house. And I heard you run a boutique? We'd love to stop by. Whenever you're ready to reopen, of course."

Quinn raised her eyebrows but accepted the card and gave hers in return. "That would be great. I planned on staying closed for the next week, out of respect for Yvonne, but Judy insisted that wasn't necessary. She knew that keeping busy would help me, so I'll be opening as usual tomorrow."

"Quinn Taylor?" the cop called again, taking a very obvious glance at the clock on the wall.

With one last nod, Quinn headed over to the police officer and disappeared into the back with him.

I waited until they were out of sight before rounding on Detective Park. "OK, spill. How did you get involved in this case? Officially, I mean."

Detective Park glanced over at the reception desk to make sure no one was listening in. "Mayor Reyes and Mayor Gunderson had a bit of a blow-up yesterday. She thinks he cares more about preserving the town's image and his reputation than he does about finding her wife's murderer."

"Well, he does," Elena and I said in unison.

Detective Park nodded. "She's a smart woman. She also knows better than to leave such an important case to the SPPD, so she called me this morning. Said I could use her name if she thought it'd bring some weight to my investigation."

"Oh, so that's why you told me who hired you. Normally you wouldn't," I realized.

"Exactly. She doesn't want her involvement to be a secret. She's hoping it'll light a fire under Mayor Gunderson and the SPPD since they wouldn't want to lose out to me."

"Professional competition. She knows exactly how to motivate them," Elena said approvingly.

I leaned toward the detective. "Does she think Adeena did it?"

Elena sucked in a breath as if I'd punched her in the gut. I knew she wouldn't like that question, but it was important—how smoothly our investigation did or did not go would be heavily influenced by the mayor and her cooperation. I felt way better about Adeena's prospects now that I knew Detective Park was officially on the case, but I couldn't leave it all up to him. I couldn't take any chances when my best friend's life was on the line.

Detective Park sighed. "I did my best to persuade her that the SPPD were being hasty, as usual. She doesn't think Adeena did it, exactly, but she doesn't want to take any suspect off the table so early. I promised her I wouldn't let my personal connections get in the way of a fair investigation."

"Wait, so you *are* looking at Adeena as a suspect?" Elena asked.

Her voice was so sharp, Detective Park flinched as if her words had cut him. "Elena, it's not like that. I will do my due diligence and collect information about Adeena, but only to prove that she's innocent so that the mayor is comfortable with me taking her off the list. It won't help Adeena if it looks like I'm covering for her because we have a personal connection."

And he was right. Of course he was right. But that didn't mean it didn't hurt. Just like in the past, when he was still with the Shady Palms Police Department and he went after me and my family for the various crimes we were accused of. Just doing his job.

I put my hand over Elena's, which was gripped in a fist so tightly it was trembling. "We get it, Detective Park. We do. We just . . ."

There was a long, awkward silence where I debated putting into words what I was sure he already knew.

Finally, he said, "I should get going. Let me know if you find any leads."

There was a pause where he looked at the two of us, waiting for us either to agree or to cuss him out. When we did neither, he continued. "And I'll do what I can to share what I find. As long as—"

"It doesn't violate your client's privacy or compromise your case. We know," I said.

He studied us. "Adeena will be fine. Don't worry."

"Of course she will," Elena said, raising her head defiantly. "I'll make sure of it."

A complicated look swept across his face as he calculated how to respond to that. In the end, he just said, "I'm sure you will."

And as he headed out the door, he turned to give us this unnecessary bit of advice: "Be careful."

Chapter Seven

It had been thirty minutes and neither Adeena nor Quinn Taylor had emerged from the back rooms yet. When I asked Elena what she'd been up to that morning, she gave a vague reply of "errands" and went back to her silent pacing.

Elena wasn't as much of an open book as her girlfriend, but I was used to her being a little more forthcoming than that. Despite Adeena being our shared bond, over the year-plus we'd gotten to know each other, she'd quickly become one of my best friends and a trusted business partner. I couldn't help but be a little hurt that she was shutting me out. Then again, if I were in her shoes and imagined Jae being the one accused of murder, maybe I'd be in my head as much as her (OK, let's be real, I'd be a much bigger mess) and would want some quiet thinking time to myself.

I was in the middle of texting the aunties for a status update on the cafe when Adeena and Amir emerged from the back. Elena beelined to her girlfriend and gave her a big hug. I'd normally join in on the group hug, but something about the way the two clung to each other made me feel I should give them a little privacy.

I turned to Amir. "What's going on?"

He sighed and rubbed the space between his eyebrows. "Where to even begin. Let's move somewhere else though. I'm sure Adeena wants to get out of here."

I looked over at my best friend. "Are you hungry? I can ask Tita Rosie and Lola Flor about hosting another meal."

"Can I let you know later? I'd love some of Auntie's good food, but I honestly just want to go home, take a shower, and nap for the next month or so." Adeena attempted a weak smile, but the corners of her lips immediately drooped back down as if she didn't have the energy to keep up the façade. "I don't know if I can stand one of our long investigation dinners tonight."

"Our parents are also being even stricter than usual right now. With her getting called in to the station again, they might not let her leave the house other than for work," Amir said. Adeena covered her face with her hands and groaned, so he added, "But they're not going to want people over either. Too much shame. We might be able to convince them to let you out if it'll help with the case. I'll see what I can do."

Amir was the golden boy of the family, so if he vouched for Adeena, he might be able to stop his parents from placing their grown daughter under house arrest.

I hugged Adeena. "Go rest. If you can't make it, I'll let you know what's up in the group chat. If nothing else, I'll force Detective Park to come over for dinner and tell me what he knows. Mayor Reyes hired him to investigate."

Adeena's eyes widened. "Whoa, how'd that happen?"

"We probably shouldn't discuss this here," Amir reminded us. "Lila, I'll make sure to come over to update you all on the case. I'd like to touch base with Detective Park as well. With him as part of the investigation, I'm feeling a lot better about how this will all shake out."

"Elena, you'll be joining us, right?"

She glanced at Adeena. "I'm going with Adeena and Amir back to their parents' house. If she's up for it, I'll go."

"Don't worry about me, babe. You know I'm gonna be stuck listening to a lecture and then passing out for a while. You should go home. Or at least check on the cafe."

Elena tucked one of Adeena's unruly curls behind her ear. "I promised you I'd be by your side through all of this. I'm not going anywhere."

I smiled at my disgustingly cute friends. "Let me know if you're coming over tonight, and no worries if you can't make it. If you want, I can bring some food over to your place later and keep you company for a bit. But right now, I've got to head back to the cafe and make sure my godmothers haven't scared away all our customers."

The three of them swiveled their heads in my direction. "You left the aunties in charge of the cafe?"

"Leslie couldn't handle it alone and I needed to get to you. They were doing just fine at the festival and Ninang June is a great baker, so I figured they could fill in for a few hours."

Adeena turned to her brother. "Amir Bhai, we need to stop at the cafe before we head home. I'm not saying I'm worried they burned down the shop, but I'm not *not* saying it either."

"Plus, we have to apologize to Leslie," Elena said.

"For leaving her alone at the shop?"

"For leaving her alone with your godmothers."

. . .

The shop wasn't on fire, but it was packed with the gossipy aunties from the church outreach group who had come straight from church to share what they'd heard with my godmothers.

"Whoa, what's all this?" I asked.

It wasn't unusual for a few members of the group to stop by the cafe after having lunch at Tita Rosie's Kitchen, but the last time I saw this many of the aunties together, it was to help my godmothers after their laundromat had been vandalized. Every single one of the tables was packed, and my poor displaced regulars hovered on the sidelines in the hopes that one of the tables of middle-aged Filipino, Mexican, and Polish women would vacate and they could reclaim their usual spots.

Ninang April was hard at work at the register and Ninang June was assisting Leslie in preparing the various orders while Ninang Mae wandered around the cafe, stopping at each table to ask how each customer was doing, checking if anyone needed any refills, bussing the dirty dishes, and very obviously eavesdropping on all the conversations. Well, it was obvious to me, anyway, but I doubt anyone else noticed. People tended to ignore service workers—not always purposely, but servers and other staff were often relegated to background noise, sometimes to the point you forgot they were even there. Until you needed something, of course.

"Adeena!" Leslie hurried out from behind the counter. "Are you OK? Do you need anything? Do you want your usual lavender chai latte? Or I could make you one of the seasonal drinks. Or maybe I—"

"Whoa whoa, chill, Leslie!" Adeena laughed and put her hands on their shoulders. "I'm doing just fine, thanks. And sorry to abandon you earlier. Has it been OK working with the aunties?"

"Uh, for the most part? Ms. June has been great at helping with the drinks and making more snacks to fill the cases and everything. And Ms. April might be even better at sales than Elena."

"I'm going to remember that, Leslie," Elena teased.

"What about Ninang Mae?" I asked, trying to hide my smile.

Leslie glanced over their shoulder at Ninang Mae as the table she was at erupted in laughter, some of the women pounding the table with their hand as they hooted and hollered. "She's kept the atmosphere very . . . lively? I guess? It's been interesting watching her work the room. I think our customers like the individual attention."

I filed away that bit of information for later. "Did you have a chance to walk Longganisa? Sorry to dump that on you."

Longganisa was my adorable dachshund and the Brew-ha Cafe's unofficial mascot. Since we were a dog-friendly coffee shop, I brought her with me to work every day, where she spent most of the time lounging in my office when she wasn't out doing promo with me.

"We went on a quick walk, but she hasn't had a chance to greet the customers since I had to get right back to work."

"Thanks so much, Leslie. I'll take over from here." I waited until they were back behind the counter before turning to Adeena, who was responding to a text. "You heading back home now that our beloved cafe is safe?"

Adeena smiled and slipped her phone back in her pocket. "I'm gonna make myself a drink and say hi to a few of our regulars first. Murder suspect or not, we do have a business to run."

"Well, that, and you don't want to deal with your family."

"It can be two things."

I laughed and headed to my office to check on my baby. Longganisa was curled up on her bed beneath my desk but stood up to greet me. Today, she was outfitted in a leaf-patterned hoodie that bore the Brew-ha Cafe logo. Cute, simple, and practical since Longganisa hated the cold. I clipped on her leash and led her around the cafe. Her usual admirers surrounded us, and we spent some time on pets and belly rubs. When we got to the front of the shop, Leslie was helping Adeena bag her order.

"Longganisa, show your Tita Adeena some love."

Adeena was more of a cat person, but she loved my little wiener dog almost as much as I did. Longganisa adored her as well, and Adeena was the only person other than me and Jae who was allowed to pick her up. Even Tita Rosie didn't get that privilege.

Adeena snuggled Longganisa close to her chest, and Longganisa rewarded her with a few licks. "Oh, my bestest girl. Your kisses will sustain me through all my family lecturing."

She dropped a few kisses on the dog's head and gently set her down. "My mom's been blowing up my phone, so I need to leave for real."

Elena started to follow her out, but Adeena stopped her. "I told you, I want you to stay here. I don't need you getting caught in the family crossfire and Lila's going to need help with a crowd this size."

"But I—"

"Babe, seriously. Do some sleuthing here if you really want to help, but you coming to the house right now will only make things worse." Adeena started to say more, but her phone rang and she swore after glancing at the screen. "It's my mom again. I've gotta go. I'll see you both tomorrow, OK? Love you."

Adeena dropped a quick kiss on Elena's lips and ran out. Elena took a few steps after her, then shook her head as if coming out of a trance. "Lila, can you leave cleaning the kitchen to me? I don't think I can handle being on the floor right now."

I stared at her. Elena loved being on the floor. How else would she convince our customers that, sure, they had just come in for a quick coffee, but what they REALLY wanted was a potted plant, some herbal tea, a few bath bombs, and a set of hand creams? Oh, and maybe a box of muffins while they were at it.

But of course I didn't say all that. I just said, "Yeah, no worries."

Which didn't feel like enough. So I followed it up with a very supportive "Uh, let me know if you need my help. With anything. 'Cause, like, I'm here for you. You know?"

That at least made her smile, even if it was because she was laughing at my awkwardness. "Got it. Thanks, Lila. Go talk to your godmothers. Auntie Mae looks like she's about to burst from all the gossip she's holding back."

With that, Elena disappeared into the kitchen and Ninang Mae grabbed my arm and dragged me back into the office. Poor Longganisa strained against her leash to follow after Elena, who was in charge of making the organic pet treats at our shop and always fed Longganisa the samples.

"I called that boutique after you left. I wanted to talk to that Quinn woman, but the person who answered said she was out. One of the church members told me that the boutique takes reservations for personal styling, so I set up an appointment with Quinn for you. I told the employee you were attending Mayor Gunderson's fancy soiree and needed a special outfit."

"Ninang Mae! I mean, points for quick thinking, but you know there's no way Mayor Gunderson would invite me to that event. First of all, I'm not in the right tax bracket. Second, he kind of hates my family. Plus—"

Ninang Mae waved her hand. "Don't worry about it! I already talked to April and June, and we agreed to pay for the dress. Besides, it's just an excuse to get some alone time with her. It doesn't matter if you're going to the soiree or not. This is just a way to get on her good side and gain her trust."

A free fancy outfit and a legit excuse for one-on-one time with the victim's best friend? I had to hand it to my godmothers—they didn't wait for opportunities; they went out and grasped them themselves.

"Thanks so much, Ninang Mae. When's the appointment?"

"Tomorrow at two p.m. She said to bring multiple bras and make sure you include a strapless one."

I made a note on my calendar and started texting Adeena and Elena about tomorrow's mission. Ninang Mae headed to the door, saying she wanted to gather more info from our customers.

She must've realized she'd gone this whole exchange without one backhanded comment, because as she stepped back into the cafe, she looked over her shoulder and said, "Choose something slimming, OK?"

I sighed as I watched her help herself to a cookie from the pastry case and reminded myself that she'd gone above and beyond today.

I also reminded myself that she promised to pay for my outfit tomorrow and looked forward to choosing the most expensive dress in the shop.

Chapter Eight

"You don't like it? Your godmother was very clear on what kind of dress she was looking for."

Quinn Taylor met my eyes in the full-length mirror, worry creasing her brow. Of course this dress was Ninang Mae's idea. My godmothers, lovers of all things floral, had been after me for years to add more color to my wardrobe. Ninang Mae in particular has never met a color or pattern that she didn't try to force together, fashion sense and color theory be damned.

Which explained the poofy, bright yellow tulle monstrosity I was wearing. It reminded me of the dress Belle wore in *Beauty and the Beast*, which, to be fair, was absolutely gorgeous and magical in the movie. On me, it looked like I was trying to cosplay at the prom. It also reminded me of the fancy gowns my mom forced me to wear as a kid so I could live out her beauty queen dreams, which was a little triggering, to say the least. None of this was Quinn's fault, of course, so I tried to be delicate.

"It's not quite my style. I, um . . ." I couldn't stand to look at her disappointed face or my haunting reflection, so I turned to Jae to help me out.

"I thought Mayor Gunderson's soiree was black tie? I think Lila would look great in something a little sleeker. Maybe in black or a dark burgundy?"

Quinn's expression cleared and she nodded her head. "I did think it odd that she requested a bright princess look." She gave me a quick once-over. "She said no black, but if it's not all black, I'm sure it'll be fine considering the occasion. I've got a few dresses that I think would be perfect on you. Just give me a minute to set everything up."

She hurried away and I moved toward my beautiful boyfriend to thank him for the save, but the skirt was so poofy, I couldn't actually get close enough for a kiss. "Bringing you along was definitely the right decision. I need to change out of this immediately. Be right back."

"Do you need help?" He grinned at me, his eyes glowing with a wicked light.

I pointed at him. "Behave. Last thing I need is Quinn reporting back to the Calendar Crew about . . . you know."

His laugh followed me into the dressing room where I carefully removed the dress (everything about the outfit was so delicate and expensive!) and changed back into my clothes. Bringing Jae really was the right move, despite his teasing. Originally, Elena wanted to join me, but she was torn between coming to find information that might clear Adeena's name and staying and working at the cafe to be by Adeena's side. Luckily, Jae had stopped by the cafe that morning at his usual time and volunteered himself for the trip.

"The new dentist I hired is working out well, so I actually have today off. I can go with Lila as backup and do some snooping of my own."

Decision made, Jae and I had arrived at Quinn and Yvonne's shop, Blue Violet Boutique, with coffee and pastries in hand.

Quinn came back with a slinky, silky burgundy dress with a halter top and loosely draped neckline, a cocktail-length black dress with a crochet insert at the chest that added detail and depth to a classic design, and a jumpsuit with an off-the-shoulder fitted black top and flowy black and white patterned bottom. I loved every single item and, judging by his expression, as he tried to discreetly and respectfully check me out, so did Jae. Each outfit suited me perfectly and they were such different looks, I couldn't choose one.

"The jumpsuit is more your style, but I don't think it's dressy enough for the mayor. It's perfect for my parents' anniversary dinner next month though. How about I get the jumpsuit for you as a gift and you choose between the dresses?" Jae suggested.

I held back a squeal because I'd had the exact same thought. The jumpsuit was something I'd actually wear, even if I knew it was wrong for the soiree (which I had to remind myself I wasn't actually going to, but it was important to keep up the façade) but a glance at the price tag had me rethinking Jae's generosity.

"You're providing all the desserts for their anniversary party for free," Jae added. "This outfit would be my thanks."

Well, if he put it that way . . . "Sold! Now I just have to choose between these dresses . . ."

Quinn stepped in. "We also carry matching shoes and accessories. Maybe seeing a complete look will help you make up your mind?"

Oh, she was good. That was a total Elena move because *of course* I wanted to check out the shoes and accessories. With Jae's help, I chose the burgundy dress ("Not to echo your aunties, but you already own so much black and you look really sexy in this"), and Quinn's expertise paired the most amazing velvet heels and chunky earrings with the dress. The gold and green jade necklace that I always wore, a memento of my deceased parents, matched well enough and I could always borrow some bangles from Adeena.

Quinn rang up my purchases and Jae handed over his and Ninang Mae's credit cards (she'd given it to me the other day for this mission). Trusting him to get the conversation going with Quinn, I wandered around the boutique to get a better feel for the place Yvonne had owned. That gossipy woman at the festival told the aunties that Yvonne was the face of the business and Quinn did most of the work. I wondered what being "the face" entailed. Did she model the designs? Appear in the ads? Handle the networking? Design the boutique's layout? Or was she the money while Quinn was the labor?

Whoever had designed the boutique had done an amazing job. The light, creamy walls spoke of understated elegance and allowed the lovely wares to stand out. The lighting was neither harsh nor dim. Shoes, jewelry, purses, and other accessories lined the back wall and several tables. The formal wear was in its own section, and we had beelined straight to that area since I was supposed to be looking for something specific, but now that I could wander the rest of the shop, I saw that the clothes ranged from casual pieces with quality workmanship to business professional and everything in between.

The areas weren't labeled, but I was in the section that must've secretly been called "Garden and Yacht Parties," based on the styles, when Quinn and Jae joined me.

"See anything else you like?" Quinn asked.

I laughed. "Not in this section. The fabrics are lovely, but my style is less Martha's Vineyard and more 'sexy grandma,' as my best friend dubbed it."

Quinn raised her eyebrows. "I didn't realize that was a look."

"Loose, chunky knits that are cropped or drape to show off your shoulders and décolletage. Flowy cardigans over silky camisoles.

Cute crocheted tops. Soft, luxurious-feeling fabrics. Everything very cozy but made to highlight your best assets. Things like that."

My love of soft, sexy knits was why I vastly preferred colder weather—hard to look good while you're sweating through your sleeveless sweater dress.

Quinn's eyes lit up with understanding and she nodded. "Yes, I love it! I understand your aesthetic perfectly. We just got a shipment of cashmere sweaters. Why don't you—"

I followed Quinn to the sweater table and she had reached out to grab one when she faltered. She stood there for a moment, hand suspended in the air, and it wasn't until Jae nudged me that I noticed she was fighting back tears.

"Quinn? Are you OK?" I asked.

She nodded, blinking rapidly. "Sorry about that. It's these sweaters. They were Yvonne's favorite. She had them in every color and pattern and cut. She looked absolutely amazing in them, of course. The supplier said she was their best customer and would send us free samples all the time. They're going to be devastated when they find out what happened to her. Just . . . devastated."

"I'm so sorry for your loss," Jae said. "Do you need a moment? Lila and I will be fine browsing out here alone. Or we can leave if you'd like."

Quinn waved her hand. "No, no, it's fine. Somehow it all hit me as I looked at those sweaters. That she's not going to waltz in here, late, of course, and fill the room with noise and chaos and . . . light. She had a real presence, you know? Vibrant. That was how Judy always described her."

Interesting that she was on a first-name basis with the mayor but considering the mayor had been married to her best friend, it made sense that they were on intimate terms. I made a note to ask her more about the mayor and Yvonne's relationship some other time. Didn't want to risk raising her suspicions.

"You two ran this shop together, right?"

"Yvonne wasn't involved in most of the day-to-day stuff. I have two part-timers that help me with that. She was in charge of marketing, networking, finding suppliers, things like that."

"Was she in charge of designing and stocking the store? Whoever handles that has impeccable taste."

She swelled with pride. "That was one of the few things we collaborated on. I also have some of my original designs here. Yvonne knew I always wanted to be a designer, so every season I was allowed to come up with something new for the store."

Jae and I glanced at the section she indicated, and Jae hurried over when he realized there was menswear as well. He'd spent most of his life not really caring about clothes, so he was still trying to find his style. With my help, of course.

"These are great! You do personal shopping for men too, right? Can you help me out? I've been getting invitations to more professional and formal events and I think it's time to upgrade my wardrobe."

Quinn riffled behind the counter for a moment before handing him a sheet of paper. "Absolutely! Just fill out this survey to help me better understand your taste and needs and bring it with you to your next appointment. We can work from there."

"Cool," Jae said, taking the paper. "Did Yvonne also help with the personal shopping? I remember both she and her wife were dressed pretty sharp when we met them at the festival. I wasn't surprised when I found out she owned a boutique."

"Yvonne catered to our more select customers, so her bookings were limited. I want as many people as possible to enjoy my clothes and learn how fun fashion can be, even if they don't have a yacht docked in Lake Michigan."

So there really was a yacht and garden party crowd that shopped here.

"It's nice that your boutique caters to a wide range of people," Jae said. "Very smart. Very egalitarian. Your shop must be really successful."

Quinn straightened some folded shirts until they were perfectly aligned. "We do OK. Though there's no way I can fill in the gap Yvonne left behind. I'll need to hire more staff, but what Yvonne did for our store isn't something that can be taught, you know? Her connections, her presence, her taste . . . that was all Yvonne. There'll never be another like her."

There was a long silence, then Quinn took a deep breath and forced a smile. "Enough of that. Jae, I'm assuming you're Lila's date to the soiree? At our next appointment, would you like my help choosing a complementary outfit or do you already have something at home?"

"A complementary outfit would be great! Would it be possible to reserve an extra-long slot since I'll need your help with both formal and casual wear?" Jae asked.

"Of course. Let me look at my calendar and I'll send you some days when I can accommodate a longer shopping experience. Is there anything else I can do for you today?"

Jae and I looked at each other, his eyes searching mine to follow my lead. There was still so much I didn't know about Yvonne and wanted to ask about. But I'd learned from my previous investigations that you can't be too direct with your questions. Not in the beginning. Not before you've earned the subject's trust. You had to play the long game with some people, and with Jae's next appointment, we could start to ask the tough questions. Until then, I didn't want to push my luck and scare off an excellent source.

"We wanted to grab a late lunch before heading back to Shady Palms. Do you have any recommendations?" I asked.

"The Wily Cow Emporium has the best burgers if you're looking for something casual. They also do salads and stuff if you want something lighter. You can also try . . ."

And she started to list other places, but I cut her off. "A burger sounds great, thanks! And thanks again for all your help. I can't wait to come back and check out more of your designs. I'm also looking forward to what you've got planned for Jae. His closet is absolutely dire."

Quinn laughed. "Looking forward to it."

Jae and I waved and headed to his car. After putting my bags in the trunk and sliding into the driver's seat, he said, "You're hoping Chuy is working today, aren't you?"

Chuy Torres was a bartender at the Wily Cow Emporium that Jae and I had gotten to know over the past year. I'd met him briefly the first time I went to the Wily Cow Emporium, back when I was following my cousin's now-girlfriend Izzy in connection to a murder investigation around Christmas (it's a long story). The burgers really were as good as Quinn said and they had an extensive cider menu, so Jae and I had become regulars since then. Chuy was also one of Elena's many cousins, and an excellent fount of information regarding people in both Shelbyville and Shady Palms since the neighboring towns were so close.

"Well, that, and Elena told me one of the specials this month is a spicy elote burger, in honor of the Corn Festival. Might as well mix business with pleasure, right?"

"I mean, that's how we got together, isn't it?" He grinned at me as I flushed.

We parked in front of the cow mural painted on the side of the pub and walked in. The hostess recognized us and called out a cheerful greeting as we walked up to the podium.

"Is Chuy working today?" I asked after greeting her.

She glanced at the schedule. "His shift starts in about forty-five minutes, but you can sit at the bar and wait for him. If you're hungry, it's between the lunch and dinner rush, so I can seat you right away."

"Can we get a booth, please? I absolutely have to try the spicy elote burger."

"Great choice! Don't worry, Dr. Jae, we have some non-spicy specials today as well." She grabbed a couple of menus and led us to our favorite table. "Enjoy! I'll let you know when Chuy gets in."

"Perfect. Thanks!"

Jae and I were just finishing our delicious and leisurely late lunch when the hostess stopped by our table to let us know that Chuy was there. I handled the check while Jae headed to the bar in the back to warm up Chuy and try to chat up anyone else who might be at the bar. Considering he was excellent at small talk and people loved telling him oddly personal things, Jae had quickly become indispensable to my investigations. I hadn't wanted him to get involved in my cases before because it was too dangerous (I know, I know, but rules for thee, not for me), but when I saw how happy it made him to be included, the relief it brought him knowing I was safe since he was by my side, I couldn't keep being selfish about it all.

"Hey, Chuy! What do you recommend for today? Low alcohol since I have to go back to work after this," I said, sliding onto the stool in front of him.

"Lila! Always good to see you, beautiful. You know I always gotta talk up my cousin's drinks. That group over there also has to go back to work soon, and they're drinking the Shady Palms Brewery's chai apple cider. If you like it, I might have to offer it as a lunch special. 'The Office Worker's Brew' or something like that."

He pulled the draft and set it in front of me, watching for my reaction. I took a deep sniff, taking in the scent of apples and spices (and a few bubbles up the nose) before sipping the orange-brown beverage.

Crisp, lightly sweet, very autumnal. Oh my gulay, this was good. I gave him a thumbs-up and he smiled, noting something down on a pad near him.

Jae was already chatting with the group that he'd pointed out, so I decided to stay on my stool and see what Chuy knew about the recent murder and the people involved. "I'm guessing Elena told you about what happened the other day? And what's going on with Adeena?"

Chuy shook his head, not to refute what I'd asked, but in disbelief. "That's wild, man. There's no way Adeena did it, so I promised Elena I'd keep an eye out. Let her know if anything interesting comes my way."

When I asked if anything interesting had come up yet, he shook his head again, so I asked, "What can you tell me about Yvonne? She was a little . . . abrasive when we met her. Did anyone here have problems with her?"

He laughed. "You've learned tact. 'Abrasive' is a good way to describe her. Or was, I guess. Yvonne was a woman who spoke her mind. I respected her for it, but not everyone was a fan. You know how it is around here. She had a good heart, but people would rather you be nice than kind. It didn't help that she was married to the mayor."

"Were people homophobic about that?"

"Not as much as you'd think. I mean, there was definitely some very vocal hate, but Shelbyville's gotten a lot better about stuff like that."

"Then what was wrong with her being married to Mayor Reyes?"

Chuy tilted his head, searching for the right words. "How would you describe the wife of your mayor?"

"Mrs. Gunderson?" I raised my eyebrows. "I don't know. I've never really thought about her before. She's just kind of there, you know?"

"Exactly. A politician's wife is supposed to be seen, not heard. Or at least, that's how people around here see it. Her role is to be the quiet support, holding charity drives, judging the local bake sale, and, I don't know, cutting ribbons while wearing a matching sweater set and pearls. You know, respectable or whatever. The fact that she's Mexican and queer made that even more important. Mayor Reyes is smart and knows how to play the game, but Yvonne wasn't about that."

Ah, respectability politics. Of course. Guess I shouldn't have been surprised, but considering Shelbyville was progressive enough to elect a queer woman of color as their mayor, I'd hoped they wouldn't fall into that trap. Silly me.

"Anyone who was particularly vocal against her?"

"The mayor's assistant, oddly enough. His name's Zack and he's a regular here. After a few drinks, his lips get a little loose, you feel me? Not about anything important, mind you. Mostly just complaining about Yvonne and how she was a PR nightmare. His words, not mine."

"You said he's a regular? Can you text me next time he's in?"

"Don't have to. Dude likes his routine. He's here every Wednesday night for our happy hour special: endless chips and queso and our prime rib French dip. Plus, all drinks are only five dollars during that time. Zack's a big fan of my Micheladas."

Chuy's grin let me know what he was really saying—and what the next step in my investigation was.

"Endless chips and queso, huh? Guess I should let Jae know we've got dinner plans on Wednesday."

Chapter Nine

Chuy described Zack as a creature of routine, which I appreciated. One, it made investigating way easier. Two, I also believed in the power of routine. Adeena thought having set habits was boring ("You're only twenty-six and you live your life according to a color-coded calendar!") and a manifestation of my need to control everything (which, ouch), but considering how off the rails my life had been the last couple of years, could you really blame me?

It was why I embraced my friend Sana's Sangria Sundays, and breakfast every morning with my aunt, grandmother, and the Park brothers, and my evening run with my dog, Longganisa, and . . .

Wow, I really was stuck in a rut, wasn't I?

That being said, I was fully ready to add Wednesday Happy Hour at the Wily Cow Emporium to my weekly schedule. The endless chips and queso were amazing, meat-lover Jae actually moaned after biting into the prime rib French dip, and the five-dollar drinks brought me back to my college days (though no Chicago Handshakes, thank goodness). They even had vegetarian specials for Adeena and Elena to indulge in. It was almost too easy to forget that the four of us weren't crammed into a booth for a fun double date, but that we were on a mission.

I hadn't planned on bringing my fellow Brew-has (Zack seemed very protective of the mayor and I wasn't sure how he'd react to seeing Adeena), but Elena overrode my decision.

"I get what you're saying, but Adeena and I can do our own bit of investigating. My cousin will help us talk to the staff and regulars while you and Jae chat with Zack."

According to Chuy, not only could Zack be counted on to show up to Wednesday Happy Hour every week, but he always arrived at the same time and sat on the same stool at the bar.

We'd gotten to the pub before happy hour started and had the hostess seat us at a booth with a clear view of the entrance to make sure we saw Zack in case he arrived early. We made it through three orders of chips and queso before my alarm alerted me that Zack would be arriving any minute. After a quick chat with the server to ask them to bring more chips and queso to the bar, Jae and I picked up our nearly empty glasses and headed to the back to stake out stools next to Zack's usual spot. Chuy had been clued in to our plan and was hard at work at the tap, ready to set things in motion the moment he spotted Zack.

Right on schedule, Zack sat on the stool next to Jae as Chuy slid two Micheladas across the counter.

Jae looked at the spicy beer cocktail in front of him, the frosty glass filled with tomato juice, beer, and hot sauce, and rimmed with Tajín and a lime wedge. "Wait, Chuy, I didn't order this. Only Lila wanted one. I asked for the chai apple cider."

"Sorry about that! I'll get your drink right away. You can have that one on the house."

Chuy moved back to the tap and Jae turned to Zack. "Excuse me, would you— Hey! I know you. Zack, right? We met at the Corn Festival."

Zack looked startled but reached out to shake Jae's hand. "You were at that booth with the great coffee, right? Nice to see you again."

Jae gestured to the Michelada in front of him. "Do you want this? I don't do spicy, and Lila can only handle one of these."

At that mention, Zack finally noticed me and gave a nod of greeting before taking the drink. "Don't mind if I do. I always get a Michelada when I come here, so this is perfect timing."

"I don't usually drink these, but Chuy said they go great with the chips and queso, so I took him up on it. Cheers," I said, holding up my glass.

Zack leaned around Jae and clinked his drink against mine before taking a deep swig. "Oh man. Is there anything better than that first drink after work?"

Jae sipped at the cider that Chuy handed him and sighed in satisfaction. "You're right about that. How are you doing, by the way? Things must be a little . . . hectic right now."

Zack helped himself to the chips and queso the server set down. "That's putting it mildly. I'm doing my best to support the mayor during this tough time, but it's hard. Elections are coming up and we were gearing up for that, but now everything's ground to a halt. Instead, I'm booking flights for Yvonne's family and trying to find accommodations even though everything's full up thanks to the Corn Festival."

Wow, was he seriously looking at organizing Yvonne's funeral as an obstacle getting in the way of election planning? I hoped he didn't cop this attitude around the mayor, because talk about insensitive. Though it did give me a lightbulb moment.

"If you're looking for a place for her family to stay, I know a guy.

My friend Xander has a vacation home that he sometimes rents out as a B&B. He's not planning on coming to Shady Palms until the last weekend of the festival, so he might be willing to rent it out to Yvonne's family in the meantime. You want me to ask?"

His eyes lit up. "Absolutely! And please explain the circumstances to him. We can't pick a date for Yvonne's funeral until we know if her family can come out here."

He set his drink down and reached into his pocket for his wallet. Drawing out a business card, he added, "You're a lifesaver. I'll have to stop by your cafe sometime this week. The mayor really loved your atole and I'm sure a box of sweets would brighten things up at the office. Do you deliver to Shelbyville?"

I reached across Jae to accept his card and hand him mine. "For larger orders and catering, we do. If you want my delivery person to drive all the way out for a single coffee, you're better off ordering local."

"It would be for the whole office, so we'll make it worth your while. Thanks for this. Mayor Reyes hasn't had much to smile about lately. I'm hoping this will help."

He finished his Michelada and Jae signaled for another one. "It's on me. You must be exhausted having to handle your regular duties on top of dealing with the media and providing emotional support for the mayor."

"Thanks, man. I appreciate it." Zack grinned at him. "You know, you're pretty popular around the office. You've gotten an influx of patients from Shelbyville, right?"

Jae paused with his glass halfway to his mouth. "How did you know?"

"My older brother runs a dental clinic near city hall. He said all the younger staffers no longer go to his practice because they prefer going to the 'hot dentist' in Shady Palms."

Jae's ears went red, and he avoided my gaze to call out for more chips and queso.

"Wait, is that why you suddenly had to hire a new dentist? I thought your practice got popular because of that conference you went to earlier this year. Am I going to have to have a talk with Millie?"

I was just teasing him (though I made a mental note to actually talk to his receptionist, Millie, about this and get the gossip), but Zack didn't seem to know that since he leapt to Jae's defense.

"Sorry, I wasn't trying to imply anything! I just meant, you know, business must be good right now. That's all." He tipped back the last of his drink and turned to the bartender. "Hey, Chuy, refills all around! This one's on me."

I grinned at him. "We're not fighting, so don't worry about it. I'm not going to say no to a free drink though. Chuy, can I get my usual cider, please?"

The three of us clinked glasses once our drinks arrived and the night devolved into fun chitchat and gossip about Shelbyville politics. Despite having zero hesitation about dropping the tea on all his colleagues, he only spoke about Mayor Reyes with the greatest respect. The same couldn't be said about her wife, however.

"Yvonne doesn't deserve her. Or didn't? I guess? Whatever. Mayor Reyes loved her so much and gave her everything and it was never enough." Zack shook his head slowly, as if in a fog. "She's in so much pain. I wish I could do more for her."

"I'm not sure there's anything anyone can do for her right now. These things take time, you know? Still, it's sweet of you to want to help so badly," I said. I picked up my drink and did my best to keep my voice casual. "Why didn't Yvonne deserve her?"

"Because she didn't understand her. She thought she did, but she didn't."

I tried to get more out of him regarding that statement, but he clammed up and kept drinking. Jae and I had switched to nonalcoholic drinks after the first few, but Zack stuck with his beloved Micheladas. After it was time to settle our bills, Zack stood up from the stool and swayed.

"Whoa there!" Jae caught him as he stumbled against the bar. "You OK? Chuy, can you get him some water?"

Chuy slid a glass of water with a lemon slice floating in it toward Zack. "You can't drive home like that, man. Give me your keys."

Either this was a common enough occurrence for Zack not to question it, or he was smart enough to realize he could barely stand let alone drive, but he handed his keys over to Chuy without argument.

"Thanks for the water," Zack said as he struggled to remain upright.

"How about you sit down and drink it?" Chuy suggested. He reached under the counter and pulled out a packet of crackers. "Eat these too. You need food and your stomach won't be able to handle much more than this."

Zack obediently sat down and nibbled on his crackers while Jae and Chuy discussed what to do with him.

"This doesn't happen often, but it's not the first time either. I can just call a rideshare for him, don't worry about it."

"No way, that's too expensive. Can't you give me a ride?" Zack asked Chuy.

"Dude, I just worked a Wednesday Happy Hour shift. All I want is food, a shower, and my bed. Plus, remember what happened last time I gave you a ride?"

Zack blushed. "I thought we promised never to talk about that."

"And I promised that I'd never let you in my car again. We're both holding to our promises."

Zack started to argue but Jae cut him off. "We can give you a ride."

"Really?" Both Zack and Chuy asked, but with very different intonations.

I shrugged. "As long as he doesn't puke in the car, I don't mind."

This was the perfect opportunity to see where and how Zack lived and I couldn't pass it up. And considering how drunk he was, maybe I could get him to say more about Yvonne.

Chuy passed me Zack's keys. "Based on past experience, that's not something he can promise. Good luck."

Zack lived in a modest two-flat owned by his family. That was the only way someone like him, who was just a few years older than me and working a low-ranking government job, could afford to live alone. That's what I gathered, anyway, by the way he told us we had to be quiet helping him up the stairs to his apartment so his mom wouldn't hear us. Apparently, she'd been woken up late at night one too many times by a cabbie who'd had to drive a blackout-drunk Zack home, and she'd threatened to raise the rent if it meant he couldn't afford to go out gallivanting.

"You're the mayor's assistant, and I can tell she really relies on you. Surely you're getting paid a decent salary," I said.

"This job pays in prestige and experience, but not a whole lot in the way of money. Mayor Reyes used to give a generous holiday bonus, but the amount has become less and less over the years." Considering Zack was so drunk he had the window down and his head slightly hanging out (either for fresh air or in case he puked, I didn't want to know), he was surprisingly articulate.

"Money must be getting tighter for her. I remember hearing she came from a pretty well-to-do family though," Jae said. "Then again, just because her family has money doesn't mean she does. Especially as a public servant."

"I'm not one to talk out of turn," Zack said, which was hilarious because he obviously was, "but Yvonne was draining their finances.

They had a joint account, and, well, let's just say there were a few surprises in the last year."

"Surprises like what?" I asked.

But by then, we'd already reached his place and the next ten minutes were spent with Jae and me navigating a very drunk and constantly shushing Zack up a flight of stairs to his apartment. While Jae helped him to his room, I did a little snooping, taking in his minimalist yet somehow still extravagant living room. My ex-fiancé loved expensive technology, particularly when it came to sound systems (not that he was all that knowledgeable about music. He just wanted people to think he was cool). Because of that, I recognized the Bose speakers and Pioneer DJ equipment taking up almost an entire wall.

"Hey, babe? Can you get Zack some water?" Jae called out.

"Of course!" Now I had a reason to check out his kitchen, my favorite room in any home.

I flicked the light on in the kitchen and studied the space. It was as clean and tidy as the living room, but I could tell it was due to lack of use rather than the care he exercised for his other appliances. It didn't look like he cooked, based on the number of frozen meals I found in the freezer and the canned and instant goods on his shelves. That plus the fact he only had one pot and one pan, both of which had almost no wear and tear on them.

In the fridge, I found plastic containers full of what looked like homecooked food, which was surprising, but then I remembered his mom lived downstairs and probably gave these to him. There was also a bottle of Pedialyte and several bottles of red Gatorade. The fact that he had Pedialyte in the fridge let me know that his condition tonight was not a rare occurrence.

I grabbed the Pedialyte, one of the Gatorades, and a loaf of bread, and brought them into his room. Jae had managed to get Zack to change into his house clothes and was now helping him sit upright in bed.

Holding up the two bottles, I asked, "Which of these do you want right now?"

Zack grabbed the Pedialyte without speaking and slowly began gulping it down. I set the other bottle and the bread on his bedside table and looked around the room to find a garbage can. Like his living room, I couldn't help but notice the weird mix of IKEA chic with extravagant touches, like the combo wireless charger and air purifier sitting beside his bed that I was pretty sure cost around seven hundred dollars. The only reason I even knew something like that existed was because Amir had moved in with his girlfriend, Sana (my good friend and business coach), and needed a good air purifier for his pet allergies since she wanted to get a cat. I thought about getting them one as a present and then I saw the prices and noped out of that.

Next to a desk that had definitely been put together with an Allen wrench, there was a small wastebasket. I was slightly disappointed that it was empty, but what was I hoping to find? A crumpled confession letter? Receipts connected to Shelbyville government corruption? A passionate love letter that hinted at another potential suspect? (OK, that last one may sound farfetched, but it'd actually happened before. It was hidden in a shoe. Long story.)

I put the empty garbage can next to Zack's bed. "OK, Zack, we should probably head out. We've all got work in the morning. Anything else you need me to do?"

He stared at me blearily then pointed to the wireless charger / air purifier I'd noticed earlier. "Where's my phone? Can you charge it for me? You just have to put it on top of this thing."

I glanced at Jae, who shrugged, so I turned back to Zack. "Can I get your number so I can call it?"

He was too busy steadily eating his way through the entire loaf of sliced bread (I shuddered at the thought of all those crumbs in bed), so I pulled out the business card he gave me earlier and dialed the cell number on it. The phone must've fallen out of his pocket while he was getting dressed because I could hear it ringing under his bed. Knowing that was a typical hiding spot for belongings of a more "personal" nature, especially for guys, I made Jae get the phone for me. I tried to subtly check if he had talked to Yvonne before she died, but his phone was locked. Of course.

I set the phone on the charger and turned to Zack. "We really need to go now. Good—"

I stopped midsentence after seeing he'd already fallen asleep. I glanced at the phone and then over at him. Maybe just a peek wouldn't hurt . . .

I checked his phone again and saw it used facial recognition. Ugh, just my luck that he wasn't an Android user like me. I was really hoping for something simple, like a thumbprint reader, but that would be too easy, wouldn't it? Did facial recognition work if the person's eyes were closed? I held the phone in front of his face and . . . nothing. A quick search on my own phone showed that no, it didn't work if the person had their eyes closed. Guess I was out of luck. Although, if he was this out of it . . .

I shook Zack to see if he'd wake up, but he just grunted and rolled onto his side. A heavy sleeper, it seemed. Perfect.

"Jae, I'm going to need your help and you're not going to like it, but please don't ask questions right now."

Jae sighed and moved to my side. "What do you want me to do?"

I leaned close. "Prop him up and hold his eyes open without waking him up. I need to get into his phone."

"Lila, that's a terrible idea."

"Keep your voice down! I'm well aware of how weird this is, but we're doing this for Adeena, remember? Now hurry up."

My long-suffering boyfriend proceeded to gingerly pull up Zack's eyelids while I held Zack's phone in front of his face. I was already super tense and trying not to drop the phone on this guy's face and it didn't help that Jae was muttering, "This is so gross and so wrong, why are you making me do this, we're going to get caught and my brother's going to kill me . . ." next to me.

Zack grunted and swatted at Jae's hands as if Jae were a mosquito and Jae leapt back as if he'd just touched a hot stove. "OK, I did what you asked—can we please go now?"

"Nope." I grinned and held up Zack's unlocked phone.

I scrolled through his recent calls and saw that he'd called Yvonne several times the day she died, the latest roughly an hour or two before Adeena found her body.

I switched over to his text messages, making sure to only glance at the ones between him and Yvonne and him and the mayor to glean clues. I may have become involved in way too many murder cases (any number more than zero is too many, in case you were wondering) but I hadn't become so jaded that invading a person's privacy came without a heavy sense of guilt.

Zack and the mayor texted each other somewhat regularly, but it was mostly boring, work-related stuff. The mayor kept her texts short, usually resorting to just saying, "Call me." I wondered if it was because it was easier to discuss over the phone or because she didn't want to have it in writing. The one message that stood out was from a little over a month ago.

I'm so sorry about this. I'll have a talk with her.
Document everything but do NOT go to the lawyer about this. Do you understand?

Who was the "her" the mayor was referencing? Was it a work colleague? Then why would the mayor feel the need to apologize for them? The only person that Mayor Reyes would likely need to apologize for was her wife, who Zack clearly had issues with. But that text made it seem like something more serious than the two just not seeing eye to eye.

I switched over to see his messages with Yvonne and quickly found the texts Mayor Reyes must've been referencing.

PICK UP YOUR PHONE YOU COWARD

YOU THINK YOU WON? YOU'RE NOT GETTING RID OF
ME THAT EASILY

YOU WANT ME COMING OVER AND MAKING A SCENE
IN FRONT OF YOUR MOMMY

Jae had been reading the messages over my shoulder and let out a low whistle at the last text. "She sounds like she's ready to square up with him. I wonder what happened."

"No idea, but we definitely need to find out." I took pictures of the messages on my phone and sent them to the Brew-ha group chat. "I wonder what other evidence we can find. Should we check his photos too?"

I went to open his picture gallery but Jae stopped me. "I think you have what you need. Besides . . ."

He gestured to Zack, who'd started to stir. Not wanting to get caught looking through his phone, I set the phone back on his charger and followed Jae out to his car.

"This has been a pretty productive night! Hopefully Adeena and Elena can join us for breakfast tomorrow so we can share everything with your brother," I said as we made our way back to Shady Palms.

"They'll be there. As competitive as Adeena is, I bet she wants to beat us at the investigation and prove that she got better info than we did."

I could definitely see that. "Not that this is a game, but we'd totally win."

"You're right, it's not a game," Jae said, stopping at a red light before turning to grin at me. "But you and I are clearly the best team, so we would definitely win."

I grinned back at my partner in crime (fighting), already looking forward to the next morning's breakfast battle.

Chapter Ten

"So that's what we've got from Zack. Is there anything I'm missing, Jae?"

We had gathered for breakfast at Tita Rosie's Kitchen the next morning and I was finishing up my recital of the events from the previous night.

"No, that was pretty much it. The one thing I'll add is less like a clue and more like a feeling," Jae said. "But Zack seemed extremely loyal to Mayor Reyes. That loyalty paired with his antagonism toward Yvonne . . . it just raised some questions for me, that's all. Especially after Lila found those texts on his phone."

I glanced over at Detective Park, sure that he'd have some choice words for me going through someone else's phone. I may have fudged the truth a bit, saying that we used Zack's thumb to unlock the phone since I was pretty sure telling him that his younger brother pried open a drunk, sleeping man's eyes to do it would not go over well. He could be a real stickler for the rules, and I didn't want to deal with yet another of his lectures. Sure enough, he was frowning. But not at me.

"Detective Park, is something wrong? You look like you're trying to intimidate your bowl of lugaw."

Instead of her usual DIY silog platters, Tita Rosie had prepared rice porridge using vegetarian stock for those of us who liked savory breakfasts. For the sweet tooths, aka Adeena, there was ginataang mais from Lola Flor.

"Your aunt is worried about my diet. Apparently, I eat too much red meat, so now . . ." He gestured at the side dishes on the table. Lugaw was often accompanied by tokwa't baboy, a spicy tofu and pork dish, but today there was grilled and dried fish. There were also some simple stir-fried greens and chopped tomatoes seasoned with patis, the fish sauce adding the perfect amount of saltiness and umami to take the unassuming side dish to the next level (salted duck eggs also make a great addition, FYI).

I loved eating simple food like this, and this was how Tita Rosie, Lola Flor, and I usually ate when it was just the three of us, especially at home. But when feeding company, Tita Rosie always felt the need to go all out and cater to everyone's preferences. For the Park brothers, that meant meat, meat, and more meat. Lots of rice. Vegetables only when necessary, and that was more of a Jae thing, since he was always touting a diet that promoted a "healthy smile." (He took dental hygiene VERY seriously.)

Tita Rosie said, "I'm sorry, but I agree with your mother. I've really enjoyed cooking with her and collaborating on recipes that would be good for your father and still tasty."

"Heart disease runs in the family, Hyung. It wouldn't hurt to cut back a little and actually eat some green stuff. Besides, this is delicious. It's not like you're being deprived of anything," Jae said, piling more veggies on his plate.

"Do you not like the food?" Tita Rosie asked. "I could—"

Detective Park put his hand over hers. "No, I'm being insensitive. Everything you make is delicious, Rosie. I'm sorry. I guess I just don't want to think about my dad and . . . Anyway, let's move on. Adeena, Elena, did you learn anything from the other night?"

"The hostess said that Yvonne wasn't a regular, but the mayor is. She doesn't have a set routine the way Zack does, but once in a while, she'll take the whole staff out on a Friday night to have fun and team build or whatever," Adeena said.

"My cousin put in a word with the staff for us, so we talked to some of the servers and other bartenders too. They pretty much all said the same thing about Mayor Reyes: friendly, supportive, big eater, great tipper. She never throws her weight around and doesn't talk to the staff as if she's campaigning all the time. Zack can be a little 'on' around campaign season, but not her. Either she's very savvy about her public image or she really is that natural," Elena reported. "Yvonne would occasionally attend these Friday-night gatherings. It seems that not everyone on staff had issues with her the way Zack did. The way I heard it, she had a sharp tongue but was very generous."

"Generous how?" I asked.

"Working at city hall requires a certain standard of dress. Most interns can't really afford a brand-new wardrobe, so Yvonne offered one free outfit per intern including free tailoring. On top of that, she gave them major discounts and free shopping expertise for those who didn't know how to dress professionally." Adeena ladled more ginataang mais in her bowl and added a drizzle of condensed milk. "You've been to her boutique, so you know how expensive the clothes are there. Her offer made a big difference in who could afford to take on the internship."

"Mayor Reyes makes it a point to take on a few interns each year that don't have the traditional educational background you'd expect at city hall. Many of them are the first in their family to receive higher education, so everything about this job is a first for them. By all accounts, Mayor Reyes and Yvonne were bringing about real change in the Shelbyville community," Elena added. "I wonder if we could talk to Mayor Gunderson about doing something similar. We have a couple of clothing shops, but nothing at the same level of Blue Violet Boutique."

"That's a great idea, but you know Mayor Gunderson can be a bit of an elitist. Plus, he clearly feels threatened by Mayor Reyes. Do you think he'd be into it knowing it was her idea?" I asked.

"He's petty enough to shoot himself in the foot over this, that's for sure," Adeena said. "But if we frame it like, 'No one loves Shady Palms as much as you do, Mayor Gunderson! We know you'd do what's right for the town. You'd never let someone from Shelbyville best us at anything, would you?' while batting our eyelashes all innocent-like, I'm sure his ego would kick in and he'd have to adopt a program that's somehow better than hers."

"So devious," Elena said, gazing adoringly at her girlfriend. "I've taught you well."

Adeena preened a little before taking a sip of her tsokolate. "How about you, Detective Park? What info can you share with us?"

"Amir was having trouble getting the autopsy report, so Mayor Reyes had it rushed. According to the coroner, there was damage to the kidney, which meant she bled out fairly quickly. The time from when she died to when Lila and Marcus found Adeena with the body is rather slim, maybe thirty minutes at most. We don't know when Adeena first stumbled across the body, but—"

"Well, I'm sorry I didn't think to check the time on my phone before I fainted," Adeena said defensively.

Detective Park smiled reassuringly at her. "I just meant that it was a tight window, and you must've just barely missed crossing paths with the killer. You're extremely lucky."

"Extremely lucky would've been me not finding a dead body at all and getting framed for murder," Adeena mumbled.

"That . . . is true. I'm sorry. I was just trying to cheer you up, but you're right. All of this is unfair. Both to you and Yvonne." Detective Park cleared his throat. "Anyway, when it comes to motive, I'm having some trouble. Based on my interviews, people may not have always gotten along with Yvonne, but not with the level of animosity that warrants stabbing a woman in the back, in public, at a heavily attended festival."

"Did the mayor give you a list of suspects to talk to?" I asked.

"Yes, but there are a few I need to keep confidential. The mayor specifically told me to not let word spread about certain individuals," Detective Park quickly added, his hands up in defense. "You know I have to respect my client's wishes."

"So what can you share with us?" Elena asked. Her eyes were narrowed, and you could tell that she was not cool with Detective Park withholding information. But she was smart enough to know when to push and I guess she didn't think now was the moment.

"I mentioned Zack as a potential suspect, and she was adamant that it wasn't him. Said that he may have had his differences with Yvonne, but he'd never cross that line. Especially over something so minor."

"Of course she doesn't want to think that her assistant killed her wife, but that's not evidence. Do Zack and the mayor have alibis for Yvonne's time of death?" Elena asked. "And those text exchanges seem to say that something not-so-minor happened between them."

"Those texts messages definitely change things, that's for sure. But considering how Lila got hold of them, I'm not sure how to approach the subject yet." Detective Park frowned. "As for alibis . . . there's a bit of a snag there, considering they're each other's alibis. Mayor Reyes claims the two of them were wandering the festival after a heavy meal at one of the food trucks."

"And can anyone back up that claim?" Elena pressed.

Detective Park shook his head. "The two of them were certainly together when the SPPD contacted Mayor Reyes about Yvonne's death. But whether they were together the whole time and what they were doing is unclear. If they were just strolling the grounds, it's not like a random festivalgoer thought to note down the time and place they saw those two together. I'm talking to all the festival vendors to see if I can put together a timeline. Not just for Mayor Reyes and Zack, but for Yvonne and anyone she might've been with."

"Shouldn't the police be handling that?" Jae asked.

"I'm sure they are. But I guarantee their information won't be anywhere near as good as mine."

"Have you considered that Mayor Reyes might have been the one to kill her wife?"

"Elena, Mayor Reyes is my client."

"That's not an answer, Detective."

"Then no comment."

"That's b—"

I jumped in before my friend cussed out my aunt's boyfriend in front of her and risked getting thrown out of the restaurant (by Lola Flor, not Tita Rosie. Tita Rosie would be hurt, but she'd never kick out a member of our family). "Elena, I know you're upset about this. We all are. But don't take this out on Detective Park. You know he's on our side, but it's a conflict of interest for him—"

"That doesn't let Mayor Reyes off the hook. How can you just take his side when Adeena—"

"Can I finish?" I stared at Elena, who looked like she was gearing up for a fight. Usually, she was the cool, calm one, the peacemaker of our trio, so it was weird to be the one trying to pacify her. "As I was saying, just because the mayor is a conflict of interest for Detective Park doesn't mean *we* can't look into her. And I'm sure he'll pass along anything interesting he learns about her while he's working the investigation she's paying him for. Right?"

Detective Park nodded. "Again, as long as it doesn't violate client privilege, I'm happy to help."

Adeena put her hand on Elena's arm and gave her a look. Elena turned her eyes to her bowl, probably trying to pretend she didn't know what Adeena wanted her to do. Adeena tucked a stray curl behind Elena's ear, her fingers lingering for a moment before she turned back to her own bowl of sweet corn porridge.

Her girlfriend's touch seemed to bring Elena back to herself. "I'm sorry, Detective Park. I know you're not the enemy. It's just so frustrating to not have a specific motive or angle for us to tackle. I don't want to waste time going from person to person and place to place on a wild goose chase for information."

Detective Park's mouth curled into a wry smile. "You do realize that that's what detective work is, right? Not every victim has an obvious target on their back. You need to look into their background and the people around them and hope that a picture forms. It's slow, it's tedious, and there is nothing glamorous about it. But it needs to be done."

"That reminds me, I need to get in touch with Xander to see if Yvonne's family can stay at his place. Zack said they can't pick a date for Yvonne's funeral until they know when her family's coming over."

It was already opening time for the Brew-ha Cafe (we opened an hour earlier than Tita Rosie's Kitchen), so our breakfast party broke up soon after that. My contributions were already in the pastry case, so I went to my office to call Xander. I sat on the floor next to my desk to cuddle with Longganisa while I waited for him to pick up.

"Lila! An actual phone call? To what do I owe the pleasure? I'm hoping it's something good and not another . . . you know."

Xander Cruz was the main investor in the Shady Palms Winery, which was run by my cousin Ronnie and his girlfriend, Izzy. He'd taken a liking to Elena and her vision for a microbrewery, so he'd also helped in getting her set up in a small space on the winery grounds. He mainly resided in Chicago, but he kept the house that he'd been renovating with his deceased fiancée as a vacation home. As I'd mentioned to Zack, he also rented it out when he didn't need it. I'd planned on easing into the conversation, but since he'd already broached the subject . . .

"Actually, I am calling because another 'you know' happened here. The wife of the neighboring town's mayor was killed at our Corn Festival and Adeena is the main suspect."

"Girl."

"The victim's family is from out of town and they need a place to stay, but everything's booked up because of said Corn Festival. They can't choose a date for the funeral until they know when or if her family is coming over, so I was hoping—"

"Lila, you realize I said that as a joke, right? Like, I was expecting an uncomfortable laugh and then you tell me a collaboration idea or that it's time for another playdate for Nisa and Poe."

"Xander, sometimes my entire life since I moved to Shady Palms feels like a joke. And not the ha-ha kind either. But yeah, someone is framing Adeena for the murder. I'm talking planting the murder weapon on her and everything. So can you help?"

Xander let out a long, low whistle. "You Shady Palms folks do not mess around, do you? But yeah, of course I'll help. I'm forever in your debt for finding Denise's killer."

Like just about all the friends and acquaintances I'd made in the last year or two, we were tied together not just because he was my cousin's investor but also due to a murder investigation. He'd lost his fiancée in a much more permanent way than I had—mine just cheated on me—and was grateful that I'd helped catch her killer.

"You don't owe us anything, but I appreciate the help. Is it OK if I pass on your contact info to the mayor and her assistant? I think her assistant, Zack, is in charge of booking things, but I could use this chance to talk directly to the mayor. Detective Park is investigating the case on her behalf, so he can't tell us anything about her that might be a conflict of interest."

"Sounds messy. I'm definitely in. Do you have my business card? If not, you can get some from Ronnie and Izzy to pass on. Makes it seem more official than 'I know a guy.'"

"I thought everything in Chicago operated on 'I know a guy.'"

It was how I'd gotten in some legal trouble a couple years ago due to my ex-fiancé, but I digress.

"Yeah, but you know you small-town types don't trust us slick big-city folk."

Rolling my eyes, I said, "Us country mice just don't know what to do around a sophisticated gentleman like you. It's natural to distrust such perfection."

Xander laughed. "Tell your aunt I'll come visit before the festival is over. Chicago has some bomb-ass restaurants but none of them make me feel as at home as Tita Rosie's Kitchen."

"Let me know when you plan on arriving. I'll try to get everyone together for another karaoke party."

The first karaoke party he'd attended at the restaurant had been rather disastrous for various reasons, but over the past year since he'd started hanging out with us, he'd come to love them as much as we did.

"Who all you inviting?"

He tried to pass it off as a casual question, but I knew what he was really asking.

"Oh, you know, the usual. Me, Jae, Adeena, Elena. Ronnie and Izzy too, of course. Marcus needs to get out more, so we've got to invite him. Who else . . ."

"Lila."

"Yes?"

"Why are you like this?"

I laughed. "If you give me enough notice, I can make sure Bernadette is off that night. Is that what you wanted to know?"

"What's that? You don't want me to bring you any Malta? And I should just leave Poe at a friend's house? Is that what I heard you say?"

"Nooo, I'm sorry!"

Malta is a popular Puerto Rican nonalcoholic malt beverage that is weirdly addictive, but a bit of an acquired taste. I fell in love with it in college and suffered through withdrawal until Xander became my supplier. Xander's dog, Poe, is a pit bull mix and the sweetest pup ever. He is Longganisa's best friend, and I looked forward to their playdates almost as much as they did.

"I'll check my schedule and let you know when I can make it down. I'll also send an update whenever that woman's family contacts me, OK?"

"Thanks, Xander. You're the best."

"I know. See you soon, babe."

I hung up with a big grin on my face. Xander had that effect on people. I checked my desk and found that I actually had a couple of his business cards lying around and decided to keep it moving while luck was on my side.

I snapped the leash on Longganisa (dressed in a cute flannel with the Brew-ha Cafe logo today) and headed into the main part of the cafe. The morning rush was in full swing and Adeena, Elena, and Leslie were all running around filling orders and answering questions about our products. I decided to take a leaf out of my godmother's notebook and schmooze with our customers, making my way to each table to say hi and let them admire our little mascot. We spent extra time chatting up everyone in line so they wouldn't get too impatient with the wait. Once things had calmed down a bit, I made my way over to Elena in her corner of the shop and let her know my plans.

"Oh, that's perfect! Zack put in a large order for the Shelbyville City Hall employees, and I was going to do the run after the rush was over."

"You were going to do it on your own?"

Leslie's mother was our delivery person, but I took on the duties when the order required friendly chitchat for networking or investigative purposes. Since I was in charge of the baking, which was mostly handled in the morning, running errands was how I helped pull my weight around the cafe during the daytime. Elena was our most knowledgeable, not to mention most capable, salesperson so we always had her on the floor. It didn't make sense to have her do deliveries when my tasks were already done for the day.

I said as much, but her response was, "Well, maybe you should let us handle it sometimes. Maybe we'd like the chance to get out once in a while, too. You ever think of that?"

No, I had not. I guess I just took it as fact that our duties were split up fairly. Adeena and Elena had always been understanding of my constant running around and I assumed it was because I'd gotten my work done first, but maybe they just hadn't felt comfortable saying anything to me?

I understood that, but . . . I was the investigator in this group. And my best friend's freedom was on the line. Why would she try to do this on her own?

"I'm sorry. I didn't . . . I mean, I hope you don't think I've been taking you two for granted. But don't you think that I . . ."

As I tried to think of a tactful way to phrase my thoughts, Adeena cut in.

"Relax, she doesn't actually want to do the deliveries. She's just saying that because she wants to be the one doing the investigating this time," she said, clapping a hand on my shoulder. "Leslie and I got this, so you two should go together."

Elena started to protest, but Adeena put her finger to Elena's lips to shush her.

"It's safer and opens more opportunities. You can pick up on things she misses and vice versa. Plus you can split up and cover more ground if necessary."

Elena didn't look convinced, so Adeena added, "It's my freedom at stake, so I get the most say here. And I say I want my best friend and my girlfriend to work on this together. All right?"

Elena and I glanced at each other. Well, it's not like I was against investigating together with Elena. But was she going to be OK going along with me?

"As long as you never try and shush me like that again, then fine," Elena said. "You're lucky I didn't bite you."

"You know better than to do that in front of company, love," Adeena said, blowing her a kiss before heading behind the counter.

Ridiculous as always. But she helped defuse the weird vibes

between me and Elena (for the most part). After I dropped Long-ganisa back in my office, we managed to pack up my ancient SUV, which was way bigger than her Beetle and another reason I was the one who handled deliveries, and head to Shelbyville with few problems but a whole lot of silence.

Chapter Eleven

I pulled into the parking lot of Shelbyville City Hall and got to work unfolding the rolling trolley we used for large catering orders. Elena helped me stack the pastries and boxes of drinks that Zack had ordered, finally breaking her silence just as I was about to wheel the cart up the building's ramp.

"Hey, Lila . . . I'm sorry. About trying to leave you out of the investigation."

The trolley was older than I was (my grandmother had gotten it from an old church sale, and we shared it to avoid having to buy a new one) and the wheels a little rickety, so Elena's sudden apology had me nearly steering into a wall until she gripped the handle and helped me right it. It's not that I was surprised that she apologized. Again, out of our trio, she was the quickest to read a situation, which is what made her such an effective peacemaker and salesperson. She was also the most willing to admit her faults. But I was quickly learning that

Adeena was one of her weak spots, and I didn't expect her to realize that she was cutting me out. Was she doing it on purpose?

"I have to admit, I was a little surprised. Is there a reason you don't want me here?"

She bit her lip, staring down at the ground, and I wished I could take it back. When would I learn to never ask a question when I knew the answer would just hurt me?

"Never mind, it's not important. Thanks for apologizing though. Do we want to talk about our strategy before we go in?"

Elena looked as relieved as I felt about moving on from the topic. "You've already established a connection with Zack, so you should talk to him if he's around. You have to give him Xander's card anyway. I'll try to talk to other members of staff that we're not familiar with yet."

"Good idea. And if Mayor Reyes is around, we should talk to her together. I want to make sure neither of us misses anything important, and she's the one we need to investigate the most."

Elena hesitated before nodding and walking ahead. I adjusted the items that had shifted on the cart and followed her to the reception desk.

"Hello!" she called out. "We're from the Brew-ha Cafe. Zack put in an order for delivery."

"Good morning! I've heard such good things about your cafe! I haven't had a chance to visit, but one of my friends is obsessed with your lavender chai lattes." The receptionist smiled at us before glancing down at the clipboard in front of her. "You can take those to Meeting Room Two down that hall on the left. The staff meeting isn't over for another half hour, but I'm sure people will be popping in as soon as they hear there's snacks."

We thanked her, and as we headed in the direction she indicated, I caught her gazing wistfully at the boxes of pastries. I made a note to bring her one as well as a cup of tea once we were done setting up. As the receptionist, she probably saw a lot of what went on in this building and probably knew Yvonne as well. Plus, I assumed she couldn't leave her post very often and had to miss out on the snacking and schmoozing that happened at these meetings. A little treat would be sure to brighten up her day. It always worked for me, anyway.

The meeting room was laid out rather casually, with tables arranged in a U-shape and a whiteboard in front. It reminded me of a small classroom. There was a long table off to the side beneath windows letting a good amount of natural light into the room. I wheeled the cart over that way and set the brake so we could unload the goods.

"Ooh, what do we have here?"

Two people entered the room, neither of whom looked old enough to legally drink yet. Probably the interns.

I plastered a big smile on my face. "Good morning! We're the Brew-ha Cafe over in Shady Palms. Zack hired us to cater your post-meeting break today."

"Really? That's cool of him. I'm Ben, by the way. I use he/him pronouns," the young guy said, gesturing to his name tag that confirmed what he just said.

"And I'm Michelle. I use she/her pronouns."

"I'm Lila and that's Elena," I said, gesturing to my partner. "We both use she/her pronouns."

"Cool. Zack has us all introduce ourselves using our pronouns, in case you were wondering. He said it 'fosters a more inclusive environment.'" Ben shrugged before helping himself to a sweet corn and cheese muffin. "Makes sense to me. It takes, like, no effort and makes our queer staff more comfortable, so why not, right?"

"That's really thoughtful of him," Elena said. "You know, maybe we should have name tags made with our pronouns on them. Might make things easier for Leslie."

"Great idea! Putting that in our group chat so we don't forget," I said, pulling out my phone to send the note. Once I was done, I turned to the interns. "Where is Zack, by the way? We need him to check over everything and sign the invoice."

"He's probably still in the meeting," Michelle said, poring over the pastry selection. "It's not finished yet, but we were assigned to handle some mailing stuff, so we were able to skip it. Do you have anything savory? I don't really eat sweets."

"The sweet corn and cheese muffin that he's eating is both sweet and salty," I said. "If you eat pork, we've got longganisa rolls, which are Filipino sausage wrapped in puff pastry."

"Yes!" both Ben and Michelle exclaimed. "That sounds amazing."

I was one of those people who yelled at the screen during *The Great British Baking Show* when the contestants had too many savory challenges ("It's called *The Great British BAKING Show,* not Cooking Show!") since I was a baker and not a cook for a reason. But I had to admit, ever since I added those longganisa rolls to the menu, we'd been getting more and more requests for savory pastries. Something to discuss with my partners later.

Elena engaged in idle chitchat with the other two while I finished setting up the drinks station, which included boxes of our house blend, decaf, and house chai, along with various milks and milk alternatives plus sweeteners. Zack had ordered our deluxe drinks package, which included not only the aforementioned beverages and creamers, but also Adeena's simple syrups. Elena had proposed the idea of producing and bottling our cafe's most popular syrups for at-home and office use and they were a surprise hit. So alongside the usual granulated sugar and honey, I lined up bottles of lavender syrup, rose syrup, pistachio syrup, and arnibal, or Filipino brown sugar syrup.

By this time, more staff members had wandered into the meeting room and were helping themselves to the snacks and beverages. Zack and the mayor still hadn't arrived yet, so I quickly lined up the little signs labeling each item before mixing up a lavender chai (hope she was OK with whole milk) and grabbing a muffin and longganisa roll for the receptionist. After letting Elena know what I was doing, I made my way to the front desk.

"Special delivery! I figured you wouldn't be able to leave your post and wanted to grab you some food before it was all gone." I set my offerings in front of her and gave her a quick explanation of what they were.

The receptionist's eyes lit up. "That's so sweet of you! I know I mentioned the lavender chai latte, but I didn't expect you to actually remember."

"I'm still waiting to talk to Zack, so it's not a problem." I watched the receptionist take a big bite of the corn and cheese muffin. "What do you think? It's a new item I added for the Corn Festival, but I'm wondering if it should be a regular cafe offering."

"I think it's great! It has the perfect amount of sweetness. Not so much it feels like a dessert, but enough to match with the salty cheese." She took another bite, chewing happily. "I can see myself picking this up for a light breakfast or a nice snack."

Muffins were fast and easy enough that even Adeena could throw together a batch in a pinch. And this was an easy way to update the savory options on the menu. I made a note to add the muffins to the permanent rotation.

She'd finished the muffin and was savoring her lavender chai in a way that let me know now was the perfect time to get information out of her. I glanced at her name tag.

"So, Felice, how long have you been working here? I heard you get a lot of interns at city hall, so there must be a lot of turnover."

The receptionist looked at least a decade older than the mayor, possibly even two, so anywhere from mid-fifties to early sixties. Most of the employees appeared to be considerably younger, and I wondered if the receptionist had the most seniority among the staff.

"Yes, Mayor Reyes started the special intern program a few years ago, which led to an increase in opportunity and on-the-job training for a lot of young people. Shelbyville was losing a lot of bright minds to the city and university towns, so she wanted to create a program that gave them a good reason to come back. I've been a receptionist here for over twenty years, and I've got to say, this was one of the smartest things one of our officials has ever done."

"Oh, so you've worked under previous mayors?"

"Yes, our mayors serve four-year terms, but there's no limit to how many times they can hold office. Our previous mayor served three terms before Mayor Reyes defeated him in a huge upset. This is only her second term and she's already done more for the town than the old mayor ever did."

"Has Zack always been her assistant? He seems very loyal to her."

She nodded. "Yes, she handpicked him to be her assistant out of that year's batch of interns. Trained him well and now he's become indispensable to her. Very loyal, very ambitious. Not sure how connected those two things are."

Interesting. "You think he's just loyal to her because she can help him get ahead?"

The receptionist seemed to mull that over. "Hard to say. In the beginning, I would've said yes immediately. It was obvious he just saw the position as a stepping-stone. But I have a soft spot for the mayor, so I watch the people around her closely. I think he's grown to genuinely care about her and her vision. I don't think he's stopped striving, but I think his heart is there. It's actually been really gratifying to watch. I guess I've got a bit of a soft spot for him too."

"I'm glad the mayor has someone dependable by her side during such a difficult time. My boyfriend and I ran into him the other day and it seems like he's been really supportive, handling all the details so the mayor can focus on the necessary things."

Felice shook her head. "Tragic. Absolutely tragic. Yvonne was prickly, but she was a good person. The perfect partner for Mayor Reyes."

"Really? Zack sort of made it seem like Yvonne wasn't the ideal wife for a politician."

"And that's what made her so good for the mayor. Mayor Reyes has a good heart and a strong vision for what she wants for Shelbyville. But there are certain members of the council and the town that don't agree. The city council operates as an old boys' club, and they don't appreciate the mayor coming in and changing how things have always been done."

"I can definitely see that, but what does that have to do with Yvonne?" *Ack, you're being too obvious, Lila!* "Sorry, you just made me curious. I'm not trying to make this an interrogation."

She smiled at me, but I wasn't sure that she bought my excuse. "Mayor Reyes knows how tenuous her position is. Despite having the popular vote, there's a very vocal minority against her. So her first term, she focused on not rocking the boat too much. She needed to look and act perfect at all times. Any wrong move she made would be blood in the water. She started diluting her messages, making sure there was nothing that could be taken out of context and used against her, sometimes saying things she didn't even mean just to avoid conflict."

The receptionist finished her muffin and threw the crumpled wrapper in the trash can next to her. "Yvonne hated it. They used to fight about it all the time. Made things a little uncomfortable around here, but Yvonne kept Mayor Reyes on the right path. She didn't want the mayor to make so many compromises that she forgot what she was fighting for."

I thought back to the Corn Festival and how perfect and smooth the mayor was. She'd seemed so warm and welcoming, knowing just what to say to put people at ease. Yvonne was the opposite, the type who liked friction, who wanted to strike sparks against another person to see how they reacted. I guess opposites attract after all.

"I see what you mean. A partner like that is good at keeping you honest. Not that I'm saying the mayor was ever dishonest, but you know what I mean." A thought occurred to me. Asking it was going to make the fact that this was indeed an interrogation even more obvious, but whatever. In for a penny and all that. "You mentioned her having trouble with certain council members. Does she have any enemies on staff?"

Felice looked like she wanted to say more, but she suddenly straightened up, unobtrusively wiping the crumbs from the desk before saying, "That's right, we not only have college-age interns, but we have apprenticeship programs with our local high schools. If you're looking to expand your town's job programs, you should really meet with Kimberly Johnson. She's the head of our work-study program and knows all about our staff and council members."

"Wha—" The sudden shift in conversation threw me off, but she looked me dead in the eyes and smiled, so I played along. "Great! I still need to talk to Zack and the mayor, but I'll make sure to look her up before we leave. Where can I find—"

"I didn't realize you were interested in our internship programs, Lila." Zack suddenly appeared beside me, looking at the receptionist with a smile that didn't quite reach his eyes. "Sorry that took so long, but the mayor was on an important phone call. Elena told me you've been out here for quite a while. She was wondering where you'd gone."

More like he was wondering what the receptionist and I had been talking about all this time.

"Oh, I wanted to make sure that your receptionist got something to eat before the meeting let out since she can't leave her post. I noticed a lot of the employees looked really young, so I asked about the improved internship program that Mayor Reyes started. It sounds amazing and I wondered if we could do something similar in Shady Palms. We have even less opportunities for young people than you all do here."

Praising Mayor Reyes's program seemed to do the trick because Zack lost the suspicious look in his eyes and started beaming. "Isn't it wonderful? I'll make sure to get you in touch with the head of the program. Not that I think your boor of a mayor is capable of implementing something like this."

Mayor Gunderson wasn't incompetent—he was complacent. Our city council was no different from Shelbyville's, made up of mostly older white men who were perfectly content with keeping things the way they were. The system had always worked for them, so they felt no need to change it. However, as Elena pointed out, Mayor Gunderson loved a good pat on the back. The more public, the better. He may care about himself above all else, but he truly did want the best for Shady Palms.

"You're underestimating him, but I see why you'd think that. Anyway, let's head back to the meeting room. I need your signature on the invoice and I'd love to say hi to Mayor Reyes."

I followed Zack to the room and saw Elena chatting with the mayor, who kept glancing at her watch. When Mayor Reyes saw me and Zack arrive, she didn't bother hiding the look of relief on her face.

"There you are! I need to run. Elena here told me she found a place for Yvonne's family to stay, so could you get the details from her? Thanks." Mayor Reyes picked up a large tote bag and reusable coffee cup. "Sorry we couldn't talk, Lila, but thanks so much for catering our meeting!"

Zack watched his boss hurry out of the room and moved as if to follow her, but then he shook his head and turned to Elena. "You really found a place for Yvonne's family? Everywhere I tried has been booked for weeks, so you're a lifesaver. Can I get their contact info? I want to take care of this right away."

"Our friend Xander rents out his vacation home sometimes and he said he'd be happy to help out. Let me just find his number . . ."

Elena started scrolling through her phone, but stopped when I pulled Xander's business card out of my wallet and handed it to Zack.

"I had some of his business cards back at the cafe, remember? Anyway, we should get going. Can you let me know when the head of your internship program has time to meet? I'd be happy to drive out here again, I just need to let my team know ahead of time."

Elena and I said our goodbyes and wheeled our empty cart back out to my ancient SUV. I wondered idly if upgrading to a van should be the cafe's next big investment or if I could put it off a little longer to get the soft-serve machine that Adeena and I had always wanted.

"I lucked out with the receptionist. She was just as talkative as I'd hoped. Were you able to get anything good from the mayor and interns?" I asked as we buckled up for the ride home.

"I think so. Enough to help us plan our next moves, anyway. But we should wait till we're back at the cafe so we can discuss this with Adeena."

Elena looked out the window, putting an end to our conversation. I turned up the music and drove back to Shady Palms in silence, trying to ignore the voice in my head that was saying that one of my best friends and business partners was hiding something from me.

Chapter Twelve

T hat's everything I learned during the delivery," I said, recapping all the info I got from Felice as I packed up the last of the unsold pastries. I'd gotten better at estimating the cafe's needs so we rarely had leftovers, but on the days we did, I'd stop at the church on my way home to drop them off with my family friend Father Santiago or any of the volunteers hanging around.

"Good thing that receptionist was super chatty," Adeena said, filling a to-go box with the last of the coffee for me to drop at the church as well.

The cafe had been packed when Elena and I returned from our delivery, so we'd jumped back into work mode and hadn't had time to talk about the information we'd collected in Shelbyville. Now that we were closed, we could unwind a bit and fill one another in on our investigation.

"Don't you find that a little suspicious?" Elena asked. She'd been busy restocking the herbal teas, but apparently questioning my source was more important.

I shrugged, trying not to be annoyed. "Sometimes people like to talk. Especially to someone who's been nice to them. And she did say Mayor Reyes was important to her. Maybe she just wanted to talk it out with someone."

Elena went back to her shelf. "If you say so. I still don't trust her."

"Well, what did you find? You were in the room with the interns plus Zack and the mayor. Did they tell you anything?"

"Not really."

"Nothing? But you were talking to the mayor when I got back. She didn't say anything that could help the investigation?"

"It was just small talk, really. I didn't want to be too obvious in front of Zack."

"OK, but—"

"Wait, didn't you say they were arguing about Mayor Gunderson's soiree?" Adeena cut in. "And something about Zack not trusting him?"

Elena froze. It was just for a second, but that hesitation was enough to let me know that Elena hadn't just forgotten to tell me that. She'd *chosen* to hide that information from me.

I wasn't one for confrontation (unless it was my family, but they had a special way of pushing my buttons) but this was too much.

"Why did you try to keep that from me? And earlier, when you tried to do the delivery without telling me. Why are you trying to do all this on your own? Why are you cutting me out of my best friend's investigation?"

Elena dropped the packet of tea she was holding and whirled around to glare at me. "Not everything is about you, Lila!"

I reared back. "What does that mean? I'm not trying to make this about me, you're the one who—"

"Stop it!" Adeena stepped around the counter and literally shoved us apart. "This isn't about either of you! So if you could stop whatever the hell this is and remember that I am the one that found a dead body and that I am the one in danger of going to jail and that I am the one having nightmares every night, that would be a big help, thanks!"

Her voice got louder and more emphatic until she was practically screaming at us, and once she was done, she took a deep breath, then turned around and ran into my office, slamming the door behind her.

Elena and I stood in silence for a moment after that outburst before turning to look at each other.

"I think I messed up," she said.

"I think we both did. We should probably talk this over more later, but for now . . . Truce?"

We shook on it then headed over to my office. I knocked softly before opening the door. "Adeena? We're sorry . . ."

Adeena was lying on the floor, cuddling Longganisa, who was licking away Adeena's tears. Elena sat down, laying Adeena's head on her lap and stroking her thick curls as she murmured words of apology and encouragement. I sat next to them and rubbed Adeena's back until she stopped crying and could speak again.

"I see Yvonne's body when I close my eyes. And then I wonder . . . why was I holding that knife? I know it wasn't me. It couldn't have been me. But sometimes in my dreams . . ."

"Oh, my love . . . why didn't you tell me? You know you don't have to keep up this happy face around me," Elena said, her words admonishing, but her tone so, so tender.

I said, "How many meltdowns have you helped me through? And over ridiculous things too, like my supposed bad taste in men."

Adeena sat up and wiped her eyes on her sleeve. "You do have bad taste in men. Except for Jae. Him I approve, so you better lock that down."

"That aside, you've always been there for me. You think I wouldn't want a chance to repay the favor even a little?"

She sighed, scooping Longganisa up onto her lap. "I know, I know. At first, I just wanted to pretend in front of my family because you know how they are. They want me to have a breakdown so they can thrive off the drama of it, and I didn't want to give them the satisfaction. And of course, at work, I just didn't want to think about it, you know? This is my happy place, and I didn't want to ruin it for me or our customers."

She paused to stroke Longganisa and looked as if she was thinking over her words. "But you two . . . you're also my happy place. You know? And I know you're just trying to help. I'm not so up my own ass to not realize that. But you both keep running around trying to do stuff for me but without really including me. And, I don't know. Maybe stop that?"

It wasn't until she said that that I realized 1) she was absolutely right, and 2) it had been days since the incident occurred and we hadn't had a chance to sit down and really talk about what had happened and how Adeena was feeling about everything. Elena and I had just immediately jumped into investigation mode without taking the proper time and care to check in with Adeena. I mean, of course we texted constantly and hovered around her at work, but with her parents being so overprotective and having her stay home more and more, plus her "I'm totally fine!" song and dance she did in front of everyone, we may have talked but we never really communicated. It was kind of (OK, very) messed up that it took her screaming at us to realize just how badly I'd failed my best friend.

"I'm so, so sorry, Adeena. I'm not going to try and excuse it because I'm sure you know and I also know that's not the point. I promise not to treat you like some damsel I'm trying to save."

"That's right. If anyone here is a princess, it's you." She grinned at me, and I knew we were OK.

"I promise to be better and do better." Elena took Adeena's hand in hers before glancing at me. "So let's plan out the next steps. Together."

We decided that 1) since we were going to be running our Corn Festival booth that weekend, we should return to the scene of the crime, if not to actually find clues, then at least to have Adeena face her fears and receive some closure, and 2) since I'd gotten useful intel from Felice, the overly chatty receptionist at Shelbyville City Hall, I should follow up on what she'd told me.

The receptionist had hinted that the person in charge of the internship program had information on the various members of the staff and local council. I'd been looking into the people who might've had problems with Yvonne, but considering that she was married to a politician, maybe I was going about this all wrong. Sure, her wife was just a small-town mayor, but people were often killed for less. Yvonne might not have had any enemies (other than her beef with Zack) but the mayor certainly did. I couldn't ignore the possibility that Yvonne was a pawn to get to Mayor Reyes. Zack had sent me the contact info regarding the internship program shortly after we'd delivered that catering order, so with Adeena's blessing, I figured it was time to try a new tactic.

A few days after our initial visit, Jae accompanied me to Shelbyville City Hall—despite Elena's insistence that she should come along, so I guess she wasn't going to give up control *that* easily—since he had his styling session with Quinn that day and it just made more sense for us to go together. Plus, if we really wanted them to believe we were there to learn from the Shelbyville internship model, Jae pointed out that having two different businesses in very different fields talking to the program head would look better. Another reason to bring him along was that he was apparently well-known around Shelbyville City Hall as the "hot dentist" and his admirers might be more willing to give us information—a fact I brought up to the Brew-has when he wasn't around and that they agreed with.

His reputation definitely preceded him, because when we arrived early so that we could chat with the receptionist, Felice, she said, "No need for introductions. You're the infamous Dr. Jae, aren't you?"

"Infamous? Jae, I didn't realize your dental services had reached the level of infamy."

Jae went bright red at my teasing and his voice cracked as he greeted the receptionist, which made him go even redder. After he cleared his throat, he said, "It's nice to meet you. We brought you a snack. Lila said you really enjoyed the muffins last time."

He handed over a Brew-ha Cafe bag filled with corn and cheese muffins and a ginataang mais cupcake that I was testing out, plus a lavender chai latte.

She went straight for the cupcake. "Ooh, this is new. What is it?"

"The cupcake has a sweet corn cake base and is topped with coconut cream cheese frosting, a coconut jam drizzle, and toasted puffed rice. A new recipe I'm toying with for this weekend's Corn Festival booth menu."

Cupcakes were a little fussier than the desserts I usually prepared (I loved a gorgeously decorated pastry, but as the cafe's only baker, I had to focus on speed and taste, not appearance), but these were simple enough and impressive-looking enough that I was willing to make the effort for a special event.

I watched as she took a huge bite of the cupcake and chewed with a surprisingly serious look on her face. Was the flavor combination too out-there for her? Maybe too sweet? Not sweet enough?

Finally, she swallowed and said, "I sure hope you have an extra cupcake for Kimberly Johnson because if you're going to pump her for information, this will definitely loosen her lips."

Jae and I shared a quick glance before I said, "Why would we need to butter her up if we're just here to talk about the internship program?"

Felice gave me a *girl, please* look. "Did you think I was just a conveniently chatty city hall employee last time you were here? You didn't think that the information I shared with you was, I don't know . . . oddly specific to your case?"

"How . . . why . . ." I gaped at this woman, who knew WAY too much, just sitting there calmly eating the rest of her cupcake as if she hadn't just rocked my world.

"Your boyfriend isn't the only infamous one around here, dear. You've solved how many murder cases now? And then the mayor's wife dies in your town and suddenly you're hanging around asking questions . . . Did you really think I wouldn't be able to put two and two together?" She shook her head. "Youths."

Jae stared at her. "You're just like my receptionist, Millie. Is being oddly perceptive and knowing everything that's going on a requirement for receptionists in this county?"

"Millie Barnes? We do Aqua Zumba together every Friday and Tai Chi on Mondays. How else are we supposed to exchange information?"

There was a lot for me to unpack regarding all that, but I wanted to clear something up first. "Um, you're right that I wanted to talk to you to get more information for my investigation. But I hope you don't think that's the only reason I brought you snacks and tea. I know it looks like I'm just using you, but it's not like I had an ulterior motive. Well, not *just* an ulterior motive? I'm making this worse, aren't I?"

Felice reached out and patted my hand. "I get what you're saying, so no need to twist yourself up in knots over this. As I told you before, I'm very fond of Mayor Reyes and I was fond of Yvonne as well. If I can help in any way, don't hesitate to ask."

I sighed in relief and handed her my business card. "This has my number on it, so if you learn anything that you think will help the case, feel free to contact me. And I did in fact bring extra goodies for Kimberly Johnson, so we should probably head over there soon."

"Make sure to ask her about Councilman Foster. He used to butt heads with Mayor Reyes all the time, but lately he's been pretending to be all buddy-buddy with her and I don't like it. I definitely don't trust it. See what she knows about the situation. As the head of the interns, she's better placed than me to get all the gossip since she's involved with every department here. She treats the interns well and they're very loyal to her." She smiled meaningfully at us.

Jae and I thanked her and made our way to the second floor, which housed most of the employee offices.

"I can't believe she knows Millie and that there's some sort of receptionist gossip group between the two towns," Jae said as we walked down the long, carpeted hallway. "I need to have a talk with her."

"About what? You're not upset that she's talking about you, are you? You know it's nothing serious. She adores you."

"I'm not upset, I'm impressed! Your godmothers are great at ferreting out information, but most of their connections are in Shady Palms. If Millie has access to the Shelbyville rumor mill, she'd be a great asset in our investigations."

I smiled at that. "*Our* investigations? And to think, not all that long ago, you were begging me to not get involved in these cases."

"Well, things are different now. Adeena needs you. As long as you're safe, I don't mind you helping out. And the best way to ensure your safety is to be here with you. So yeah. *Our* investigations."

He really was too good to me, wasn't he? If he could get involved in my interests, as weird and dangerous as they were, then maybe I should learn more about his.

I reached out and gave his hand a squeeze. "When we've got time later, why don't you teach me that trading card game you love so much?"

He looked at me as if I'd announced that Michael Jordan was coming out of retirement to play a charity game with Jae's amateur basketball league.

"We are on a mission right now, so I need to focus, but I love you and how willing you are to try new things for me. You're the best."

Now it was my chance to stare at him. Did he seriously just drop the *L*-word? For the first time ever? In response to me wanting to learn a card game?

At this point, we'd reached the internship program office, so I decided to obsess about that later so I could focus on the present task.

I knocked on the closed door and entered after a voice said to come in. Kimberly Johnson was a short Black woman in her late forties. Her desk was covered with folders and stacks of documents arranged in a way that was messy but still organized. The dark wood of the bookshelves matched her desk and the shelves were equally stuffed with an array of binders and folders as well as several rows of books. I was dying to take a peek at the titles, but that seemed way too forward for a first meeting, so I dialed down my nosiness and pasted a professional smile on my face. After a brief greeting and introduction, she got down to business.

"Thank you so much for coming all the way out here to inquire about our internship and job placement programs. I consider it a huge compliment that neighboring towns have recognized the impact these programs have had in Shelbyville and that you want to implement them in your own communities." She handed us each a pamphlet. "I don't know how much Zack told you, but these are the basics. Look them over and I'll be happy to answer any questions you might have."

"Thank you for taking the time to talk with us. I brought you some snacks from my cafe. Feel free to enjoy them now while Dr. Jae and I read these pamphlets, or save them for break time with your interns later."

Jae set down the boxed coffee and assorted pastries on the table she indicated, and we both started reading the information she'd handed us. Even though this meeting was mostly an excuse to find out more about the different players in Shelbyville City Hall and see who had it out for Yvonne, Mayor Reyes, or both, I had a genuine interest in developing this program for Shady Palms.

Shady Palms High already implemented an apprenticeship program that allowed students to work part-time for school credit and real-world experience. This program was how we'd found our previous employee, Katie, who'd left to attend college and had recommended Leslie in her place. There was talk of opening a technical college in Shady Palms, and a program like this would be perfect for those future students. Not every kid wanted or needed a university education, and this program would help those looking for alternatives.

I looked up from my reading material to ask Kimberly a question and noticed her studying the open pastry box in front of her rather intently. "Would you like me to explain the different items? You don't have any food allergies, do you?"

"No food allergies, thankfully. They just all look delicious, so I wasn't sure where to start. The minute my interns find out there's free food in here, they'll converge like a swarm of locusts and pick this box clean. I need to choose before they get here."

I'd packed all the seasonal items as well as the staples, so I explained what was in each dessert. "I recommend them all, of course, but the items I created for the Corn Festival are only available this month. Those cupcakes are my latest experiment."

Like the receptionist had predicted, Kimberly went right for the ginataang mais cupcakes. "Before I shove this in my face, do either of you have any questions for me?"

While this was going on, Jae had taken out his notebook and been jotting down questions. "Yes, actually. I know that this program was Mayor Reyes's vision, but how long did it take from planning to actual implementation? And what issues did you run into in the beginning?"

"It took about fifteen months from the initial planning stage to our soft test run of five new interns. Zack was part of that inaugural class. And I'd say it took roughly three years for it to grow and reach the stage where we could add the additional job placement program for our interns who graduated, as well as other qualified individuals in the area. As for issues . . ."

She let out a huff of annoyance. "Just the usual things to expect. Funding battles. Spreading the word about the new initiatives to the people and areas we most want to help. Convincing the townspeople that the programs are important enough to the town's economy to justify raising taxes. And of course, having to deal with the older members of the council who were happy with the way things have always been. Who wondered why we needed a new initiative when we already had interns helping out. Quite a few of them complained that our new interns didn't have the right 'pedigree' to be working in politics. Their words, obviously, not mine."

"Pedigree?" I repeated. "They're not dogs competing for a blue ribbon."

Kimberly's lips quirked at that. "Mayor Reyes basically said the same thing and then asked if they thought *she* had the right pedigree to work in politics. That shut up all but one of them. But Councilman Foster has always been the type to say the quiet part out loud and not care about 'woke nonsense.' Though apparently, he finally realized that nonsense was popular with the constituents, so he's been backing all her programs lately. Total one-eighty from before, but I'm not going to complain about him finally getting on the right side of history."

I tried not to look too excited about that bit of information. This was the guy that the receptionist had mentioned earlier.

"Oh, that's interesting. So the guy who started as the biggest opposition actually switched sides and became one of the mayor's main supporters? I wonder what changed his mind."

"I don't want to imply anything about our current mayor, but with her predecessor, there were rumors that he had various methods of coercing the members of the council to vote his way. This council member in particular was known as someone who could be easily bought, though there was never an actual accusation let alone an investigation into those rumors. It could all be talk, but let's just say this wouldn't be the first time the councilman voted against his original stance."

"Oh wow. Thanks for sharing that with us, but aren't you worried there will be repercussions for you talking about this?" Jae asked.

She shrugged. "Mayor Reyes is my boss and the only person I answer to. I haven't said anything negative against her, talked about anything confidential, or provided evidence for or against the rumors I mentioned. Also, I hate that guy. So it doesn't hurt me none."

I could see why the receptionist had wanted me to talk to Kimberly. She wasn't going to sneak around and pass me confidential documents, but she knew enough about the people involved to point me in the right direction. The importance of a person like that couldn't be overlooked—they were absolutely crucial for someone like me, who relied on connections and community for my investigations.

We chatted a bit more and I contemplated asking Kimberly about Yvonne or if she had insight regarding Mayor Reyes's personal life but decided not to push my luck. She'd already given us a wealth of information and I knew better than to push my sources too hard and make them suspicious.

We exchanged business cards and Jae and I promised to follow up once we'd put together a proposal to bring to Mayor Gunderson's attention.

After stopping at the reception desk to thank Felice for her help, Jae and I made our way to Blue Violet Boutique for his personal styling session with Quinn. The boutique was closed when we got there, but we were a little early for our appointment so decided to wait in the car and go over the information we learned.

"Obviously our next step is to talk to Councilman Foster. If he's been one of Mayor Reyes's biggest detractors yet suddenly started backing her on her most important issues, there might be strings attached to his support."

I nodded. "I have no idea how we can connect him to Yvonne, but if nothing else, he might be able to point us in another direction. I just wonder how to approach him."

"We don't live in Shelbyville, so we can't pretend to be concerned constituents that he has to listen to. I wonder if we can get Zack or Chuy to help us out."

We batted around ideas for a while until we noticed that Quinn was late. "Should we give her another few minutes?" Jae asked.

"Why don't you text her? If something came up, better we know now so we don't waste more of our time. I need to get back to the cafe to help close, and I was hoping to get a little more time in the kitchen to finalize the menu for the weekend."

Jae sent Quinn a quick text and his phone started ringing almost immediately. Seeing that it was Quinn calling, he put her on speaker-phone.

"Jae! I'm so sorry I'm late. I had to take my dog on an emergency vet visit and we're just getting out now. Is it—"

"Oh no, is your dog OK?" I'd planned on just listening to their conversation, but hearing about a sick pet made it difficult for me to stay quiet.

"Lila?" Quinn sounded confused for a moment. "Oh, you have me on speakerphone, you're probably driving. Anyway, Cleo's OK, thank goodness. But I'm a little behind schedule. Do you mind waiting an-other fifteen minutes or so until I arrive? Or would you prefer to re-schedule?"

Jae glanced at me, probably since I was the one who needed to get back to work. It was still pretty early, so I said, "We're already here, so we might as well do it today, if that still works for you. And no need to rush. I'm glad your dog's OK."

I heard her sigh with relief. "Thanks for being so understanding. Be there soon."

Exactly fifteen minutes later, Jae and I saw Quinn pull up in an old but well-taken-care-of sedan. We got out at the same time she did, and I squealed when I saw her dog.

"Oh my gulay, you have a doxie too?!"

Quinn, who had the dog wrapped in a soft blanket, kissed the top of the dog's head. "This is my baby, Cleopatra Louise, but she goes by

Cleo. We had a bit of a scare earlier, but now I know she's learned how to take the lid off a plastic container of chocolate-covered almonds. Won't be making that mistake again."

Cleo was a brown short-haired mini dachshund just like Longganisa, but she seemed to be considerably older since there was a bit of gray around her muzzle. She wore a cute bandana printed with sparkly crowns, and peered out from her blanket burrito with a calm, queenly expression. I asked if I could pet her and held my fingers in front of Cleo after Quinn said yes. After a quick sniff, the dog bowed her head and let me pet her. What a good girl.

"Let me drop her upstairs and we can get started on your styling session, Jae."

"Could she be with us during the appointment? I'd be happy to watch her while you're helping Jae."

Quinn hesitated. "Yvonne didn't like having her in the shop since she was worried that she'd get dog hair on our clothes. And she's getting up there in age, so if she has an accident in the store . . ."

"I could carry her, if that helps. I'd love to spend more time with her. She seems so sweet, and I already spent too much money on my last shopping trip, so it'd be nice to have a distraction while Jae shops."

She smiled. "That would actually be a big help. I want to keep an eye on her for the next few hours in case her condition changes and we need to rush back to the vet. Just make sure not to set her down and keep an eye out if she needs to potty."

"Why don't I give her a quick walk before we head into the shop? Just in case. You and Jae can get started without me."

Quinn unwrapped Cleo and set her down, handing me the blanket (which I was pretty sure had been hand crocheted using the softest yarn in the world) and Cleo's leash with a handy poop bag attachment on it. "I appreciate it. She can't move the way she used to, but she loves a good walk."

Same, girl.

Jae followed Quinn into the boutique, and Cleo and I strolled around the neighborhood, enjoying the crisp fall air. Cleo's jaunty bandana added style points to her look, but not a lot of warmth. Considering she was older and sick, I wondered if she'd appreciate something warmer. I used the spare key Jae gave me to pop the trunk, remembering that we'd recently picked up an order of the screen-printed tees (for both pets and humans) that Naoko, our cafe's merch designer and the daughter of my friend Yuki, had just prepared for us to sell at the Corn Festival. Would Quinn think it too forward of me to dress her dog? Well, if either she or Cleo didn't like it, we could just remove the shirt.

After sifting through the designs, I settled on the shirt with a chibi Corn King and Corn Queen holding hands with a sentient cup of coffee bearing the Brew-ha Cafe logo. Cleo must've been used to wearing clothes because she didn't put up a fuss when I slipped the shirt over her head and front paws, adjusting the bandana so it hung over the front of the shirt. Properly clothed, the two of us set out on our walk.

The boutique was situated on a street with several other upscale-looking shops: an antique store, jewelry store, and perfumery all sat next to the boutique, and farther up the street was a store that seemed to sell only olive oil and olive oil–related products. Cleo paused in front of the olive oil shop, and I wondered if she was familiar with the store or owner. Sure enough, the bells above the door tinkled and an older Black woman greeted us.

"Well, hello there! Is that little Miss Cleo I see?"

Cleo walked over to the woman slowly, her fiercely wagging tail the only sign of how excited she was to see the shop owner. The woman stooped down to pet Cleo, her knees cracking and a slight "oof!" showing her discomfort.

"Are you OK? Would you like me to hold Cleo up to make it easier for you to pet her?"

The woman chuckled, waving her hand at me. "Give it another ten years or so, and your knees will sound just like mine, believe you me. I don't believe we've met before. I'm Gladys Stokes, the proprietor of the Olive Oil Emporium. We've got the finest selection of olive oil and artisanal goods in town," she added with a wink.

I smiled. "Nice to meet you, Ms. Stokes. I'm Lila Macapagal, and I co-own the Brew-ha Cafe in Shady Palms. I'm just taking Cleo on a walk while Quinn has a styling session with my boyfriend."

"Call me Gladys. Glad to see that Quinn's staying busy after that nasty business. I was worried she'd have to close the store after losing Yvonne."

Interesting. This woman clearly knew Quinn and Yvonne, which meant I may have finally found an objective outsider who could tell me more about them. I just needed a way to get her to talk without sounding too ghoulish or nosy.

I fixed a concerned look on my face. "I hope not. She's been really great, and I think she has some fun designs. She said she'd have to hire more help, but there was no replacing Yvonne."

Gladys sighed. "I'm sure she thinks that. Wish she had more faith in herself."

At my questioning look, she said, "I've known Quinn and Yvonne since they opened that boutique almost twenty years ago. The Olive Oil Emporium has been going strong for over forty years, so I take it upon myself to get to know the new shops and help them out if I can. You said you co-own a cafe? Then you should know how tough it is to run your own business."

"The only reason my cafe could even get off the ground is with the support of my business partners. And don't even get me started on how much I need them to deal with the day-to-day." I thought about what it'd be like trying to run the cafe on my own and shook my head. "Poor Quinn. My co-owners are also my best friends, so whenever I try to put myself in her shoes . . ."

I couldn't even imagine the horror. The strength it would take to just get out of bed, not to mention having to put on a brave face and return to the place you built together and try to keep it going.

"Those two were quite a duo. Quinn had the talent and Yvonne had the ambition. That store wouldn't have lasted this long without both of them giving it their all. But as Yvonne became more involved with her wife's career, she had less and less time for Quinn and the store." Gladys shook her head. "Quinn has more experience running that boutique on her own than she thinks. But she'd gotten so used to deferring to Yvonne, she doesn't think she has what it takes to carry on without her."

"That's a shame. Does Quinn have any family or close friends who can help her with the shop?"

She shook her head again. "Quinn doesn't talk much about her family, but from what I gather, they're not close. Yvonne had a falling-out with her own family when she moved out here, so for the longest time, they were each other's only family. I had the two of them over to dinner so many times over the years, I consider them part of my family as well. But Mayor Reyes reached out to Yvonne's parents recently and got them to reconcile. I know Yvonne had siblings because she told me she was excited about getting to know her nieces and nephews. One of the last times we talked, she told me she was planning a trip back home around Thanksgiving. Tragic to think that'll never happen now."

Gladys and I quietly petted Cleo as that statement hung in the air between us.

"I appreciate you sharing all this with me, but I have to ask why. I mean, we just met. How do you know I'm not going to be running my mouth about this?"

Gladys caressed Cleo's head and Cleo nuzzled against her ankles in response. "Quinn trusted you with Cleo. That's basically like trusting you with her life."

"She doesn't even know me like that. She was just—"

Gladys held up her hand. "Trust me. Cleo is not just a pet to Quinn. Especially now that Yvonne's gone."

"Because of the comfort and company?"

"Because they adopted Cleo together after they moved to Shelbyville. She was their baby. I wouldn't be surprised if she looks at Cleo and the store as her last links to her best friend."

Quinn and Yvonne adopted a dog together? Did that mean . . .

"Were those two ever . . . I mean, do you think . . ."

She smiled. "No, they were never lovers. They just—"

"Excuse me. I'm sorry to interrupt, but are you open?"

A voice behind me suddenly cut into our conversation, making me jump. "Oh, sorry about that. I didn't mean to block the entrance."

A middle-aged Latine woman dressed in a puffy coat that was way too heavy for fall gave me a tight smile. "It's fine. I didn't mean to interrupt, but I didn't want you to think I was eavesdropping since I was kind of hovering here."

"Welcome to the Olive Oil Emporium," Gladys said, stepping aside so the woman could enter. "I'm the owner, Gladys Stokes. Please let me know if you need help with anything. I'll be right in in a second."

The woman thanked her and swept inside, and Gladys gave Cleo one last pet. "Well, duty calls, and Queen Cleo here is still waiting for her walk. I hope you come by again. Since you run a cafe, you should check out my various olive oils. Excellent for cooking and baking."

I grinned at her. "I'll be sure to stop by with my partners on our next day off. We're always up for trying out local products and experimenting with our offerings. Thanks for the talk, Gladys."

"Tell Quinn to bring Cleo over for dinner sometime. I got something special I want them to try." She gave Cleo one final caress and smiled at me. "Stay safe, honey."

Chapter Thirteen

After bidding us goodbye, Gladys waved us off and returned to her shop. Cleo trotted alongside me as we made our way around the block, not heading back to the boutique until she'd taken care of her business. I cleaned my hands with the wipes I carried in my purse then wrapped Cleo in her blanket and entered the store. "How's it go— Whoa."

Jae stood in front of the full-length multisided mirror in the back as Quinn fussed with his outfit. He was dressed in a slim-fitting maroon suit that somehow highlighted all of his best assets and drew attention to ones I didn't even know he had.

He met my eyes in the mirror. "You approve?"

It took everything in me to not shout, YES, ABSOLUTELY, BUY IT NOW AND WEAR IT OUT OF THE STORE, so I just nodded like a bobblehead on the dashboard of a car hitting every single pothole on a Chicago street.

"I agree, he looks wonderful. But do you think this is a little too matchy-matchy with your dress? If Mayor Gunderson's soiree is meant to be black tie, wouldn't a tuxedo with maroon or burgundy accents be more appropriate?" Quinn tilted her head from side to side, analyzing Jae's appearance. "Though this suit would be an excellent addition to any wardrobe. Last time you were here, I remember you mentioning an anniversary dinner?"

"That's right! I'll be wearing the jumpsuit Jae bought me, and if I pair it with the burgundy velvet shoes from the soiree outfit, it'd be a nice complement to this suit. What do you think, Jae?"

"I think I need any outfit that has you eyeing me the way you did when you entered the store," Jae said with a grin. "What, did you think I didn't see you? Thanks for the compliment, by the way."

"Someone's a little full of themselves, aren't they, Cleo?" I asked the tiny dog in my arms, who gave a big yawn in response. "Yes, I know he's right, but that's not the point here."

"You two are really cute together, you know that?" Quinn handed Jae a tux on a hanger. "We don't carry a wide selection of tuxedoes, so if this doesn't work for you, we can go through the catalog together and have something shipped here."

Jae went back to the fitting room and I brought up my meeting with Ms. Gladys Stokes. "By the way, Cleo and I had a nice chat with one of your neighbors. The woman who owns the olive oil store?"

Quinn's eyes lit up. "Gladys! Isn't she amazing? She's been running that shop almost as long as I've been alive and I don't see her stopping anytime soon. You have to try her Meyer lemon olive oil, it's so delicious. And her soap is fantastic, too."

I made a mental note about the bath products at the store since Elena would definitely want to check that out. And Meyer lemon olive oil would probably pair well with calamansi. Hmm . . .

"Yeah, she seems like a real powerhouse. I'm sure she was a huge help when you first set up shop here. It's not easy being an entrepreneur, especially when you're new in town."

Quinn stopped fussing with the clothes she'd hung on the rack for Jae to try on. "She told you all that?"

"Only because I asked how she knew you. She said something about wanting to have dinner with you soon, that she had something special for you and Cleo to test."

Quinn's expression smoothed out. "Oh, of course. She's working on a new pet care line of olive oil–based products for all the 'bougie pet owners' in town. Her words, not mine. She has me bring Cleo by to test whatever she's whipped up that day. Cleo and I love being her guinea pigs. Whether it's for our hair or skin or to fill our stomachs, Gladys never disappoints."

"It's nice that you have someone nearby looking out for you. Does your family ever come to visit?"

Quinn reached out for Cleo and I handed her over. "Cleo and Yvonne and Gladys are my family. They're the ones who matter."

Gladys had said that Quinn seemed to be on bad terms with her family and she was definitely right. "I'm sorry. That must make losing Yvonne extra tough."

My family was my biggest source of stress but they were also my greatest supporters. I couldn't imagine not being able to lean on them during my darkest times. And now Quinn's tiny found family had become that much smaller.

Quinn didn't respond to my statement, instead remarking on Cleo's clothing. "I just noticed Cleo's shirt. Did you put this on her?"

"Yes, it's a little chilly outside and I wanted to make sure she was comfortable during our walk. Is that OK? Sorry if it was weird for me to dress your dog without asking."

"Not at all. Thanks for being so thoughtful. And this T-shirt is so cute! Do you sell these at your cafe?"

"My friend's daughter is a young up-and-coming artist. We commission her to design most of the merch we sell at the shop."

"So you not only have delicious food and drinks, but you sell cute merch like this? I need to stop by sometime."

"We also sell herbal teas, bath and beauty products, seasonal plants, and other things like that. At least once a month we hold special events and workshops, plus we have a liquor license, so we stock drinks from the local winery and brewery." I grinned at her. "The Brew-ha Cafe's got a lot going on. And best of all, we're pet-friendly. I'd love for you and Cleo to stop by. You could meet my doxie, Longganisa. She's our shop's unofficial mascot."

"And people don't mind having her in the store?"

"Nope. We keep her away from the kitchen and other food prep areas, she sleeps in her bed in my office most of the time, and when she is in the cafe, I keep her leashed and wait for the customers to come to us if they want to pet her. We don't approach anyone we don't already know in case they're allergic or uncomfortable. Plus, there's a designated area for pets, and they're only allowed in that specific spot. It's not perfect, but it's worked so far. We also plan on installing air purifiers eventually."

"I wonder if my customers would warm up to the idea of Cleo being a shop dog. Now that she's getting on in age, I'd prefer to have her close to me. And without Yvonne, my hours are even longer than before. I don't like leaving her alone for so long."

"You could keep her behind the counter or in your office, like I do. Having a designated space that keeps her near but away from the customers has worked surprisingly well for me."

"Thanks, Lila. That gives me one less thing to worry about,

especially after our little health scare." Quinn kissed the top of Cleo's head. "Now what's taking your boyfriend so long?"

"I'm just finishing up! Sorry, I'm not used to wearing a bow tie, so it took me a minute to figure out," Jae said, emerging from behind the curtain. "What do you think? I can't tell if the bow tie makes me look fashionable or ridiculous."

I read lots of romance novels and always admired the authors' ability to describe the physical attractiveness of the love interest in a way that was both eloquent and desirable. I, sadly, lacked that particular talent. Words failed me as I took in the sheer hotness that was Dr. Jae Park in formal wear.

Before I could bumble my way through an inappropriate compliment (inappropriate both in the subject matter and in how it couldn't come close to describing how good he looked), a long, low whistle interrupted us. The three of us turned to the front of the shop to see Mayor Reyes and Zack making their way to us. Mayor Reyes was the one who'd whistled, and she stopped in front of us with a grin.

"You look amazing, Dr. Jae! Is this for Mayor Gunderson's soiree?" At our nods, she said, "That's why I'm here. I was hoping Quinn would work her usual magic and find an appropriate outfit for me."

"You're still going?" Quinn asked. "Even after . . ."

"The mayor may be in mourning, but she can't neglect her duties," Zack said, warning Quinn off. "It's not like she's going to have fun. This is a work obligation. Don't make this—"

"Zack, it's fine. Of course it looks bad that I'm attending a party so soon after Yvonne's passing," Mayor Reyes said, putting a hand on his shoulder. The two exchanged glances in a silent conversation before Zack sighed and stepped away from Quinn. Mayor Reyes turned her strong gaze back to her deceased wife's best friend. "But trust me when I say I have very particular, very *personal* reasons to want to be at this soiree. And to pull it off, I need the perfect outfit. Something powerful. Something that shows that I will not let them win."

Quinn studied the mayor for a moment before nodding her head. "I've got you. But I'm going to need to order a few things since our selection is limited right now. I'll call you when they arrive."

"Thanks, Quinn. I knew I could count on you," the mayor said. She turned toward me and Jae. "Are you two almost done here? I'd love to treat you both to lunch to thank you for handling the accommodations for Yvonne's family. I got off the phone with your friend Xander shortly before this and he is absolutely delightful."

Quinn handed Cleo back to me and moved toward Jae, bending down to mark the places the tux needed to be taken in. "I just need a few minutes to finish this, and they'll be good to go."

"Excellent. Zack, can you go ahead and put in a reservation for four at the Little Gem Cafe? I'll wait and walk over with our guests."

Zack left and Mayor Reyes turned her attention back to Quinn. "I'm sorry for his overprotectiveness. You know how he is. But considering what you're also going through, he had no right to talk to you like that."

Quinn kept her eyes on the pin she was carefully inserting in Jae's pant leg. "Like you said, this is nothing new for him. Though considering how disrespectful he was to Yvonne, you could stand to be a little more forceful with him."

There was a long, uncomfortable silence that remained unbroken until Quinn inserted the last pin.

"There we go." She stood up and checked over her work. "What do you think?"

"I think I can't wait to pick up my finished outfits," Jae said with a grin. "Thanks so much, Quinn. I'll take all the casual wear now and put a down payment on the tux and suit."

While those two handled the transaction, Mayor Reyes gave Cleo a friendly pat. "Queen Cleo seems to have taken a liking to you. She's a good judge of character, so that says a lot about you."

"I have my own doxie, so she must sense my love," I said, giving her a snuggle. "I hear that Quinn and Yvonne adopted her together. Do you have any pets, Mayor Reyes?"

"Unfortunately, my schedule can be rather unforgiving, and I didn't feel right bringing one home when we were out so much. Yvonne was an animal lover, so even though she was disappointed, she understood. She would just visit Quinn and Cleo when she needed a fix." Mayor Reyes smiled, but I didn't miss how her eyes watered at the mention of her deceased wife. "I always told her we'd get an entire menagerie once things calmed down at city hall, and we'd lie in bed imagining the little animal haven we'd build on our grounds. Guess I shouldn't have kept putting it off."

She sniffled and dropped her gaze to root around in her purse. "Excuse me, the pollen is really strong today, I need to find a tissue."

I shifted Cleo to one arm and pulled out a packet of tissues from my purse for the mayor. "Here you go. Allergy season has been so rough this year."

"Tell me about it." Mayor Reyes dabbed at her eyes and turned away to blow her nose. "I think I need some fresh air. I'll wait for you and Jae outside."

I watched her throw out the tissue in the wastebasket by the register and head out the door without bothering to say goodbye to Quinn. Either she was an amazing actress, which meant she should shoot to the top of my suspect list, or she was exactly what she seemed to be— a woman dealing with the tragic loss of her wife, a woman who couldn't allow herself to grieve publicly due to her position. I hated having to pry into a person's secrets during such a vulnerable time, but I also couldn't dismiss the possibility that she was involved in her wife's death in some way.

Murder investigations were so much easier when I didn't like the people involved. Here's hoping our lunch with Zack and Mayor Reyes would answer some questions and allow me to cross the mayor off my list. But still, I couldn't let myself sympathize with my suspects too much. Not when Adeena's freedom was on the line.

Chapter Fourteen

R eady to go?"
    Jae's voice broke into my thoughts. He shifted all his shop-
ping bags to one hand to pet Cleo. "I hope Nisa doesn't get jealous
that we've been cheating on her with another dog."

Jae and I gave Cleo one last pet before I handed her back to Quinn.
Cleo, who'd been super chill inside her blanket burrito the whole
time, suddenly started whimpering and wriggling in Quinn's arms,
trying to get back to me.

"Seems like she really enjoyed your walk," Quinn said, staring
down at her dog in awe. "She always loved a little stroll, but now that
she's gotten older, she's usually happy to just sit next to me on the
couch and watch TV."

Same, girl. Cleo and I had a lot in common.

"Sorry, Cleo, but we've got to go. Mayor Reyes is waiting for us
outside. And if I'm going to make it back to the cafe in time, we should

get moving," I added, glancing at Jae, who'd been petting and cooing at Cleo the whole time.

Jae reluctantly gave the dog one last pet and said his goodbyes. "She'll be here when I pick up my altered tux and suit, right?"

Quinn laughed. "She'll be here. And you're free to visit anytime in between then. In fact, please come. Cleo could use the company and I could use the business."

"Both of you should stop by the Brew-ha Cafe sometime, too. I'd love to introduce Cleo to Longganisa."

"Sounds like a plan." Quinn picked up Cleo's chubby paw to wave to us.

"See you soon, ladies. Take care now!" Jae and I waved goodbye and the sounds of Cleo whining for us followed us out of the store.

"Way to make another Shelbyvillain fall in love with you," I said as we joined the mayor on the sidewalk.

I waited for Mayor Reyes to comment on the term "Shelbyvillain," (the not-so-flattering term that some people from Shady Palms used to refer to people in Shelbyville), but she was staring down the street, a look of alarm and confusion on her face.

"Mayor?" I asked. "Are you OK?"

She suddenly seemed to notice we were there. "Oh! Sorry. It's just, I felt like I was being watched and I obviously wasn't, but then I saw someone . . ." she trailed off. "Anyway, it's nothing. Just my eyes playing tricks on me."

"If you feel like you're being watched, you should let my brother know," Jae said. "We still don't know if you're also a target and—"

"Good idea. I'll be sure to let him know later. But right now, I'm starving and Zack is waiting for us."

The mayor was good at putting on a brave face, but even she couldn't hide how shaken up she was. Still, her tone let me know she wouldn't appreciate us pushing any harder, so I made a note to bring it up to Detective Park myself later.

I gestured for her to lead the way. "What kind of restaurant are we going to?"

"It's called the Little Gem Cafe! It's on the next block and is absolutely darling. Yvonne discovered it, and it became our favorite place to hold business lunches. They also do a lovely date-night special," she added as she guided us into the cozy space.

The restaurant wasn't very large, but it managed to feel light and airy yet warm and comfortable at the same time. Similar to the Brew-ha Cafe, there was quite a bit of greenery sprinkled throughout the room, which perhaps led to the feeling of freshness, and the lighting was soft but not dim. The small tables were covered in red gingham cloth, and the mismatched plates and cutlery somehow looked charming rather than cheap (a look that Tita Rosie's Kitchen, with our literal bargain basement goods, hadn't managed to pull off until we commissioned Elena's mom to make all our tableware).

After a quick greeting to the hostess, Mayor Reyes led us to a semi-private booth in the back where Zack was waiting. He stood up until everyone was seated and gestured to a waiting server, who placed a breadbasket and dish of butter on the table before filling Zack's and Mayor Reyes's wineglasses.

The server held up the bottle. "Would either of you care for some wine? This is Mayor Reyes's favorite rosé."

Jae and I both agreed to a small pour. The wine was crisp and bright and deliciously fruity. It had just a touch of sweetness, but not enough to taste like a dessert wine. The bread had a crisp crust, and a curl of steam escaped when I broke it in half. The insides were soft and lightly dense, a perfect match to the salted butter on the table. I already liked the place.

After poring over the menu, Mayor Reyes and I both went with the French onion soup. "It's not very graceful to eat, but this place has the best French onion soup I've ever had," Mayor Reyes said. "Lunch is on me, so no need to hold back. They have lovely crostini and salads as well."

I chose another of her recommendations to go with my soup, the roasted heirloom tomato salad with burrata cheese. Jae was craving something simple (but not so simple that he'd actually choose a salad as a meal), so he went with Zack's suggestion of a BLT with a side of truffle fries. Zack and the mayor both ordered the restaurant's signature salad with added protein, chicken for him and salmon for her. After the server took our order and poured water for everyone, Mayor Reyes got to the point of our lunch meeting.

"I'm not going to beat around the bush," Mayor Reyes said, laying her napkin on her lap. "I know you don't have an invitation to Mayor Gunderson's soiree. I know this because I've seen the guest list and you two aren't on it. So there must be a reason you lied to Quinn about needing clothes for the party and I'd like to know what it is."

I should've known that little white lie wouldn't get past her. Did I tell her the truth? If so, how much of it? I glanced over at Jae, who nodded to indicate that he'd follow my lead, and then studied Zack and the mayor. There was something about Zack that was slippery; something told me that honesty was a bargaining chip, not a policy for him. But Mayor Reyes didn't seem like that. She was smooth, but she wasn't slick like him.

My gut said that she'd respect me for speaking the truth. Besides, it's not like I'd gain anything from lying to her. Her receptionist already told me that my investigation skills (some would call it meddling, but potato potahto) were known here in Shelbyville, after all. And she was employing my aunt's boyfriend as a private investigator. She must have some idea of what I was doing. Here's hoping I was right about all that (and also, you know, that she wasn't the killer), otherwise she could prove to be a huge obstacle.

"I'm sure you've heard that I've been involved in several investigations in Shady Palms. What I'm about to say isn't because I'm biased, or at least not entirely because of that. But Adeena is not a killer. She's my best friend, so of course I'd say that, but that also means I know her better than anyone. She had no motive to kill Yvonne. She was only in the corn maze because we were competing against each other for fun. Elena and I were with her that entire day right up until then and there was no hint of her planning the murder of a woman she literally met that morning. It just doesn't make sense for Adeena to be the main suspect."

Mayor Reyes smiled at me. Not in amusement or condescension, but almost like a challenge. "Murder rarely makes sense, my dear. As for motive, Yvonne was flirting with Adeena's girlfriend, wasn't she? What's her name . . . Elena? They could have gotten into an argument over that, and it ended tragically."

I set my wineglass aside. "If you're using Yvonne's flirting as a possible cause for her death, you realize that means you also had a motive, right? Your wife was chatting up another woman right in front of you. I'd say you would have more reason to kill Yvonne than Adeena."

"Watch yourself," Zack warned. "Mayor Reyes is above reproach. Don't you dare—"

"Enough, Zack. No one is above reproach. And she has a point. If I'm going to assert that Adeena had a motive because of Yvonne's flirtation, of course that line of reasoning could easily be turned around on me. It's not true, of course," Mayor Reyes added. "But I see what you're saying."

"Putting the motive aside, what if it wasn't planned?" Zack asked. "Yvonne could be very provoking. What if they argued and fought and Adeena killed her in the heat of passion?"

"Adeena doesn't carry a knife. Her father and brother think it's too dangerous, so they gave her pepper spray and an alarm for self-defense." I took a sip of water. "She may have had the opportunity, but she had no means or motive."

"You weren't kidding when you said you've done your fair share of investigating." Mayor Reyes took a sip of wine, mirroring my movement. "But let's say Yvonne and Adeena had gotten into a verbal altercation and Yvonne felt threatened, so she pulled out a knife. Unlike your friend, she did carry one for protection, and for various things at work. Things escalated and Adeena ended up killing my wife in self-defense. A terrible twist of fate."

"Wait, are you suggesting that your wife attacked Adeena first?" I asked.

"I'm not suggesting anything. I'm just listing possibilities. Which is more than your town sheriff has done," Mayor Reyes added bitterly.

"That doesn't make sense though. What could they have argued about that made Yvonne so jumpy that she'd pull a knife? And even if we pretend that's what happened, why would Adeena lie about it? She could claim self-defense like you said."

"Maybe she was worried no one would believe her since the victim was married to a well-respected politician," Zack said. "So she decided to pretend she fainted and has no idea what happened."

Jae helped himself to more bread and put another roll on my plate as well. "Not Adeena. Even if it were in self-defense, she's not the kind of person to avoid the fact that somebody died as a result of her actions. She would own up to it. And if nothing else, her brother is one of the best criminal defense attorneys in the county. She may not trust the system, but she absolutely trusts her brother."

Zack looked like he was gearing up for another rebuttal but then our server arrived with our food. It had been hours since my rushed breakfast of ginataang mais, and the intoxicating smell of savory beef broth and sweet caramelized onions wafting from my bowl of soup was enough to get my stomach growling. That noise, embarrassing as it was, smoothed the crease between Mayor Reyes's brows and a softer look appeared on her face.

"Let's table that conversation for now and enjoy our lunch. Bon appétit!"

Mayor Reyes kept the conversation light for the rest of the meal, asking questions about the cafe and how I come up with the recipes, teasing Jae about his popularity amongst her staff, and telling us more about the internship program that she founded. Well, Zack used the word "founded," but that wasn't quite right since there had always been interns at city hall. I guess "revitalized" would be the more appropriate word.

He made an excellent hype man, always ready to jump in and talk up the mayor whenever he felt she was being too modest. For her part, Mayor Reyes was complimentary without gushing, funny without making it seem like she was putting on an act, and exuded a warmth and genuine curiosity that loosened us up after that rather intense conversation premeal.

As I savored an excellent cup of coffee and split a slice of flourless chocolate cake with Jae (I always had to end a meal with something sweet), Mayor Reyes gestured for the check. "You two can take your time, but Zack and I need to head back to the office. And expect a visit from Detective Park either later today or tomorrow, depending on how fast he works. I sent word to Mayor Gunderson to add you two to the soiree invitation list as part of my party."

That sudden statement distracted me so much, I bit down on my fork. Hard. "Ow! Mother eff . . ."

"Are you OK?" everyone asked, all different levels of worried.

"I'm fine. You just surprised me, that's all."

"Let me see." I tried to wave him off, but Jae would not be deterred from his dental duties. After a quick examination he said, "I was worried you chipped a tooth, but you seem to be fine."

"Never mind that. Why did you add us to the guest list?" I asked Mayor Reyes. "What's your game?"

"No game. I just figured if you're this adamant that your friend isn't the killer, you might actually find out who is. You've done this before, and you seem to be better at it than your town's police department, at the very least. I figure between you and Detective Park, there's a chance I'll find out what happened to Yvonne and why. That's what I really want."

"And you'll be happy with that? That's all you need?"

She studied me a moment before gesturing to Jae. "If someone took him from you, would you be happy with just the who, what, and why? Would them going to jail be all you needed to move on?"

When I didn't answer, she said, "Exactly. Now if you'll excuse me, I've got a town to run."

Chapter Fifteen

"T his has been an extremely long day and the sun hasn't even set yet."
Jae and I were making the drive back to Shady Palms and talking over all the information we'd learned, especially from Ms. Gladys Stokes since he hadn't been around for that.

"She seems like an excellent source of information on Yvonne, so I'm hoping the Brew-has and I can plan a trip to her store and maybe poke around a bit more. If nothing else, I'm sure they'd appreciate a chance to check out a possible new supplier."

I was right. After Jae dropped me off, I worked the last few hours of my shift, restocking small amounts of our bestsellers, bringing Longganisa around to greet our customers, handling admin duties, and all the usual day-to-day things it takes to run a cafe. But once our last customer left and Leslie switched the sign to CLOSED and locked the door, I filled everyone in on what I'd learned as we all relaxed with Adeena's drinks and the leftover pastries.

Elena said, "I've been wanting to make olive oil soap but haven't found a bulk supplier I'm happy with yet. I'd love to check out the shop with you!"

"I had no interest in those trendy olive oil lattes before, but if it'll help with the case, I'd be more than happy to give it a try and see if it's worth adding to the menu," Adeena said. "Love a good tax write-off/investigation combo."

"An olive oil cake might be a nice addition. I know citrus pairs well with olive oil, so maybe adding some calamansi to the cake itself and topping it with a calamansi glaze or serving it with calamansi marmalade would—"

A knock on the front door cut our planning short, and we turned from our position at the counter to see Detective Park waving at us. Leslie, who'd been sweeping the floor (so diligent) to let us converse privately, went to go let him in.

I stood up to greet him. "Hey, Detective Park. We just closed but we've got some leftover sweets. Would you like anything?"

Detective Park waved away my offer. "I'm having dinner with your aunt soon. I just stopped by because I've got your invitations for the soiree."

"Dang, you work fast. I wasn't expecting to see you until tomorrow at the earliest."

"It was good timing. I was already speaking to Mayor Gunderson when I got the request."

Elena perked up at that. "Did he have any useful information for your investigation?"

"He mostly railed at me for being a traitor to Shady Palms, and he can't believe I left the force to help a woman like Judy Reyes, etc., etc." Detective Park chuckled. "You should've seen his face when I told him Mayor Reyes wanted you and Jae to attend his soiree as her special guests. He thought I was joking until he saw her message. It's the little things that make this job worth it."

"I'm surprised he didn't refuse. Make up some excuse about the guest list being too full," Adeena said, wiping down the counter and passing dirty items to Leslie. "Sorry, Leslie, can you put these in the wash? Thanks. Anyway, he is the pettiest of petty benches. Which I can respect in a way, but you know. Not at times like this."

"He actually did pull that excuse. You know him well, Adeena. But his wife was also there since I wanted to question both of them, and she appealed to his better side. Said Mayor Reyes was already going through a difficult time and putting in a public appearance so soon after her wife's death meant she could be afforded some grace. And that if having you and Jae there would make her happy, there was no reason not to accommodate her." Detective Park smiled. "I'll say this for them. Mrs. Gunderson doesn't speak much, but when she does, he listens. So you have her to thank for this."

"You said you wanted to speak to both of them about Yvonne's murder. Are they suspects?" I asked.

Detective Park tilted his head side to side. "Technically. One of the reasons Mayor Reyes hired me is because Mayor Gunderson is a viable suspect, and she doesn't believe that the SPPD will actually look into him. It's my job to make sure there's as little bias as possible during this case."

"Shouldn't your job be making sure there's *no* bias in the investigation whatsoever?" Elena asked.

He shook his head. "Investigations are run by human beings, so there will always be bias involved, whether we're aware of it or not. A good investigator acknowledges that and does their best to work past it."

"Do you think the Gundersons did it? Just, you know, off the record," Adeena said. "Mayor Gunderson is full of himself, sure, but a murderer? I can't picture him wanting to get his hands dirty with something like that. His wife even less so. She's supportive, but you know, in that 'behind every successful man is a woman' kind of way."

"I think anytime a politician or someone close to them is killed, the possibilities are . . . messy. Were they killed for personal or political reasons? Both? Neither? Does the fact that it was a spouse mean Yvonne was the intended victim or was it meant to strike a blow against Mayor Reyes? Did she learn something that could've dethroned someone in power? Was she a threat in any way? These are the questions we have to answer if we want to find the truth."

"That would make sense if Mayor Reyes and Mayor Gunderson were, like, big-city politicians. But Shelbyville's population is roughly the size of a big university like UIC and Shady Palms is even smaller. Not like being the mayor here brings that much power," I said.

"Power is power, and the people who wield it rarely want to give it up. Whether it's over a company, a town, a family, or even just a single person, people have killed to keep what little they have," Detective Park said. "I get what you're saying, I do. But even with all you've seen these past couple years, I don't think you understand just how ugly people can get."

"Besides, Illinois politicians getting up to shady stuff? Like we should even be surprised by that possibility?" Adeena pointed out.

Considering the track record of the state's governors, she most definitely had a point.

"Do the Gundersons have alibis for the time of Yvonne's death?" I asked.

"Mrs. Gunderson does. She was helping out at the historical society booth and there were plenty of witnesses that placed her there. Mayor Gunderson's alibi is trickier. He claimed he was in one of the festival buildings at that time, to repair damage to his Corn King costume. The staff working that particular building can corroborate that they saw him, but no one is sure of the time."

"I was hoping to avoid Mayor Gunderson at the soiree, other than a quick greeting, but I guess Jae and I will have to make a point to talk to him and his wife. Even if she already has an alibi, she might know something important. I wonder if having Mayor Reyes around for the conversation will make it easier or more awkward."

"Speaking of which . . ."

Detective Park reached into his bag and handed over the invitations, the envelopes surprisingly heavy. The invitations themselves were printed on thick paper that somehow felt silky, with gold script on a background color that was too pretentious to be called light yellow. It probably had some bougie name like egg yolk or marigold or duckling. I said as much, and my partners gave their two cents.

"Pretty sure that's sunshine," Adeena said. "What do you think, babe?"

Elena peered at the invite. "You're close, but I think it's actually cornsilk. Which would be fitting since it's Corn Festival time."

"Oh, you're right. What a nice touch. That color choice is really quite brilliant, and the font is . . ."

This talk went on way longer than I thought possible and I regretted making a snarky art comment in front of my art-loving friends since what had started as a few facetious comments on their part had somehow spiraled into a legit conversation on color theory.

Adeena must've noticed my and Detective Park's eyes glazing over because she said, "Sorry, that started as a joke and then our art geek sides came out. All that aside, I can't believe you get to have a sexy, dangerous ballroom dance mission! I claimed dibs on that months ago."

"That's only if we got involved with an art heist, remember? And it's not like I want to go. Jae and I got caught in a lie and it just ended up working out like this. At least it'll be a good way to question people we normally wouldn't have access to. I'm hoping that shady councilman will be there."

Detective Park furrowed his brows. "What shady councilman?"

I checked my phone notes. "Uh, his name is Councilman Foster. A source told me that he was Mayor Reyes's main opposition but did an about-face in her second term."

"Isn't that a good thing?" Adeena asked. "Maybe he learned from her example and realized she was right. Rare, I know, but possible, right?"

"That would be the ideal scenario, but apparently there are rumors of him voting whichever way brought him the most money. At least, that's how it was with Mayor Reyes's predecessor. Nobody seems willing to accuse her of bribery, but the rumors surrounding him still get around."

Detective Park took out his notebook. "I haven't heard about this. Who's your source?"

I almost told him until Elena nudged me and gave me a meaningful look. Right, I finally had a bargaining chip! "You know I can't reveal my source. Unless, of course, you have information you'd like to trade. Something we wouldn't have come across in our own investigations, maybe . . . ?"

Detective Park's trademark glare, so piercing most people physically recoiled when it was directed at them, bored into my eyes, trying to get me to give up my source. But I wouldn't let him intimidate me (much)! I needed to win his little staring contest for Adeena, so I just glared back until he sighed.

"Either I've gone soft or you're too used to me by now. All right, what do you want to know?"

"Give me a second." I gestured to Adeena and Elena to follow me behind the counter for a huddle. "What should I ask? We may not get another opportunity like this, and I don't want to waste it."

"I'd like to take the lead on this, actually," Elena said. "If that's OK with you, Adeena."

Adeena shrugged. "I don't mind. That cool with you, Lila?"

The two of them turned toward me with very different looks in their eyes—Adeena, worried but confident that Elena and I could handle it, while Elena's gaze held a bit of a challenge. *Are you going to push back on this?* her eyes seemed to ask. My first instinct was to fight it. I was the one with the source. I was the one who knew Detective Park best. Adeena was *my* best friend. But then I looked at Adeena, whose eyes were ping-ponging back and forth between me and her girlfriend, and I realized how ridiculous I was being.

We weren't being scored on this. I wasn't trying to get an A+ in some Investigations fieldwork course. I wanted to save my friend. We both did. So I made a *be my guest* gesture and we followed Elena back to where Detective Park was patiently waiting.

"Mayor Reyes believes Adeena is a possible suspect since Yvonne was seen flirting with me during the Corn Festival," Elena said. "But that holds true in reverse, too. As a wife and political figure, wouldn't Mayor Reyes be more upset at her spouse's come-ons? Isn't it more likely that she's the one who confronted Yvonne in the corn maze and stabbed her? I'm not saying she planned it; I'm just saying it's possible."

"I don't think Mayor Reyes is a suspect."

"Why not?"

Detective Park did that stone-faced *I'm a hard-ass detective* expression he always used when he didn't want to answer.

Elena crossed her arms. "Detective, if you want us to give up our source, you have to give us information, remember?"

Oh OK, suddenly it's *our* source even though I was the one who actually connected with them. Just like she was the one who supposedly secured lodging for Yvonne's family despite me being the one who'd contacted Xander. Cool cool cool.

Not that I needed to be acknowledged as the one who did those things or anything like that. I was already past this. As long as we proved Adeena innocent, it didn't matter who got the acknowledgment. If she's happy then I'm happy. Right? Right.

Detective Park sighed. "What I'm about to say doesn't leave this room, do you understand me?"

Here he glanced over at Leslie, who'd just emerged from the kitchen.

"Um, all the dishes are in the washer, and I did the sweeping. Do you want me to hang around until you're done so I can mop or . . . ?"

"I'll handle the mopping, you can head home. See you tomorrow," I said.

They grabbed their belongings from my office, gave us all a tight smile, and hurried outside, locking the door behind them. Adeena, Elena, and I all turned our attention back to Detective Park.

"As I was saying, this is confidential for a number of reasons, but . . . Mayor Reyes and Yvonne were getting a divorce."

"What?!"

"Are you serious? But everyone made it seem like they were so in love!"

"Doesn't this give Mayor Reyes a stronger motive?"

"You're right, normally, I'd say it would give the mayor a stronger motive, but not in this case," Detective Park said, responding to Elena's question.

"Why not?" I asked. "This way she doesn't have to pay alimony or a divorce attorney. And as someone who cares about appearances, not only does she not have to go through the public mess of a divorce, she gets sympathy from her constituents for losing her wife in such a tragic way."

Elena nodded. "It's ghoulish, but it is a bit of a win-win for Mayor Reyes, isn't it?"

"Not in this case. Mayor Reyes comes from a wealthy family, who insisted on Yvonne signing a prenup before they'd agree to the marriage. She's not hurting for money, and she wasn't in danger of losing any either. Plus, it seems like the divorce was more of a political strategy than irreconcilable differences."

"What makes you think that?" Adeena asked.

"She basically told me. Not in so many words, but she implied that while she and Yvonne loved each other very much, being together wasn't good for her political career. She's the one who requested the divorce, by the way."

Something about Detective Park's explanation niggled at me until I glanced at my notes and remembered a previous conversation. "Wait a minute, Detective. You said Mayor Reyes wasn't hurting for money, but that contradicts something Zack told me. He mentioned Yvonne draining their joint account."

Detective Park looked impressed at my knowledge of the situation. "Yes, Yvonne did take out large chunks of money from their joint account, so there were some losses there, but they also had separate personal accounts. Mayor Reyes was hurt by Yvonne's deception, but she still remained a very wealthy woman. It wasn't the money but the betrayal that led to their divorce."

"And the fact that it could lead to a scandal, I'm sure. How did Yvonne take it?" I asked. "If it's true that they still loved each other, Yvonne didn't seem like the type to let it go without a fight. What if she confronted the mayor in the corn maze and Mayor Reyes killed her in self-defense?"

Detective Park shook his head. "She eventually accepted it. I've talked to the lawyers that were representing them and both said that it seemed mutual and cordial. Yvonne even went on the record as saying she was at fault for the divorce, and Mayor Reyes was doing what was best for both of them."

"You said 'eventually.' Which means that she didn't at first."

Suddenly, I remembered the texts that Yvonne sent to Zack. "Wait, was this before or after Yvonne messaged Zack?"

Detective Park rubbed the back of his head and I knew I was onto something.

"Zack told the mayor something about Yvonne that led to those screaming texts. I'm guessing they're also what led to the divorce since Zack cares so much about Mayor Reyes's image."

Detective Park looked away and I had to stop myself from fist pumping. I looked over at Adeena and Elena, who seemed to be thinking the same thing.

Elena smiled. "Good thing we all love queso. Because I think we all know what our next move is."

Chapter Sixteen

This is so weird. Why am I on a date with my big brother?" Adeena grumbled, using two tortilla chips to sandwich an ungodly amount of queso.

Adeena, Elena, Jae, and I had all come to the Wily Cow Emporium during Wednesday Happy Hour to talk to Zack again, but this time we were accompanied by Amir and his girlfriend, Sana Williams. Amir was good about gathering info and sharing it with us at my family's dinners, but he never came to investigate with us. As a respectable lawyer, he had clearly defined boundaries of what he was willing and able to do.

"You realize that makes it sound like we're the ones dating, right? Which is extremely creepy?" Amir wiped his hands on a napkin, as if trying to scrub away the grossness of that statement.

Sana laughed. "Sorry to barge in on your fun. I guess going on a triple date with your brother isn't your idea of a good time."

"Don't get me wrong, I'm always happy to see you, Sana," Adeena said, grinning at our friend and business coach. "I just don't see why he feels the need to babysit me."

"He didn't tell you?" Sana turned worried eyes to her boyfriend, who was shaking his head vigorously.

"It's not important, don't worry about it," he said. He picked up a menu, trying to change the subject. "What's good here? I need more than melted cheese to sustain me."

"Amir Bhai."

"The burgers seem to be popular."

"Amir. Bhai."

"Ooh, they have goat. I wonder if it's halal."

"Amir!"

Our whole table stopped and stared at Adeena. My cousins and I always used honorifics with our elders but didn't usually bother with that naming hierarchy for ourselves anymore. Adeena's family was a lot stricter when it came to that, and I'd never known her to talk to her older brother without using his title.

Sana put her hand on Amir's. "Tell her."

"Why should I—"

"Despite how your family treats her, she is an adult and deserves to know."

Amir sighed. "Amma and Abbu told me that there's been too much talk about you. Their friends said it made you seem guilty to be out gallivanting with your friends all the time after such a serious accusation. They were going to make it so that you weren't allowed to go anywhere that wasn't work or the police station. No classes at Sana's, no hanging out at Elena's, no dinner with Lila's family . . . just work and home."

"But what . . . how . . . ?"

"The only reason you were able to come out tonight is because I negotiated with them. You can go out for fun or investigations if you want, but . . ."

"But you have to chaperone me."

Adeena's voice was dangerously flat, but all Amir could do was nod in response.

Elena reached up to rub her girlfriend's back, and Adeena stiffened before shaking off Elena's hand.

"Excuse me, I need to go to the bathroom."

Adeena fled in the direction of the restroom with Elena right behind her. I started to get up too, but Sana grabbed my wrist.

"Maybe you should let Elena handle this."

"But she's my best friend. Why shouldn't I go comfort her too?"

Sana smiled at me kindly. "Adeena is probably, rightfully, angry. But I think she's also embarrassed. Maybe even ashamed at how little her parents trust her and stand up for her. And how often Amir's had to come to her rescue lately. I don't think she'll appreciate a crowd right now. Not with the expression I saw on her face."

I must've looked hesitant because Jae said, "She's right, Lila. Besides, Adeena hasn't just been relying on Amir this whole time. She's been leaning on you and your investigative skills. You're the one who's been going out every day, putting yourself at risk to clear her name. I wouldn't be surprised if both she and Elena are feeling a little helpless. I think they need each other right now."

But they don't need me?

You can't help your thoughts. I know that. But that selfish voice in my head filled me with guilt. Why did I have to make everything about me? Elena had asked me that and I had no idea what she meant until this moment. Looking back, it was definitely a bad habit of mine, but still. I wasn't prepared for the loneliness that came with being the third wheel with my best friends. I knew Adeena didn't value Elena more than me. She just loved and needed us in different ways. Logically, I knew that.

Didn't make it hurt any less.

Luckily, I didn't have time to wallow in those toxic, invasive thoughts since Zack walked in at that moment.

"There he is."

The four of us watched him weave through the crowd and head toward the bar. Adeena and Elena weren't back yet, but we didn't need them for the first part of the plan. We weren't sure how Zack would react to seeing Adeena and couldn't risk him leaving right away, so the idea was that Jae and I would loosen Zack up and then Adeena and Elena would join us. Hopefully, the element of surprise would work in our favor and we could use that to pry details of the mayor's divorce out of him.

I sent a message to the Brew-ha group chat as Jae and I made our way to the back. Elena had told Chuy our plan and he said he'd have a table for five set aside for us. Sure enough, when Jae and I made eye contact with Chuy, he gestured toward a table tucked into a corner near the end of the bar where Zack was sitting. There was a sign that said RESERVED on it, but Chuy sent a server our way who greeted us and removed the sign.

"What can I get you two?"

After putting in our order, the server left and Jae headed to the bar to set our plan in motion.

"Hey Chuy! Thanks for reserving that table for us. Elena wanted to let you know that she might not make it tonight. Her mom was having some trouble at the restaurant, and she went to help."

Chuy added an orange slice to someone's beer glass and passed it over before saying, "Is my aunt OK?"

"She's fine. Nothing that Elena can't handle. But she still wanted me to tell you since you were supposed to discuss the next delivery from the winery."

"Thanks for the heads-up. So now it's just you and Lila at that table?"

"For now, yeah. They might still show up, but we're not sure."

"Well, until then, you got that table and I know someone who could use some company. Zack!" Chuy called out. "You mind moving over to their table and making some room at the bar?"

Zack, who had been staring moodily at his basket of tortilla chips and hadn't seemed to notice Jae right next to him, jerked to attention at Chuy's voice. "Oh, Dr. Jae! What's up?"

"I'm pawning you off on him and his girlfriend so I don't have to worry about you drinking too much again," Chuy said with a grin. "Now get up. That woman looks like she could use a seat. Be a gentleman and let her have it, yeah?"

Zack glanced at the young twentysomething in stilettos who was hovering by his seat and looking like she was dying to sit down. "Oh, sure. Sorry about that."

Jae helped him carry over his chips and queso while Zack brought over his plate of sliders and his drink. "Sorry for crashing your date, but you know how Chuy is."

"No worries. We were actually supposed to meet our friends here, but they might not be able to make it after all. At least with you here, we don't look like jerks hogging a big table all to ourselves." I smiled at Zack. "I thought you always ordered the same thing here. What's with the sliders?"

"Chuy said I had to eat more and drink more water if I wanted him to keep serving me drinks." Zack shrugged. "He nags worse than my mom sometimes but he's still right. At least the food is all half off right now. And these sliders are awesome."

I looked at the menu and saw that the sliders were mini versions of all the burgers they served and decided to put in an extra order for me and Jae to share. As I sipped my cider, I studied Zack over the rim of my glass. He had deep circles under his eyes and seemed worn out in a way he hadn't when we'd had lunch together a few days ago. "Are you doing OK? Is the mayor overworking you? No offense but you seem a little . . . burned out."

Zack had been slouching in his seat, absently nudging his queso back and forth with a chip, but he straightened up to glare at me. "I'm doing just fine. And I'll have you know the mayor would never make her employees work too hard. I'm just upset that there haven't been any breakthroughs in the case and have been staying up late doing all I can to help around the office."

"Have the police or Detective Park given her any updates?" I asked.

"Nothing worthwhile."

"How about Yvonne's family? When are they coming to town?"

He made a face. "They've been nothing but a thorn in my side since the beginning. Mayor Reyes was so excited to finally meet Yvonne's family, and then she found out Yvonne's sister refuses to come. Apparently, the sister was the person Yvonne was closest to, so the mayor is taking it personal that she won't be here for the funeral."

He sighed and took another gulp of his drink. "The rest of the family arrives day after tomorrow. Mayor Reyes is taking the day off to pick them up from the airport and drive them to their accommodations."

"Oh wow, that's at least four hours round trip, more if she hits traffic. Though I guess it makes sense that she'd be the one to pick up her in-laws rather than make them rent a car or something like that."

"I told the mayor that I'd gladly do this for her, that it was my job to handle these kinds of errands, and she damn near bit my head off.

'Picking up my grieving in-laws is not a task to check off your to-do list, Zack. This isn't my dry cleaning, it's my dead wife's family,'" he said, perfectly imitating Mayor Reyes's cadence. His head drooped down and he stared sadly into his Michelada. "I was just trying to help."

Oh my gulay, was this grown man pouting? He would hate me so much if he knew what I was thinking, but I couldn't help hiding a smile at how adorable he looked. I mentally shook my head. This man was still a very viable suspect in Yvonne's murder, and I really needed to stop looking at the people on my suspect list as potential friends and business associates. "Adorable" was not the word I should be using to describe a possible murderer. Adeena didn't kill Yvonne and it's highly possible that I'm acquainted with the killer. *Come on, Lila. Where's that sense of self-preservation?*

"She knows that, Zack," Jae said, breaking into my mental scolding. "She's just under an immense amount of pressure right now, that's all. I'm sure it's making her act in ways she normally wouldn't. She's still grieving, you know."

"I know she's still grieving. Why do you think I'm trying to take so much off her plate?" Zack said. He chugged the last of his beer cocktail and slammed the empty glass on the table. "I've been running point with her housekeeping staff to make sure that the house is always clean, her clothes and meals taken care of, and her beloved garden tended to. I've canceled any unnecessary meetings, rescheduled projects, and am handling all minor office tasks. What more could I possibly do?"

"Maybe that's your problem, buddy. Maybe you're trying to do too much. People handle their grief in different ways. You're being extremely kind and practical by handling all those errands for her. But maybe she wants to keep busy and bury herself in work and you're not letting her do that," I observed. "Did you ask her what she needed, or did you make those decisions on your own?"

"Well, no, but—"

"It could also be that you're helping in a practical way, which, don't get me wrong, takes a huge burden off her shoulders," Jae added. "But maybe what she needs is emotional support. Does she have close friends or family that she can lean on for that?"

Zack made a face. "I'm definitely not the person for that, especially at the office. That's Felice's job."

"The receptionist? Why her?"

"Felice is her godmother. She was her mother's best friend and has been looking out for her since high school, after Mayor Reyes's mother passed away."

So that explained why she was so interested in the mayor's relationship and so willing to share important information with me. It wasn't gossip. It was maternal affection and concern. She was trying to help Mayor Reyes in her own way, by making sure that I had the necessary information to move my investigation forward. You'd think my big-headed self would love that people in Shelbyville knew about me, but honestly, it was just weird. And kind of inconvenient since I couldn't go incognito or anything like that. At least people knew to come to me if they wanted to help though.

"If you're not good at emotional stuff, then just ask the mayor what she needs."

"She'll just say 'nothing,' and I know that's not true."

"You spend a lot of time with her. You know her personality, her likes, dislikes, strengths, and weaknesses. Maybe instead of trying to do everything for her, you can just fill in the gaps for the tasks you know she hates or isn't good at."

He sighed. "She's really bad at taking time for herself. So maybe it's good that she's in charge of Yvonne's family. I know they're not here for a vacation, but they'll be staying at your friend's place for at least a week, she said. Maybe I can convince her to take them hiking at Starved Rock or make the drive to the Botanic Gardens. They both loved hiking and strolling through the gardens. It would be nice to show Yvonne's family places that were special to them."

I took a sip of my apple cider. "For someone who didn't like Yvonne, you seem to know her pretty well."

"It's not like I hated her. We just had very different ideas on what was best for the mayor. I don't doubt that Yvonne loved her. I just didn't think she was good for her, that's all."

"Is that why you passed on dirt about Yvonne to the mayor? To push her into a divorce?"

Zack whipped around to see Elena and Adeena standing behind him.

"Sorry we're late," Elena continued, as the two of them slid into the remaining seats. "But I'm glad to see such interesting company joining us."

Zack gaped at her like a goldfish, mouth opening and closing silently as he struggled to respond to her accusation. "Where did you hear they were getting a divorce?"

"We can't reveal our source. But we know that you're involved. The fact that the papers were filed shortly after you received some rather threatening texts from Yvonne can't just be a coincidence."

"How do you know she was threatening me?!"

"Again, we don't share our sources. But we are very well-connected, so I wouldn't suggest lying to us."

Dang. I knew I was getting all up in my feelings about Elena taking my place in the investigations, but maybe I should've utilized her more in the past. We'd make an excellent good cop, bad cop team. She's the sweetest and most chill of our trio, but she's also the one best able to home in on people's weaknesses. For the millionth time, I was glad she was on our team.

Zack narrowed his eyes at us. "You're not with the press, are you? I'm not paranoid enough to think you're in cahoots with the opposition, but I wouldn't be surprised if you tried to sell this story to the papers. I've seen the schlock that the *Shady Palms News* team prints."

"Paranoid much?" I said. "We just want—"

"If you don't want word of the divorce to spread, I suggest you talk. The owner of the *Shady Palms News* is obsessed with Lila. They'll listen to anything she says." Elena took a long, leisurely sip of her beer. "What did you have on Yvonne?"

"I don't have to listen to this," Zack said, getting up.

Before he could leave, Elena pulled out her phone and selected one of the contacts before putting it on speakerphone so we all heard the person on the other line say, "*Shady Palms News*, Wilson Philipps speaking. What've you got for me?"

Zack hit the end call button before Elena could respond. "Not cool!"

"Then talk."

He ran his hand through his hair in frustration. "Look, I can't go into detail, but Yvonne had dealings with a certain council member that were not aboveboard, shall we say."

I raised an eyebrow. "Yvonne was having an affair?"

"No, nothing like that. I thought so at first, but I don't think . . . I don't think their relationship was of that nature."

"Then it was something illegal. Something that threatened Mayor Reyes's position," Elena said.

"Mayor Reyes had nothing to do with her wife's actions. She didn't ask or even suggest that Yvonne do what she did. I just want to make that clear."

"And what exactly did Yvonne do?"

"Come on, I can't . . . You've got to understand you're putting me in a difficult position. Some of this information isn't mine to tell. It's personal. And I don't want to risk my job or the mayor's by sharing confidential information."

"You're putting it at risk by not helping us out," Elena pressed. "We're not interested in you or your boss unless you're the ones who killed Yvonne. We just want to clear Adeena's name. She had nothing to do with this. So either you talk or we will. That's not a threat, that's a promise."

I stared at Elena, barely believing this was the same sweet peacemaker friend I'd worked with every day for over a year. She met my eyes briefly, but they flicked over to Zack before I could read their depths.

Zack took a deep breath then leaned close so no one outside our table could overhear him. "Yvonne bribed one of the opposing council members to start supporting Mayor Reyes's initiatives. Not all of them. Just the ones that the mayor cared about the most."

"Like the internship program?" I guessed.

He nodded. "And affordable housing. More bike lanes and reliable public transportation. Public green spaces. Things that focused on quality of living and not just the economy."

Adeena laughed. "Her opponents must've hated that. But didn't everyone get suspicious when that guy started supporting the mayor?"

Zack studied her, clearly not willing to give her up as a suspect even if the mayor did. "He'd append things to her proposals and make it clear that he didn't believe in her position, but he was looking out for the best interest of his supporters. He'd say things like, 'I don't approve of this hippie BS, but if it means I can get XYZ through, then might as well let this woman do the work for us.'"

"Sounds like a real winner," Adeena said with a grin. "How'd you find out Yvonne was bribing him?"

"I caught them arguing in his office. I had some documents I needed him to sign and when I walked in he had his hands on her and I just . . . I thought they were having an affair. I dropped the documents on his desk and walked out without saying anything. Yvonne ran after me."

"And she admitted what she was doing?" I asked.

"At first, she tried to deny that anything was going on. But then I accused her of cheating on Mayor Reyes and she laughed. She called me 'simple' and 'naive' for not having more imagination than that." He closed his eyes as if remembering the scene. "I'm sorry, I think I need another drink. Could I—"

"Jae, tell Chuy to make him another Michelada. And a pitcher of water for the table," I instructed. "Go on, Zack."

But he wouldn't speak until Jae had returned with drinks for everyone. Zack took a big gulp of his beverage and wiped his mouth with the back of his hand.

"She pulled me into an empty room and admitted what she'd done. Said she'd thought that I'd approve since I was so desperate to make Mayor Reyes's time in office a success. Said that she and I were the ones most invested in seeing Mayor Reyes happy, and that's why we should keep what I saw between us."

"But you didn't," Elena said. "You ratted her out to the mayor."

"It wasn't right!" Zack had just lifted his glass but he set it down with a clatter. "Mayor Reyes was so happy because she thought she was finally getting through to those old fools! She thought she was finally good enough, smart enough, persuasive enough to get the people on her side. She was palling around with that asshole, thinking that he was now her ally, and all this time he'd been laughing at her! Stealing from her! Using her to push his own agenda. She deserved to know."

"Zack, I can see where you're coming from, but don't you think it was a little cruel to tell her that?"

He glared at me. "She needed to know. She needed to know how her wife had betrayed her, had set her up so that if anyone found out, her career would be ruined. Everything she ever worked for could be gone in an instant because her wife thought it was OK to take a short-cut. 'The greater good,' she said. But if she knew her wife even a little bit, Yvonne would know that the mayor wouldn't have stood for it. Would've hated the very idea of it."

"So what happened after you told Mayor Reyes? I know Yvonne threatened you, but did it go any further?"

"She came over to my house and made a big scene in front of my family. My mom wanted to call the cops, but that would just cause the mayor problems, so I had Mayor Reyes come over and handle it." Zack was quiet for a moment. "I think that was just one thing too far. When I first told the mayor about the bribery, she said she would put a stop to it and have Yvonne make up for it somehow. But after that incident, she saw what a loose cannon Yvonne was and knew it wouldn't work. I didn't mean to break up their marriage. I didn't mean for any of this to happen. I just wanted Mayor Reyes to be happy."

Was that a confession?

"What do you mean, Zack?"

"It's my fault Yvonne was wandering around alone. I insisted that she go off on her own to enjoy the festival while the mayor and I did our rounds. She'd already argued with Mayor Gunderson several times that day, so I told her that she was messing up our networking opportunities and making Mayor Reyes look bad. If I hadn't selfishly tried to separate them, then Yvonne would've stuck with us and none of this would've happened. She'd still be alive."

He angrily wiped his eyes with the backs of his hands, the tears threatening to spill out rubbed away before they could fall. I wanted to insist that it wasn't his fault, that he didn't know what was going to happen, but, well, even if it really wasn't his fault (I wasn't going to scratch him off the list just because of one tearful display) there was a certain truth to his statement and nothing I said would convince him otherwise. So the rest of us sat quietly while Zack pretended he wasn't crying.

Jae broke the silence. "The councilman that Yvonne was paying off . . . what happened with him? I'm assuming he didn't like losing that money stream. Did he try to get the mayor to take over the payments?"

Zack shifted in his seat. "The mayor told me that she was handling things and that he wasn't my business anymore. She would never pay someone off for her own gain, though. That's all I know."

"Have the police talked to the councilman as part of the investigation?"

"No, and they're not going to," Zack said sharply. "Even if it was Yvonne who was paying him off, if anyone finds out about it, it's going to be a huge scandal. You can't tell anyone about this. Promise me."

My friends and I all looked at one another.

"You have to promise me! He's not connected to the murder, he can't be!"

"Why not?" Elena asked. "What makes you so sure he's not involved? A man like the councilman would be upset about losing such an important source of money. And you were the one who said he had his hands on her. You never know, he could've been trying to coerce her to sleep with him and she turned him down."

"Rejecting a man can be dangerous. Sometimes fatal," I said, continuing what Elena set up. "A powerful politician being turned down by the wife of his political opponent . . . I bet he was outraged. Who's to say he wasn't at the Corn Festival that day?"

Zack didn't answer, just kept drinking his Michelada until he'd drained his glass. He raised his hand for another, but Jae cut him off and slid a glass of water in front of him instead.

"You've had enough. It's been a long day and I don't want to drive you home again. Plus, I don't think you're going to find the solution to the mayor's problems at the bottom of your glass. You need to get it together if you're going to help her."

I expected Zack to get angry, and braced myself for a fight, but instead Zack grasped Jae's fingers and squeezed. "Thanks, man."

Jae placed his free hand on top of Zack's and looked him in the eyes. "It's gonna be OK, Zack. We just want to help, I swear."

Zack let go of Jae's hand and gulped down his water. "Look, I still don't like the idea of involving that council member. But if you can give me some solid evidence that he was involved in Yvonne's death, I'll convince the mayor to give up his name as a suspect. And I'm not talking about vibes here. I need something concrete. Proof he was at the festival the day Yvonne died. His fingerprints on the weapon. A phone recording of him hiring a hit, I don't care. But if you can't make the connection, you promise me that no one else will know about this."

"Um, how about us plus Detective Park?" I asked. "He's not with the police force so he doesn't have to report this. But he has resources I don't, so if there's any evidence to be found, he'll get it if I can't."

Zack sighed. "The mayor trusted him enough to hire him, so fine. If he doesn't already know about the councilman, it's probably because the mayor was worried about a scandal. So make sure he knows not to tell anyone. Otherwise, you're banned from city hall and I'll make sure that no one connected to the case talks to you ever again. Are we clear?"

I doubted he had the power to put that into effect, but considering how much he was helping us, I might as well humor him.

I held out my hand. "It's a deal."

Chapter Seventeen

"Can you three get a little closer? Perfect!"

Leslie snapped a million pictures of me, Adeena, and Elena fake smiling in front of our booth at the Corn Festival before checking the results on their phone.

"Um, could you all maybe look happy to be here? I don't think I can post any of these to our social media . . ."

It was another Corn Festival weekend, and we all decided it would be best to close the cafe and have all the full-time staff work the booth. Mostly because we'd be stretched too thin otherwise, but also because we wanted to make sure Leslie had a chance to enjoy the festival while still getting in their hours.

However, as Leslie pointed out, the Brew-has and I were a little less than enthused to be here. Adeena had insisted that today was the day she was going to get back in the corn maze and face her fears, and while Elena and I would normally be supportive of that, we both had our doubts as to whether Adeena was truly ready.

For one thing, Adeena was the type to become extra exuberant to cover up her anxieties, and when that didn't work, she'd get super pissy and irritable since I guess snapping at your best friend was way easier than admitting you were worried about something (not that I'd know anything about that). Because of that, we'd had to deal with Adeena swinging from singing show tunes during working hours and convincing a few of our regulars to join in, choreography included, to her yelling at me because I pointed out that she'd accidentally used salt instead of sugar for the simple syrup she was making. And then she got mad at herself for messing up and also for yelling at me, so she stayed silent the rest of the day for fear of snapping at anyone else. And that was all just on Thursday. We had to deal with more of the same the rest of the week until it was finally Corn Festival weekend.

On top of that, while Elena and I agreed Adeena was pushing herself too hard, we both had very different ideas on how best to handle it. I'd known Adeena for over a decade (doing the math on this actually hurt; dear lord we'd known each other for a long time) and I knew the best thing to do when Adeena got like this was to gently point out her behavior and let her talk through her problems while you nodded and made sympathetic noises so she knew you were actively listening. Active listening was very important to her. Then once she'd reached a conclusion on her own (she didn't actually want anyone else's opinions, she just needed a sounding board while she worked through things herself), she could make a decision in a much clearer frame of mind.

Elena's solution was basically to wrap her up in warm blankets and protect her from the world. Which, fine, I could understand that method since obviously it was painful to see the person you loved the most hurting. But if she understood Adeena at all, she would know that enabling Adeena by pretending everything was OK was just prolonging the inevitable and not actually helpful. I couldn't believe I was actually saying this (it felt too much like something Lola Flor would say), but Elena was coddling her. And anytime I tried to suggest anything other than indulging Adeena's whims, Elena accused me of being cold and unsympathetic.

Since none of us could agree on how to handle the situation (heck, Adeena wouldn't even acknowledge there *was* a situation), tempers were running high and everything was weird and tense and kinda fake between the three of us, and I hated it. Leslie could sense it too, being way more empathetic and emotionally intelligent than I'd expect at their age. Despite their maturity, they were still the resident young person on our team and because of that, Leslie was in charge of our social media platforms and newsletter—yes, I realized I was technically young, but there's a difference between an adult in their midtwenties and someone fresh out of high school. Anyway, it was their job to make us all seem like one big happy family. Or at least a semi-happy team with amazing drinks and baked goods.

Once the requisite promo stuff was done and their posts approved, Leslie grabbed the flyers advertising our special Corn Festival discount and offerings and made their way around the festival to hopefully draw a large crowd to our booth. Thanks to our success on the festival's opening weekend, the Brew-has and I had been ambitious when it came to how much stock we brought with us, and I was a little nervous. I was usually conservative with my estimations for events like this since I didn't want us stressing ourselves out to prepare a huge amount on time, end up going overbudget, and then be stuck donating hundreds of dollars' worth of product to the church program since we only sold fresh goods.

On top of the fifty million other things I was stressed about, another reason I wasn't looking forward to Adeena's plan to come to the Corn Festival today was that I remembered how nosy everyone had been about the murder the day after. I didn't need anyone asking insensitive questions and setting Adeena off. I mean, I'd gladly take their money, but the moment their questions got inappropriate, Elena and I had to be ready to spring into action. Luckily, the festivalgoers who came to our booth seemed genuinely interested in our goods and we kept up a steady, comfortable pace for the first few hours.

I knew our luck couldn't hold for too long though, and sure enough, shortly after Leslie returned from their lunch break, Wilson Philipps of the *Shady Palms News* team sauntered up to our booth. I tensed as soon as I saw him and I could feel Adeena beside me do the same.

Elena glanced at us and took the lead, probably hoping to guide the interaction. "Mr. Philipps! What can I get you?"

"Half a dozen cookies, a large black coffee, and a comment from Adeena about the death of Yvonne Reyes."

Adeena had gotten started on his order but froze as soon as he said that last part. Elena and I jumped in.

"How dare you approach us like that—"

"Completely unprofessional—"

"Both she and her lawyer have been very clear—"

"Do you need me to talk to Detective Park about this?"

At my threat to bring in someone he counted on as a source, Wilson Philipps held his hands up in surrender. "My apologies, ladies. You can't fault me for trying though, right?"

We sure as hell could. None of us said it out loud, but our silence and expressions must've spoken for us since he pulled out his wallet to finish his transaction. "Suit yourselves. How much do I owe you?"

"Thirty bucks," Leslie said, preparing to ring him up.

Wilson Philipps blinked. "But your flyer said there was a discount—"

"Not for people who harass my coworkers. Those customers pay full price," Leslie said, looking him dead in the eyes. "Also, I'm not a lady. Is that going to be cash or card?"

He scowled but tapped his card on the card reader and accepted his coffee and bag of cookies. "You keep using your connection to Detective Park as a Get Out of Jail Free card, and people are going to start questioning if you've got something to hide. You might want to think about that before you start throwing his name around all willy-nilly."

He turned to leave but Leslie called out, "No tip?"

"If you don't take the time to shape the narrative, others are going to do it for you. How's that for a tip?" he threw out over his shoulder as he stalked away.

"Well handled, Leslie," I said.

"I still remember how he treated us during that thing with the Miss Teen Shady Palms pageant. I didn't like him then and I don't like him now, even if he's less of a bully than he was before." Leslie turned to Adeena. "Are you OK? Do you want to take your lunch break now? I can handle things on my own for a bit."

Adeena stared after Wilson Philipps, lost in her own world until I poked her in the side. "Oh, sorry. I was just . . . Do you think he's right? Should I have talked to him?"

"When has Wilson Philipps been right about anything?" I asked.

She bit her lip. "Usually I'd agree with you, but maybe he's actually got a point this time. A broken clock and all that."

"Please don't tell me you plan on going after him for an interview," I said.

"Don't worry, I'm not that foolish. Though I will tell Amir about today and see what he thinks. I promise I won't act on my own. Not like I want to give my family any more ammunition against me," she said, a bitter smile marring her usually cheerful face.

Elena took one look at Adeena's expression and jumped in. "Leslie shouldn't be alone at the booth, but Adeena needs a break. Lila, can you stay with Leslie while I take Adeena out for lunch? We can bring you back something if you want."

Unlike her previous attempts, I didn't get the feeling that she was trying to shut me out. She probably just saw how shaken up Adeena was and wanted a little quiet time with her girlfriend. So I pushed down my petty urges and smiled at them.

"Yeah, of course. Just bring me back a large serving of whatever you're having. Leslie and I will hold down the fort."

A small family chose that moment to approach our booth, so Leslie and I waved Adeena and Elena off and focused on our customers. Once the family left, though, Leslie turned their attention to me.

"Are you OK?"

"I'm fine."

"'Fine' as in genuinely all right, or 'fine' like that cartoon dog drinking coffee in a burning room?"

"... The second one."

"That's what I thought." Leslie moved to help another customer, glancing over their shoulder at me as I prepared the customer's drink. "The three of you really need to sit down and talk. You know that, right?"

"I know."

"Are you going to?"

"Probably not."

They sighed. "That's what I thought."

. . .

Adeena insisted on re-creating the same conditions as that fateful day, so the three of us waited until the sun was setting and the air cold and nippy before we stepped into the corn maze. Despite a murder taking place so recently, the maze was packed with excited festivalgoers of all ages ready to take on the second-largest corn maze in Illinois.

When the sun was out, its light was enough to bathe the whole festival in its gentle warmth. But now that it was setting, my oversize cropped cardigan wasn't enough to fight the chill that creeped in. On top of that, I couldn't shake the feeling that we were being watched. It had been happening on and off all day, but I assumed that was because people knew Adeena was a murder suspect and wanted a vicarious thrill.

I wrapped my arms around myself and surveyed the area, trying to spot anyone acting weird or out of place. Other than a vaguely familiar woman wearing a puffy jacket that was way too heavy for this weather (it was chilly, sure, but she looked ready for a polar vortex) hovering awkwardly near the entrance of the maze as if waiting for someone, nobody seemed out of place.

Still, I wanted to get this over with already. "Do you want to take the route as you remember it, or would you rather we work together and solve the maze?"

I hoped that igniting Adeena's competitive spirit would have her rethink her scheme, and for a moment her eyes lit up in excitement before becoming subdued.

"I think we should retrace my steps. I know that the chances of us finding a clue after all this time are practically zero, but maybe I'll remember something."

I was tired of being the Debbie Downer of the group, and even though I didn't think we'd find anything, it wouldn't hurt our case and might bring Adeena the closure she needed. That was what my therapist said when I brought it up during our session. Or did she say catharsis? Whatever, some important *C*-word that therapists love.

"Sounds good. Lead on," I said, gesturing her forward.

Adeena took a deep breath, threw her shoulders back, and marched ahead. For all my many complaints, seeing her now, her bravery and determination on full display, I couldn't help but swell with pride and platonic love. That was one thing I'd always admired about Adeena—when she said she was going to do something, she did it. She never let fear hold her back, the way I always did.

So I copied her—I took a deep breath, threw my shoulders back, and followed her to the scene of the crime.

This is it."

Adeena had led us to a random aisle that seemed just like any other in the maze. The spot was no longer considered a crime scene since the police had already gathered what little evidence there was, so they'd taken down the crime scene tape a while ago. There were no blood stains or broken stalks of corn indicating a struggle. There wasn't a second murder weapon or locket bearing the initials of the killer buried in the dirt. There wasn't even an eerie aura hanging over the place that we could vibe on. In other words, there were no signs, visible or otherwise, that we'd actually found the area where Yvonne's body was discovered. But Adeena was sure.

"This is it," she repeated. "I feel it. This is where it all happened."

Elena and I took our time searching the area, trying to spot any clues or identifying markers that would contribute to Adeena's confidence, but couldn't find any. After half an hour of crawling around on our hands and knees (drawing the weirdest looks from people passing by) and coming up empty, I glanced at Elena and she shrugged at me. Pretty sure she cared less about finding evidence and more about what this field trip would do to make Adeena feel better. Either way, we were currently oh for two since there were zero clues to be found and Adeena didn't look any more at peace than she had when we'd started.

I didn't want to hurry Adeena along or anything, but it was getting really cold, and if coming to this spot didn't help Adeena at all, our time was better spent reaching the end of the maze and heading to Tita Rosie's Kitchen for a warm meal.

"Has coming here helped at all?" I asked, glancing at my watch. If we didn't hurry, it was going to be pitch-black soon, and even though there were flood lights to keep the maze safe, I didn't want to stay in this creepy labyrinth any longer than I had to.

"Why do you always do that?" Elena demanded.

"Do what?" Startled, I looked up to meet Elena's angry eyes.

"Rush everyone along at your pace. You said you want to be there for Adeena, so just BE THERE. Stay still for a minute. Let her handle things in her own time."

"I'm not trying to rush her! She just does better when she verbalizes her thoughts, so I'm asking questions to help her with that."

"Well, the way you're asking questions makes it seem like you're pressuring her. Like if there are no tangible results, then it was a waste of our time."

Well . . . wasn't it? Wasn't the whole point of this exercise to get results of some kind? But something told me that was the wrong thing to say.

"I'm not trying to pressure her. Again, I just know the way she thinks and I wanted to—"

"Because you always know what's best, right? You don't think I know her well enough to—"

This back-and-forth between me and Elena could've gone on forever if Adeena hadn't decided to cut off our petty bickering by sucking in a deep breath and screaming at the top of her lungs.

Elena and I both flinched and whipped around to look at her.

"Babe, what's wrong? Are you—"

"Adeena, are you OK? What's—"

The sound of footsteps stampeding toward us cut off me and Elena, and eventually Adeena stopped wailing like a banshee.

"What's going on over here? Is somebody hurt?" Two people wearing Shady Palms Corn Festival Security T-shirts ran over to us, the beams from their flashlights so bright, I had to throw up a hand to cover my eyes.

Adeena turned to face them with a sheepish expression now that the moment had passed. "Sorry about that. I know it wasn't the smartest move, considering what happened here, but I needed to release some tension and that's what felt right in the moment. I didn't mean to scare anyone."

"So this was a prank?" The older of the two security members gave her a harsh look. "I don't appreciate you girls fooling around like that. Like you said, after what happened here, you should know better. Our whole team is on high alert for the rest of the festival and we don't need you making it worse."

"It wasn't meant to be a prank. More like . . . therapy? I really am sorry. Are you going to kick me out?"

The security team studied Adeena's earnest face and after a quick glance at each other, they dismissed us. "Don't let it happen again."

"It won't." Adeena watched the security guards walk away and gestured for Elena and me to follow her. "Let's get out of here."

She led the way in silence for a few minutes and probably wouldn't have said anything at all if I didn't suddenly blurt out, "Adeena, are you going to tell us what that was all about?"

She turned and looked me in the eyes. "What do *you* think?"

I stopped short. I wasn't expecting her to throw it back at me like that. "Something about releasing tension?"

"And?"

"It was therapeutic?"

"Kind of the same thing, but sure. What else?"

I sighed, knowing she wouldn't stop until I admitted my part in all this. "Because Elena and I were fighting yet again about you even though we promised we'd stop?"

"Bingo! Give the woman a prize. You have a choice between this plaque to your hero complex or this booklet of coupons you can redeem each time you keep a promise for once. Which will it be?"

"Adeena . . ."

"And don't think you're off the hook," she said, turning to her girlfriend. "You also get a booklet of coupons and a plaque to your mothering complex."

"Thank you?" Elena said.

"I don't mean 'mother' in the cool ballroom way! I mean you try to act like my mother in the way you're so overprotective. I am a grown woman. I need you to support me, not cover me in bubble wrap and fight all my battles."

Elena looked as ashamed as I felt. "I'm sorry, babe. I know I was being a bit much, but I was just so frustrated not being able to fix everything and make it all OK for you."

"Same," I admitted. "I guess I got used to being the person that solves things, and the longer I couldn't do that for you, the worse I got. I'm sorry I didn't support you the way you asked before."

Adeena sighed. "I know you two mean well. And I should've known that having that one conversation wouldn't fix things. Like, just because we talked about our feelings once doesn't magically make everything better. We've all been trying. But I just couldn't anymore. And I don't want us to have to do this a third time. Agreed?"

Elena and I both nodded.

"Good." Adeena took Elena's hand in one hand and mine in the other. "Now let's get out of here. I'm freezing and you both owe me a very expensive dinner."

Chapter Eighteen

It had been a few days since that (rather unnecessary yet emotionally cathartic) trip to the corn maze, and the Brew-has had taken a short break from the investigation to focus on all the extra business the Corn Festival was sending our way. I was refilling the pastry cases after the cafe's usual morning rush when the tinkling of the bells above the door had me turning to greet our new customer.

Quinn stood just inside the doorway with Cleo, who was wrapped up in yet another hand-crocheted blanket.

"Hey, you two! Welcome to the Brew-ha Cafe." I walked over to give Cleo head scratches. "I'm so glad you could finally visit. How are you both doing?"

"No emergency vet visits, which is always a good thing. The boutique is closed today, so I figured Cleo and I could go on a little field trip to your cafe. It looks amazing, by the way."

"Thanks! Let me give you a tour." I led the way to Elena's corner, which was full of plants, herbs, and bath and beauty products. "Elena's our best salesperson and she's in charge of this area."

"Nice to see you again. And who do we have here?" Elena smiled down at Cleo. "Can I pet them?"

Quinn moved part of the blanket so Elena could get a better look at her dog. "This is Cleopatra Louise, but you can call her Cleo. And she loves attention, so go ahead."

Elena held out her hand and Cleo bowed her head to accept the pets. "Aww, aren't you the sweetest? You look like you need a pup cup. The ones Adeena makes are way healthier and tastier than the chain ones, so make sure to check them out. I also make organic treats for cats and dogs, so make sure to tell your friends about us."

"You're right, she is good," Quinn said to me. Turning back to Elena, she asked, "Do you have pet-safe moisturizer? Now that she's a little older and the weather's getting cold, her skin and coat have been a little dry."

Elena raised her eyebrows. "I've never thought of making one, but that's a good idea. Give me a week to research this and I'm sure I'll have something that's perfect for Cleo. Does she have any allergies?"

"Not that I know of. I'll be back to check on her moisturizer, but what would you recommend for me? I want . . ." The two of them started discussing the merits of the various herbs and essential oils Elena used in her concoctions. Once Elena was done convincing her to fill her basket with herbal goodies, I took her over to the pastry cases and explained everything we had on offer.

"They're all good, if I do say so myself, but I always suggest checking out our seasonal items since they might not come back," I said. "Ginataang mais butter mochi is my newest addition. I came up with them this morning to fulfill a request for a gluten-free seasonal treat, and honestly, they might be my new favorite."

I hadn't expected much when I threw together what ingredients I had to fulfill my friend Valerie Thompson's request, but the results blew me away. The dense, chewy texture paired with the unique flavor combination of corn and coconut was out of this world. I had my aunt, grandmother, and godmothers test my creation that morning at breakfast and all of them bestowed upon it the highest honor an Asian person can give a dessert: "It's not too sweet!"

"Then that's what I'll have. And the house blend coffee, so I can focus on the flavors of the butter mochi. And where are the dog treats?"

I led her over to Adeena and introduced them once it was Quinn's turn at the counter. "This is my best friend and other business partner, Adeena Awan. This is Quinn Taylor and her dog, Cleo. She owns the Blue Violet Boutique."

Adeena raised her eyebrows and reached out a hand. "Nice to meet you, Quinn. And you too, Cleo."

Quinn stared at her, not bothering to shake Adeena's hand. The look on her face wasn't hostile, but it wasn't friendly either. Then it hit me that Quinn must've heard that Adeena was the main suspect in Yvonne's murder. Of course she wouldn't be all smiles around the person who might've killed her best friend.

An awkward beat passed, and then another, and finally Adeena lowered her hand and said, "What can I get you today?"

Quinn glanced at me before putting in her order, and I guided her over to the dog-friendly side of the cafe. Should I comment on the Adeena thing? Or would that make it more awkward? I decided to let it go for now since anything I said in her defense would obviously seem biased. "Give me a moment, I want to grab Longganisa from my office."

As usual, Longganisa was napping under my desk and did not appreciate being roused for a social event. "Come on, Nisa, I need you to help me smooth over an extremely awkward situation. Besides, you need more friends than Poe, and Cleo is a doxie, just like you. Don't you want a big sister?"

I clipped the leash to her collar, and she followed me over to Quinn and Cleo's table. Quinn was making quick work of the ginataang mais butter mochi, but she stopped mid-bite when she saw us. "Oh. My. God. Are the two of you wearing matching cardigans?"

I had gotten so used to Longganisa dressing in cutesy outfits and doing multiple costume changes in a day that I had to glance down at her to remind myself of what she was wearing. "Yeah, Adeena has been obsessed with crochet lately and made these for us. It was Longganisa's birthday last month and this was her present. Well, one of them."

Adeena, who loved colors and patterns as much as Ninang Mae did, had also been trying to get me to incorporate more color into my wardrobe. The chunky burnt orange cardigan with oversize buttons was a nice compromise for us, and looked absolutely adorable on Longganisa as well. She knew I couldn't turn down a cute matching outfit.

Longganisa cautiously approached Cleo, who hadn't moved from her position at Quinn's feet. There was something regal about the older dog, as if she were waiting for Longganisa to present herself and curtsy. The two sniffed each other for a moment and, after a quick glance at me, Longganisa kneaded the blanket that Cleo was lying on into a little nest before curling up next to her. Cleo must've accepted her because she just laid her head on Longganisa and the two of them promptly fell asleep. Cue me and Quinn whipping out our phones to take pictures and trying not to sob from the cuteness.

"I've never seen Cleo take to another dog so quickly. Usually, she ignores the other dogs at the dog park. She barely even tolerates humans, let alone other animals," Quinn said in amazement. "I don't know what it is about your Longganisa, but we need to set up a play-date. I think it'll be good for her."

"That would be great! Longganisa was better socialized when I lived in Chicago and could drop her off at doggy daycare, but now her only friend lives in Chicago and visits Shady Palms a few times a year."

"Does her friend also wear matching outfits with their human?"

"No, that's definitely a me and Longganisa thing," I said with a grin. "I used to buy cute clothes for us online once in a while, but now that I have so many artistic friends here in Shady Palms, I'm getting a little bit spoiled."

"You, spoiled? Who would ever say that," Adeena said, plopping down next to me with a giant mug of lavender chai. "I wanted to make matching beanies for both of them but ran out of that yarn and my family has banned me from buying more until I use up what I have. Maybe I can sneak some for Lila's birthday though." She paused to take a sip of her drink and sighed in satisfaction. "I know I already sat down, but mind if I join you for a bit? Leslie's covering the register."

Quinn hesitated, and I could practically see the battle in her eyes of wanting to talk to another crocheter but not if that crocheter was involved in her best friend's death. The silence went on long enough for Adeena to get the hint, though.

"On second thought, I should probably make my rounds to greet our other customers. Hope you enjoy your stay, Quinn."

Quinn and I watched Adeena approach customers at another table, who were much happier to receive her company. They were soon laughing and chattering away, and I couldn't help smiling in relief.

"Sorry about that." Quinn spoke so quietly, I had to lean in to hear her.

As upsetting as it was to see Adeena get the cold shoulder, it's not like I could pretend that I didn't understand why she reacted that way.

If our positions were switched, I'd probably do the exact same thing. (Let's be real, I'd be way ruder.)

I said as much, and Quinn smiled and quickly changed the subject.

"I like crochet, but I started recently and can only make simple things. Cleo's blanket was a baby blanket pattern, and I sometimes make shawls and scarves. Mostly just to keep my hands busy while I watch TV, though I do sell some of it at the boutique." Quinn studied Longganisa's and my cardigans more closely. "You know, if you're interested in being the go-between, I'd be happy to sell your friend's stuff on consignment. This is quality work. And if you have more matching owner/pet outfits, even better. People in Shelbyville love spoiling their pets."

I perked up. "I'd have to ask her, but I think that's a great idea! I know she has tons of finished projects with nowhere to put them and no interest in selling them online. But if you're willing to handle all that, she might change her mind."

"I can understand not wanting to sell them online, but why not here in the cafe?"

"Elena had actually suggested that before, but Adeena insisted she just wanted to enjoy her hobby without turning it into a capitalistic thing. That made sense, so we let it go, but maybe there can be a compromise," I said, then added, "She's not going to be interested in commissions or anything like that, but if the cafe sets up an artist corner, where local artists can put up already finished pieces to sell, she might be OK with that. Any sales on her projects can go toward funding her hobby. Adeena wasn't kidding when she said she was banned from buying more yarn—she once spent almost her whole paycheck at the local craft store."

I babbled on like this a bit longer before I noticed Quinn staring at me. "Oh, sorry! Didn't mean to talk shop so much, but you gave me a great idea. Thanks for that."

"It's not a problem. I was just thinking that you know your friend and how she operates so well. How did you meet?"

"We went to different grade schools, so we didn't become friends until freshman year of high school," I said. "We were in the same homeroom and had a bunch of classes together.

"One of the things we bonded over was that both our families refused to let us buy school lunch, so we brought lunchboxes they packed," I added. "It was kind of embarrassing at first, but looking back, there was no way those soggy cafeteria pizzas were better than anything her mom and my Tita Rosie made. They were doing us a favor."

Quinn propped her chin in her hand and smiled, gesturing for me to keep talking, so I did. I wondered why she wanted to hear my nostalgic rambling—was she trying to suss out more info on Adeena or was she genuinely interested?—but considering I needed her to do the same, I figured it was fair play.

"Sharing lunch with Adeena was the best," I continued. "We never really ate out when I was a kid since it was expensive, and my grandmother would insist that our family could make it better anyway. The only times I got to eat food that my family didn't make were during church potlucks and from Adeena's lunchbox."

"That's so nice. Reminds me so much of me and Yvonne. We met freshman year of high school too," Quinn said. Her smile was nostalgic and a touch bittersweet. "I don't think my parents ever packed a lunch for me, not once. It was fine in grade school since my parents gave me money to buy lunch, but they stopped in high school."

I furrowed my brow. "But then how did you eat? Did you learn to cook for yourself?"

Quinn shrugged. "A lot of peanut butter sandwiches. Yvonne took notice after a while and started bringing a second lunch for me. Her family fed me well, at least."

"How did you two meet? I'm assuming you were in class together."

"We sat next to each other in Home Ec. Do schools still teach Home Ec? Anyway, we were both obsessed with fashion even then. We learned how to sew in that class, and I started making my own clothes and accessories for friends and that's how our dream started. We knew we'd open a shop together someday."

Two best friends realizing a high school dream together. They really did sound like me and Adeena.

"What made you decide to open your boutique in Shelbyville? Midwestern small towns aren't exactly known as fashion havens."

Quinn laughed. "Yvonne and I are from a small town in California that no one's heard of, so it's not like we were Hollywood or anything like that. I wanted to get away from my family, so I found a cheap school that offered me financial aid and had fashion merchandising programs. That's how I ended up in Illinois. Yvonne was originally going to skip school and go straight to work at her family's business, but she met Judy while visiting me and decided to stay."

"I'm glad you two were able to make your dreams come true. Even if it was cut short like this." I was quiet for a moment. "I'm really sorry for your loss, Quinn."

The bittersweet look that had been on Quinn's face when she reminisced about her school days with Yvonne lost all trace of sweetness and became as bitter as the black coffee in her cup. "I still don't believe it sometimes. I wake up and grab my phone to see what ridiculous message she sent me late at night, or I'll turn around at the boutique expecting her to be there and she's just . . . not. I don't know what to do anymore."

I put my hand on her arm. "You said you were close to Yvonne's family in high school, right? They should be in town by now. Have you reached out to them or Mayor Reyes?"

She shook her head. "Yvonne had a falling-out with her family since they were opposed to her marrying Judy and staying out here. She was supposed to join her family's company and they were furious that she would abandon them so quickly. She and Judy only knew each other for a month before they got engaged after all."

My eyes widened. "A whirlwind romance! My aunt told me it was the same for my parents. But Yvonne wasn't their only child, right? Why make such a big fuss about the family business?"

"She wasn't the only child, but she was the oldest. I guess they just expected she would do what she'd always promised to do, and when she didn't, they overreacted. They eventually reconciled, but it wasn't the same as before. And of course, if Yvonne wasn't getting along with them, it meant I couldn't contact them either."

"Well, what about now? I'm sure they'd love to spend time with you now that they're in Shelbyville. I bet Mayor Reyes would be happy to have you join in their plans."

Quinn made a face then tried to quickly cover it up. "I don't want to get in the way. Judy has been wanting to get close to Yvonne's family for years and this is her chance."

"Are you sure? They're staying at my friend Xander's place, so I can give you the address if you want. I bet we could—"

"Drop it, Lila."

This sharp statement came from Adeena, who must've stopped by to check on us. She must've seen how much it startled me because she added an unspoken warning with her eyes. *Look at Quinn. She can't handle any more right now. Let it go.*

I glanced over at Quinn and saw that her trembling hands had a stranglehold on her mug, clenched so tight that her knuckles were white.

"Sorry. People always tell me I'm too nosy, that I need to stop meddling in people's business."

"And I'm sorry for intruding on your conversation. I just wanted to see if either of you needed anything since it's time for me to get back behind the counter," Adeena said.

"Maybe something with no caffeine? I must've had too much coffee earlier, I'm a little jittery." Quinn tried to laugh off her reaction to my prying questions.

"Got it. I'll have Elena prepare one of her special tea blends. You'll love it," Adeena said, smiling at Quinn before heading behind the counter.

Quinn and I watched Adeena sneak up on Elena, who was at the register, and grab her around the waist. Elena jumped and laughed, leaning into her girlfriend's touch. Adeena tucked a loose curl behind Elena's ear before leaning close and whispering something—whether it was sweet nothings or Quinn's order, I didn't know, and when I finally looked away from them, I saw Quinn studying me.

"They're cute together. Still in the stage where everything is roses and romance," Quinn observed. "Something about them reminds me of Judy and Yvonne. What's it like working with the lovebirds?"

"It's fine," I said, because it was fine. "They're careful not to make me feel like a third wheel and we're all equal partners. Well, the cafe is *slightly* more Adeena's and mine since Adeena invested the most money and the deed is in my name, but we don't think about it like that."

"Of course not."

I didn't like the knowing look she threw my way and didn't know what else to say, but I needed an escape. "Let me go check on your tea."

I got up and slowly made my way toward Elena, careful to control my strides so it didn't look like I was running away.

Once I was behind the counter, my sense of control returned to me and I took a deep breath, inhaling the rich fragrance of whatever Elena was preparing. "What've you got there? It smells great."

"I'm preparing the Chill Vibes blend," Elena said, measuring out the tisane into a glass teapot. "It has lavender, peppermint, rosemary, and lemon balm. Soothing without being a sleepy-time tea. Though if she's looking for a tea to help her sleep, tell her to let me know since I have a few blends that may work."

"Thanks, Elena." I leaned against the counter while she worked. "How's it been today? Good business? Good gossip?"

"The PTA Squad was in earlier complaining about the lack of job opportunities for their kids. Apparently one of the members has a son that called her last week to let her know he wouldn't be coming home after college, so they were all consoling her about that."

"Ooh, we should talk to them when we get a chance. If we include testimonials from other Shady Palms citizens in our proposal, Mayor Gunderson can't dismiss it so quickly."

"I thought the same thing. I'll make sure to bring it up next time they're in."

The electric kettle had reached the boiling point, but according to Elena, it had to cool slightly before pouring it over the tea.

"Anything else?" I asked, waiting for the water to reach the correct temperature.

"Business has definitely picked up since the Corn Festival started."

That kind of statement would normally be something she'd say with glee since she was the one most interested in increasing our customer base. But today she said it nonchalantly, like she couldn't care less about our record sales.

I studied her face, taking in the dark bags under her eyes, the tension around her mouth. "And how are you doing?"

"Me?" She looked bewildered, as if she couldn't imagine why I'd ask that. "I don't know. Doesn't really matter right now, does it?"

I was reaching for the electric kettle but stopped to stare at her. "Doesn't matter? Of course it does. Things are tough for you too right now."

"Sorry. I know you're right, but my instinct is to just . . . Anyway, after our talk in the corn maze, I promised myself I'd be better about this. Still a work in progress, I guess. But I don't think I can honestly say I'm doing OK until I know Adeena is safe." She shrugged. "Not what you wanted to hear, right? By the way, you should go back to Quinn. See if you can get more info out of her."

I watched her walk back to her section, a prickle of unease traveling across my skin. She was acting more and more out of character the longer this investigation dragged on. I thought we'd all reached a good place after our argument in the corn maze, but I guess I was foolish to hope that everything would suddenly be back to the way it was. We needed to solve this case soon, before it permanently affected our relationships. Not to mention our mental health.

I placed the filled teapot and matching teacup on a tray and brought it over to our table. "Sorry for the wait. Elena was teaching me about the different teas and picked this one out for you. I hope you like it."

Quinn poured the fragrant liquid into the teacup, the puffs of steam surrounding us with a scent reminiscent of walking in an herb garden. She inhaled deeply before taking a sip. "Mmm, this is wonderful. I'm not usually a tea drinker but this could convert me."

"Elena grows all the herbs that she uses in our teas, and blends most of them herself. She outsources the pure, higher-grade teas, but she makes the tisanes and flavored ones," I said. "She's also great about recommending stuff based on whatever your needs are. Tummy problems, sleep issues, sexy times . . . you name it, she's got it."

"Sexy times?" Quinn raised an eyebrow. "Can a tea really help with that?"

I grinned. "Well, it's not like we've done scientific trials or anything, but I've had more than one TMI conversation with Adeena where she assured me it works."

Quinn coughed. "TMI indeed."

I laughed. "She said after years of having to listen to my horror stories about men, it was time she gave me a taste of my own medicine."

Adeena hadn't been the only queer person at our high school, but considering it was already slim pickings if you were straight, her choices had been . . . well, "dire" was a little harsh. Nicer to say that, until Elena came around, nobody was quite her type in Shady Palms. What little experience she'd had was when she visited me in Chicago, and even that hadn't been much since she hated my ex-fiancé so much, she stopped visiting a couple years into my stay (she didn't admit this until after I'd come back home for good).

Quinn hid a smile behind her teacup. "I know my feelings about her are complicated, but you seem to be a good pair. Make sure to treasure your friendship. I know owning a business together seems like a dream, but I hope you don't let anything come between you."

"What do you mean?"

"Money. Success. Love. All the things that people want have a flip side that can ruin a friendship, even one as strong as yours."

"Were you and Yvonne . . . ?" I didn't know how to finish that question without being too rude or nosy.

"We had our ups and downs, for sure. But we loved each other and believed in each other." Quinn sighed. "No relationship is perfect, whether it's family, friend, lover, whatever. But we were fine. Just fine."

That "fine" sounded a lot like my "fine" earlier and I couldn't help but feel a sense of kinship with Quinn. We sat together in companionable, if somewhat uncomfortable, silence until she'd drained the teapot.

"Thanks so much for everything today. I'll be back for more

playtime with Longganisa and more, well, everything. It was all wonderful," Quinn said, rousing the sleeping dogs. "And please make sure to talk to your artist friends about selling things on consignment at my boutique."

"Of course."

Longganisa and I walked Quinn and Cleo to the door. It was time for Longganisa's walk, so we followed them outside and almost crashed into Jae, who must've been on a quick break since he still had his white lab coat on.

"My favorite girls! I didn't expect to see you out here," he said, crouching down to pet Cleo and Longganisa.

"Am I considered one of your 'favorite girls' or does that only extend to dogs?" I asked with a smirk.

Jae looked up from his crouched-down position and I could practically see him doing the math in his head to figure out how to talk his way out of this one. "You're a woman, not a girl, so uh, different category."

"That's what you're going with?"

"That's the best I could do without my afternoon coffee, so yeah."

I laughed. "That's fair. I'll go grab your drink and you can stay out here with your girls. The usual?"

He nodded and I handed him Longganisa's leash before heading back inside to place an order for the Dr. Jae, which was similar (probably too similar, to be honest) to my special drink, except his was sweetened and had vanilla in addition to the pandan cold brew and coconut milk. He also preferred his coffee hot, which I would never understand, but to each their own.

Adeena must've seen us through the shop window because she had Jae's order ready just as I stepped up to the counter. "Here you go. I made it extra hot, just the way he likes it."

"You're the best."

"You know it! Hey, do you think he has ideas for a different variation of his drink? I was thinking we needed to change it up a little. No offense, but—"

"No, I was just thinking that our drinks are too similar. And even though he loves this combo, it doesn't really seem particular to him, does it? I'll see if he's got any suggestions."

Adeena grinned at me. "I knew you were thinking the same thing. It's like we have ESPN or something, huh?"

If we could joke around making *Mean Girls* references, maybe she was doing all right after all. As dramatic and supremely Adeena-like as her actions had been in the corn maze the other day, they seemed to have worked. I guess we all had times where we needed to let it all out. Some people had axe throwing, some had rage rooms, and others chose to scream at the top of their lungs in a (probably haunted) corn maze. Who was I to judge?

By the time I made it back outside, Quinn and Cleo were already gone.

"She said sorry to leave without saying goodbye, but she had some errands to run," Jae explained as I handed over his drink. "Mmm, Adeena made it extra hot, didn't she?"

I nodded. "Do you have some time before your next appointment?"

He checked his watch. "I've got at least half an hour before I need to be back. Can I join you two on your walk?"

"That would be great!" We walked around the neighborhood at a moderate pace, making small talk about our day and just enjoying this brief time to unwind. As we made our way back to the plaza that housed our businesses, I brought up Adeena's suggestion.

"I know you love that latte, but don't you think it's almost the same as mine? Adeena was thinking about switching things up and wanted to know if you had an idea for a different signature drink. She's got a lot of time on her hands lately, so she's been wanting to revamp our menu."

Jae tilted his head. "You know, you might be right. I thought it was cute that our drinks are so similar, but it's kind of a waste, isn't it? I mean, if I wanted to have this, I could just order your drink and have Adeena or Leslie add vanilla syrup to it. No reason to take up extra space on your Specials board."

I sighed with relief. Jae was usually pretty chill, but you never knew how someone would react when you suggested getting rid of their favorite items. We've had to deal with more than one irate customer who pitched a fit when they couldn't order an out-of-season drink or dessert, and I didn't want to hurt Jae's feelings by implying his current favorite beverage wasn't good enough for our menu.

"I know you wanted to have dinner at your place to plan for the soiree since it's coming up soon, but Jonathan and I already have plans with our parents," Jae said. "Are you OK just having your aunties and Adeena and Elena over? You can give me a rundown on the way to the party."

"That's fine, everyone else already has plans anyway. Since Chuy's been helping so much, Elena promised to fill in for a bartender tonight. Adeena's parents still don't want her going out, and Bernadette said something about Xander being in town. From what I heard, he's taking her and the Calendar Crew out to dinner."

He laughed. "Poor Bernadette. At this rate, they'll never get to have an unchaperoned date."

I laughed too. "That's what happens when you're as popular as Xander. The aunties love him and they overheard the two making plans, so they invited themselves. Can't wait to hear how it went."

We made it back to the cafe, but neither of us wanted to say goodbye. Jae's phone alarm forced the situation though. "Time for my next appointment. My schedule's packed for the rest of the week, so we probably won't be able to spend any real time together until the soiree. Make sure to save that first dance for me."

I pictured him bowing to me and asking for my hand to dance, like we were at a Jane Austen or *Bridgerton* ball, which led to me picturing him in breeches, and I almost had to fan myself, he was so hot.

I wasn't sure how, but he seemed to know what I was thinking, because he flashed that wicked grin he'd been showing me more and more and said, "Looking forward to seeing you in that dress. If we're lucky, maybe we can leave the soiree early."

Lord, please let us be lucky.

Chapter Nineteen

I've always kind of wondered how specialty stores like this stay in business, but this place is amazing."

Adeena gazed around the Olive Oil Emporium, taking in the smooth, gleaming wood tables and shelves piled high with various types of olive oil, vinegar, jams and preserves, and other products. We'd closed the cafe early to stock up on supplies for the next Corn Festival weekend (since I planned to be at the soiree Saturday night, I had to get all my weekend baking done early) and decided to throw in a Shelbyville trip since we were already out and about.

Remembering how everyone had wanted to check out Gladys's shop, we decided to head there first and then visit Quinn's boutique right before closing time. Adeena's parents were still being strict about her going out—they weren't locking her up or anything, but they asked enough questions and gave her enough restrictions that she'd mostly been staying home after work to avoid the hassle. Since this trip was technically during work hours, Adeena could enjoy more freedom than usual and we were going to take full advantage of it.

Not sure what to expect from an olive oil store, the three of us were a little overwhelmed by the amazing selection. We wandered together, not touching anything, just taking everything in, when Adeena stopped to pick up a large curved wooden tray that looked like it would make an excellent cheese or charcuterie board and tilted it to inspect the wood grain closely.

"Beautiful, isn't it? Made of polished olive wood by a local woodworker. Rustic yet chic." Ms. Gladys Stokes hadn't been on the floor when we first entered her shop, but now she was next to Adeena touting her wares. "A versatile piece for any home, but particularly nice if you like entertaining."

"My friend Sana's birthday is coming up and I think it would be a perfect gift for her." Adeena held up the tray so Elena and I could see it better. "What do you all think?"

"It's gorgeous," Elena said, running her finger across the smooth wood.

Gladys beamed. "I'll make sure to tell the artist you said that. It's my nephew," she added in a stage whisper. "Lovely to see you again, Lila. I see you've brought some friends with you."

"I promised you I would. These are my best friends and business partners, Adeena Awan and Elena Torres. This is the owner of the shop, Gladys Stokes."

Gladys shook their hands and gestured for us to follow her to a display in the middle of the shop. "Nice to meet you all. If you're interested in that tray as a present, we also have a full charcuterie set that pairs perfectly with it, as well as local honey and preserves."

"My uncle owns a local apiary and sources all the honey we use at the Brew-ha Cafe, but the charcuterie set looks great. The three of us can pool our money together and give it as a group gift," Elena said, inspecting the various items Gladys indicated. "Oh, you've got clotted cream. Lila, didn't you say you wanted to start carrying some for your scones?"

I rushed over to look at the jars in front of her. "Yes! A member of the PTA Squad wants us to cater her daughter's bridal shower and requested a fancy afternoon tea, complete with scones, clotted cream, and jam. I was going to attempt making my own, but this saves me so much time."

"Your uncle owns an apiary? I'm always looking for more local products to feature in the store. Do you have his card? Does he offer tours so I could sample his honey?"

"Yes and yes. I spent summers helping out at the apiary as a kid, so I'm confident when I say that his honey is the best I've ever had," Elena said, digging his card out of her wallet. "In return, can you tell me about your olive oil soap? And which of your olive oils you'd recommend if I wanted to try making my own?"

Gladys and Elena wandered off, throwing around terms like "saponification" and "cure times," leaving me and Adeena behind in the sample area. I felt like it had been forever since my best friend and I had been alone together and I had the unfamiliar sensation of not knowing what to say to her.

"It's been a while, huh? Since just you and I have had a chance to talk," Adeena said.

"Get out of my head, bruha! I was just thinking that."

She grinned at me. "Good to know I still have my powers. Anyway, now that it's just the two of us, we can do one of our favorite things."

I was confused until she gestured at the table in front of us, and I laughed. "Try the samples?"

"Try ALL the samples!"

"Let's do this."

My ex-fiancé had had me on his Costco account (I know, I thought it was true love at the time, too) and when Adeena came to visit us, one of our favorite things to do was hit up Costco and try the free samples. We truly knew how to live it up.

Adeena and I wandered around the shop, sipping the various olive oils and flavored vinegars, tasting the jams, and even sampling a delicious shrub made from local berries. Adeena went wild over the last item, asking the employee who'd just served us the drink how to make it.

"Oh, it's so easy! You just need overripe fruit, sugar, and vinegar, and you've got a syrup that should be good for months in the fridge, though I always drink it all up before I've had a chance to find out. It's great in cocktails and mocktails, but I mostly just top it with seltzer water when I want a pick-me-up." The employee showed us the vinegars that would work well for drinks. "You don't want distilled white vinegar, it's way too harsh. But depending on the flavor profile you're going for, you could play around with a cider vinegar or maybe a nice champagne or wine vinegar, or . . ."

Adeena quickly filled a basket with different types of vinegar for her to experiment with. "Forget olive oil coffee, this is the next drink I want to add to the menu."

"Sounds good! Can't wait to try it." I turned to the helpful employee. "She handles the drinks at our cafe, but I'm the baking person. Which olive oils would you recommend for a nice cake or dessert?"

"That's my area of expertise, so I'll take it from here, honey," Gladys said, reappearing with Elena. Like her girlfriend, Elena bore a basket full of products. Gladys was making good money off us Brewhas, and I could see how she'd managed to stay in business for decades.

"Elena tells me you're heading to Quinn's after this. Mind giving this to her for me?" Gladys asked after ringing us up. She handed me a large paper bag, the kind you'd get when ordering delivery. "I just know that girl hasn't been eating right with Yvonne gone, so I made her a little something. Tell her if she doesn't come by to see me before the weekend, she'd better be prepared for me to march into her store and make a scene."

I laughed. "Got it. I'm sure she'd love to see you though. Are you sure you don't want to be the one to drop it off?"

She shook her head. "I'm gonna trust you young people to handle it. She needs friends who aren't just her dog and an old lady who can't mind her own business."

"I don't know that three twentysomethings who can't mind their own business are any better, but we'll do our best," I promised. "We'll be back again soon. And if you ever have time, come visit us at the Brew-ha Cafe. You've got to see how we're putting your olive oil and vinegar to use."

We all said our goodbyes then Adeena, Elena, and I stopped at my car to drop off our purchases and grab Adeena's crocheted pieces before walking down the block to Quinn's boutique. I'd managed to convince Adeena to put her best finished projects on consignment by reminding her she could put the money into her yarn fund, and that it wouldn't hurt to have another reason to stop by the boutique and ask questions. I thought Adeena would want to hang back, maybe wait in the car or check out some other stores while Elena and I met with Quinn, but she refused.

"Look, I know why Quinn is weird around me. And I'm not going to pretend that I can begin to understand what she's going through. But I didn't do anything wrong and I'm tired of acting like I've got something to hide. She's the one who requested my work, so she should be ready to deal with me. If it gets too awkward, I'll bounce, but I don't want to begin this partnership tiptoeing around and having her pretend I'm not there."

My conflict avoidant tendencies aside, she was right. So the three Brew-has made our way to Blue Violet Boutique.

Since I'd only been there during personal shopping hours, I'd never met her staff or seen anyone else in the store (other than that time Mayor Reyes and Zack surprised us). Today, I got to see the Blue Violet Boutique as it usually operated and it was nice to see that, while it wasn't packed, there were enough shoppers to keep Quinn and her two part-timers busy. The three of us wandered the store while we waited for Quinn, Elena particularly excited to check out the wares. Out of all of us, the boutique's style fit Elena best—a lot of the clothes featured earth tones and neutrals, which meant not enough dark clothing for me or bright colors for Adeena.

Quinn found us in the accessories section, where the three of us were trying to figure out if any of us were hat girls. Considering we all had wavy-to-curly hair, finding the right hat was something we all took seriously, and as much as I liked the idea of hats, the reality had never quite worked out for me.

"We have some satin-lined beanies that would work for all of you," Quinn said, pointing to a pile in front of Adeena. "Also, I think hats are more about confidence than anything else. You can make any style work for you if you just lean in to it."

"You know what? I like that." Adeena picked up a wide-brimmed hat that was labeled "pencil brim fedora" in a lovely terra-cotta color. "I think it's time to reclaim the fedora. They're not just for neckbeards anymore."

If Quinn was confused by any of that (or wondered why Adeena was in her store to begin with), she didn't let on. "I'm glad you could all make it to the shop. Let me know if I can help you with anything."

Adeena held up her tote bag and the delivery bag from Gladys. "I brought some crochet pieces to see if you'd be interested in any of them. And we were just at the Olive Oil Emporium. Gladys asked us to give this to you."

After a brief hesitation, Quinn accepted the delivery bag. "Thanks for making the time to stop by. I'd love to see what you've got."

She shot me a quick look like, *What is happening? You were supposed to be the go-between!*

But I just smiled at her and said, "Elena and I are going to check out the rest of the store. Hope you two can figure something out!"

Quinn shot me one last pleading look before giving in, and while she haggled with Adeena, Elena and I split up to talk to Quinn's employees. We wanted to see if they had any insight into their former employer that others didn't—after all, I imagined those working for Yvonne had a very different relationship with her than someone who knew her on a more personal level. Elena had several items she wanted to purchase, so she went to talk to the cashier while I headed over to the young woman straightening the folded sweaters.

The woman must've heard me approaching because she turned with a smile and said, "Hello there! How can I help you?"

"Are these the sweaters that Yvonne loved? Quinn told me they were in this area." I watched her expression carefully to see if her face would give away how she felt about her deceased employer. Sure enough, a flicker of sadness came to her eyes even as she kept up her professional smile.

"It's actually this display over here." She led me to the correct section. "I didn't realize you knew Yvonne. I don't remember ever seeing you here."

"Unfortunately, I didn't know her very long before she passed away. But I met Quinn and wanted to provide support, so my boyfriend and I have stopped by to have Quinn help us with personal shopping."

The employee glanced in Quinn's direction before leaning forward. "That's so nice of you. I've been so worried about her. And Frank was saying something about the boutique maybe closing, but Quinn promised us that wouldn't happen."

She gestured at the cashier as she said this, so I assumed that was Frank.

"I'm glad to hear that. I really like this shop and would be sad to see it go." I picked up a sweater and unfolded it, pretending to study the pattern. "Have you worked here long?"

"About two or three years. I also work part-time at my family's sandwich shop near city hall. That's where I met Yvonne and how I started working here."

"Oh? Was she a regular?"

She nodded. "One day I told her that I'd stopped by her boutique and how much I wished I could afford the clothes there since everything was so beautiful. She told me that employees got a 40 percent discount and asked if I wanted a job there."

"40 percent? That's so generous," I said, not bothering to hide how shocked I was. I'd heard of people getting that kind of discount at chain retailers, but an independent boutique like this? Never. Even at the Brew-ha Cafe, the most we could offer Leslie and Helen (our delivery person) was a 20 percent discount and free leftover baked goods.

The employee smiled sadly. "Yeah, Yvonne was always super generous. Not that Quinn isn't, of course. But I think Yvonne paid for the employee and intern discounts out of her own pocket rather than the store's profits. I'm a little worried about what's going to happen with her gone."

"I'm sure the mayor has something in place to help out," I said. "Plenty of people have told me how important the intern program is to her, and I'm sure she'd want to keep this place going. Both out of respect for her wife and also for the good of the town."

The employee's eyes widened. "Wow, you really did know Yvonne well."

Oh crap, was that too much? I didn't want her to figure out who I was and what I was trying to do, so I decided to go with something vague that was still true. "Not as well as I would've liked."

I was still holding the sweater I'd picked up. "Sorry for messing up your display, but I don't think I want this sweater after all. Thanks for your help though."

"No worries! Let me know if there's anything else you need."

I surveyed the store to see where I should go next, when I noticed that Quinn was standing alone near the entrance, staring out the large window that made up most of the front wall of the boutique. I thought she was taking a moment to appreciate the sunny fall weather until I realized she was scanning the landscape as if looking for something.

I waited until I was a few feet away before saying, "Hey, Quinn—"

She gasped and whirled around, clutching the front of her blouse like I'd almost given her a heart attack. "Lila! Wha— Sorry. You surprised me. How can I help you?"

She pasted on a quick sales smile and tried to act like nothing was wrong, but I could see her chest heaving as she tried to regulate her breathing. I'd need a soft touch here.

I stepped a little closer, but not so close that I was in her personal space, and lowered my voice. "Are you OK?"

"I'm fine, I—"

"Quinn, I know things are tough right now. I understand if you don't feel comfortable talking to me, but you don't have to pretend you're OK. Do you need a moment in your office? Or I can get Gladys."

That at least had some effect on her because she said, "No, please don't tell Gladys. I don't need her worrying any more than she already is. It's just . . ." She bit her lip and glanced out the window again. "I know this is going to sound crazy, but . . . I feel like somebody's watching me. I'll be arranging a display and I'll feel eyes on me, and when I look up there's nobody there. But just now, I could swear I saw someone over by that tree."

She pointed to a small tree a few stores down. It was large enough to lean on comfortably, but not quite big enough for an adult to hide behind without being super obvious.

I must've looked skeptical because she added, "They weren't hiding. They were standing next to it as if waiting for someone, but they were staring at the store, I'm sure of it."

"I'm not doubting you," I assured her. If she thought I wasn't taking her seriously, she wouldn't open up to me, and this seemed like a good lead. "I was just thinking about how both Zack and Mayor Reyes said something similar recently. If all three of you are experiencing the same thing, it's likely the same person. Could you see what they looked like?"

Quinn looked relieved. "I was so sure I was hallucinating. I mean, being stalked isn't great news, but I was positive that I'd finally cracked."

I smiled. "Don't worry. Detective Park already knows about this and he's keeping an eye on the situation. I'll let him know to look out for you, too."

I expected her to smile back at that, but somehow that made her even more nervous. "I'm not going to have the police stationed at my store, am I? I'm already dealing with enough right now, I don't want anything that might hurt my business. Customers don't exactly love shopping at places that are being investigated."

Fair enough. "I'll let Detective Park know to be discreet. But make sure to keep an eye out and let him know if you see anything suspicious. Warn your employees, too." She looked like she wanted to protest that last statement, so I added, "It's not safe for you or anyone around you if you really are being stalked. They deserve to know."

She sighed. "You're right. I'll let them know now. Better not wait until closing time, just in case."

While she headed to the employee on the floor, I looked for my friends. Elena was at the register, and judging by the number of bags she had, Blue Violet Boutique's sales were just fine for the week. As I made my way over to her, I received a phone call from a number I didn't know. I let it go to voicemail to see if the caller would leave a message and they did. By the time I finished listening to it, both Adeena and Elena had joined me.

I must've looked as shocked as I felt because the first thing Adeena said was, "Why does your face look like that?"

"First of all, rude. Second, do you two mind waiting somewhere for a while? I have to go do something," I said, texting Jae and Detective Park to tell them what I was about to tell Adeena and Elena.

"Mayor Reyes wants to talk to me and Jae. Alone."

Chapter Twenty

Jae and Detective Park had responded to my texts immediately, but since they were both in Shady Palms, it would take them at least half an hour to arrive. At Adeena's insistence, I'd called the mayor back to get more details on why she wanted to see us, but all she said was that she wanted to discuss the soiree with us. Oh, and that she had a few questions about how I was conducting my investigation, but they could wait until I arrived.

Since I was only ten minutes or so from the address the mayor sent me, I got there way before the Park brothers. I didn't want to be alone in the house with her (she was still a suspect after all, and acting super weird), so I sat parked in front of her house while I waited for them to arrive. I played a merge game on my phone to pass the time and was deeply absorbed in earning enough tickets to plant a tree in real life when a sharp knock at my car window startled me back to reality.

Mayor Reyes studied me for a moment before gesturing for me to get out of the car, but I just rolled the window down slightly. "Uh, hi there, Mayor Reyes. I was just waiting—"

"Are you the one who's been watching me?"

"I— What?"

"I told you before, lately it feels like someone's watching me. Especially when I'm at home. Have you been staking out my house as part of your investigation?"

I was so shocked by the accusation that I was a little more blunt than I meant to be. "Mayor, I know I want to clear Adeena's name, but you know I have a job, right? And a life? If anyone's staking out your house, it's probably the cops. Or Detective Park."

Mayor Reyes looked confused. "Why would Detective Park be watching me?"

"That day we had lunch together. You said you were going to tell him that someone was following you."

She lowered her gaze. "I never told him. I guess with everything that's been going on, I wanted to convince myself I was just imagining things."

"I figured you wouldn't, so I did. Either someone is stalking you and you need to report it to the police, or Detective Park already handled it and the cops are keeping an eye on you for your safety."

She sighed. "You didn't need to do that. Anyway, why don't you come inside."

"Um, that's OK. I'll just wait here until Jae arrives."

"That's not necessary. Why don't you make yourself comf—" Her eyebrows had been all scrunched up in confusion, but they smoothed out when she realized what I was doing. "I see. You suspect me, don't you?"

"I'm just playing it safe, Mayor."

She closed her eyes and took a few deep breaths. Was she angry and needed to calm herself down? Or did I hurt her feelings and she needed to steady herself? Either way, she just said, "Fair enough. We can talk more once Dr. Jae arrives." And then she turned and walked back into her house.

"Well, that was awkward," I mumbled before returning to my game. I hoped she wouldn't change her mind about having me and Jae join her at the soiree, but it couldn't be helped. Luckily, Jae arrived not too long after and he promised to try to smooth things over after I filled him in on what had happened.

"Anyway, my brother said he got held up at the station but he should be here soon in case we need backup. I'm glad you waited for me," Jae added as we walked up the stairs.

"I do learn from my mistakes, you know."

Well, usually. Nobody's perfect.

Mayor Reyes let us in and led us to her kitchen. "Can I get either of you a drink? I was about to put on a pot of coffee."

Jae and I both agreed that a cup of coffee sounded great. Secretly, I thought that caffeine was probably a bad idea considering how jittery the mayor and I both were, but at least sipping on a drink would help me cover up any awkward silences on my part. And though I preferred iced coffee, clutching a warm mug was super comforting. Jae and I both loved specialty lattes, but when it came to regular coffee, our tastes were pretty simple: He took it black while I preferred a good splash of half-and-half. The mayor added a shocking amount of milk and sugar to her own coffee before gesturing for us to follow her into her living room.

Once we were all settled comfortably, Mayor Reyes said, "I'm sorry for all the cloak-and-dagger, but I thought you'd be more honest if it was just us. Jae, has Lila caught you up on what we discussed before you arrived?" At his nod, she said, "Do you have anything to add?"

He shook his head. "Feel free to have your receptionist check with mine, but I've kept to my usual schedule and have been spending most of my free time helping my parents. I have no reason and even less time to follow you around. I can't speak for my brother, though. Have you talked to him about this?"

Mayor Reyes sidestepped his question. "Let's table that topic for now. The soiree is this weekend and I'd like to know what your investigation plans are and if you need me to do anything."

"We mostly want to talk to Mayor Gunderson. His wife's been cleared, but his alibi's a little shaky from what I hear."

"Do you think he did it?"

I couldn't bear to see the look of naked hope in her eyes, so I dropped my gaze to my mug. "Honestly? No. Mayor Gunderson has a ton of flaws, but as far as I know, he's not out-and-out corrupt. And he's definitely not the type to get his own hands dirty. Unless Yvonne had dirt on him that was so scandalous he'd get thrown out of office, I can't picture him doing anything that heinous."

Jae agreed. "Though like Lila said, things change if Yvonne was threatening him with something. Do you think that's possible?"

Mayor Reyes shook her head. "They saw each other at functions we both attended with our spouses, but that's about it. Yvonne didn't care for how he talked to me or how he carried himself, but she wouldn't have bothered trying to dig up anything on him. She found him ridiculous. A non-threat, in the grand scheme of things."

"Then why are you focusing on him as a suspect?"

She looked into my eyes. "I have to focus on someone. I do believe that your friend is innocent. But that means we're left with no leads. And I can't bear that thought."

I gave her a minute to collect herself before asking, "I know this is a sensitive subject so I'm sorry, but I know you and Yvonne were getting a divorce. Could you tell me a little more about that councilman?"

"I knew you'd ask me about that sooner or later. Detective Park warned me you would, and yet I still wasn't ready." Mayor Reyes rubbed her hands up and down her face before letting out a bone-weary sigh. "What do you want to know?"

"How long had Yvonne been paying him off? And has he said anything to you now that she's gone?"

Mayor Reyes picked up her mug. "From what I gathered, it started around the third year of my first term. By that point, I was getting a little disillusioned. I'd started wondering if it really was possible for me to make a difference considering how few of the items I brought up got passed. But then Councilman Foster came to me with a compromise: If I included some important propositions that he wanted to get passed along with my most important proposals, he'd throw his support behind me. I was getting desperate, so I figured that if he wanted to use me, I might as well use him right back. At least that way some of my proposals had a chance of passing."

"And you had no idea that Yvonne had paid him to do that?"

The mayor shook her head. "I would've rather ended my term as a failure than stoop that low. Quid pro quo is common in politics, so I was prepared to lose my pride to get what I wanted. I was not and still am not willing to set a price on my ideals."

"Yvonne must've known how you felt. Did she ever explain why she did it?"

She looked down into her mug, gathering her thoughts. "My first couple years in office were tough. Tough on me. Tough on our marriage. I was not myself during that time and Yvonne didn't like who I was becoming. I think it scared her how all the pressures of the job were getting to me. So she tried to lighten the load the best way she knew how: by throwing money at it. That's how her family had always handled things and I'm guessing she thought that was her only option."

Her voice took on a nostalgic tone, as if she were reminiscing about something sweet despite the bitter smile on her face. "Her family actually tried to bribe her to not marry me. They were upset she was throwing away her place in her family's business for someone she barely knew. My parents were upset too, which is why they made her sign the prenup. But Yvonne didn't care about the money. Not then, anyway."

"What changed?"

"I guess she realized how hard it was to effect real change with just your ideals. She was as passionate as I was about making a difference in this town. But then she saw how difficult it was to take on an intern position if your family didn't have the means to support you. People say to dress for the job you want, but they don't talk about how expensive that is, how one's impression of what a professional looks like is based on shallow things like hair and clothing."

"Is that why she offered such generous discounts to the interns in your program?"

The mayor nodded. "That was the start of it all. All programs need funding, and bake sales and charity drives can only do so much. What you really need are sponsorships and generous donors. Yvonne was good at that part."

"How does Councilman Foster fit in with all that?"

"There's no such thing as a one-time favor. I wanted to accomplish more and more, which meant his demands became higher, for both me as well as Yvonne apparently. I cut him off after Zack told me what Yvonne was doing, though. He threatened me if I didn't continue to pay him off, but we both have enough on each other that we'd end up destroying both of our careers. So he's just been sulking on the side during all the council meetings."

"If he threatened you, do you think he threatened Yvonne as well?"

"I wouldn't doubt it. I asked her if he'd approached her at all, but she brushed it off saying she was fine and could take care of her own mess. I wish to god that I had pushed a bit more, told her that whatever happened to us, I'd always be there for her."

"You haven't told the police about the councilman being a potential suspect." It wasn't a question, but I wanted to see if she'd answer anyway. When she didn't, I said, "I understand why you didn't, but you have to see that he's the best lead we've got right now. If he's the one who killed Yvonne—"

The mayor got up and started pacing. "I know! And I'm prepared to throw my career away if it means catching Yvonne's killer. I just . . . I'm not ready yet. That's why I'm talking to you even with Detective Park doing his own investigation. I keep hoping that you two will find an alternative path."

"Again, I understand why you feel that way, but Detective Park is—"

"Quiet!"

Jae, who'd been silent throughout this entire conversation, suddenly cut us off and stood up, throwing his arm out to the side as if to shield me.

"Jae, what's—"

"I just saw someone outside the window."

Before the mayor and I could freak out, Jae put his finger to his lips and made a phone call. "Hyung? How far away are you? OK, good. There was someone peeking into Mayor Reyes's house. It doesn't seem like they're trying to get in, but—" Jae was quiet and I could tell he was listening to his brother's instructions. "So you'll head through the back? Wait two minutes and go out through the front, got it."

He hung up and turned to us. "The two of you should stay together and my brother suggests staying away from the windows. Mayor, if you want to call the police, now's the time to do it. But we're going to do our best to make sure the suspect doesn't run away. Whatever you do, do not go outside. Understood?"

The only thing Mayor Reyes and I could do with gentle Jae being this forceful was nod. No reason for us to argue and play the hero.

The mayor put in the call to a friend of hers at the police department and by the time she was done, Jae had headed outside.

We waited in silence. Mayor Reyes had requested that the police not use any sirens so as not to scare away whoever was outside, so we had no idea how close they were or what was going on out there.

Luckily, we weren't kept in suspense for long. The front door opened and the mayor and I both whipped around to see the Park brothers leading a woman dressed in a puffy coat, who looked to be in her late thirties or early forties, inside. She looked vaguely familiar and I couldn't figure out why until . . .

"Jessica?!"

"You were the woman outside of Gladys's store! And at the corn maze!"

Mayor Reyes and I looked at each other.

"You've seen her before?"

"Who's Jessica?"

The woman must've gotten tired of the mayor and me jinxing each other because she rolled her eyes and said, "I'm Jessica. Jessica Maldonado, Yvonne's younger sister."

"I thought you weren't coming. Your family told me that you'd changed your mind, canceled your flight. Why didn't any of you tell me you were here? Where have you been staying?" The mayor's voice sounded more and more frantic with each question, and Jessica held her hand up to get her to stop.

"I came separately. I wanted a chance to observe you and the people who were around Yvonne without anyone knowing."

"But . . . why . . . ?"

"I've been calling this town's police department to check on how the investigation is going. Day after day, I've been calling yet there's been no forward movement. All the police will tell me is that no one's been arrested yet. My sister was murdered, but no one will tell us anything! I figured people would act differently around me if they knew I was Yvonne's sister. Be too careful about what they say, things like that. So I came incognito."

"You're the stalker!" I blurted out. "The mayor, Zack, and Quinn have all mentioned at one point that they felt like someone was watching them. It was you, wasn't it? Trying to figure out if any of them were involved in your sister's death. Is that why you were at the corn maze, too? You wanted to check out the crime scene?"

"I am not a stalker! I was just studying them! Judy and Quinn were the ones closest to Yvonne and I heard that Zack guy didn't like my sister very much, so you all seemed like the natural choice."

"Um, why didn't you just talk to them?" I asked. "I understand not approaching Zack since you don't know him, but you know Quinn. I heard she was super close to your family. And Judy's your sister-in-law."

"My sister-in-law who I've never met because Yvonne chose her over our family," Jessica reminded me. "And Quinn, I don't know. I haven't seen or talked to her since she left for college almost thirty years ago. We're not the same people anymore. I wasn't sure if I could trust her."

The mayor started to ask a question but was interrupted by a knock at the door. At her nod, Detective Park checked the door security cam before opening it up. A Shelbyville police officer stood on the porch.

"Hey there, Jonathan. Mayor Reyes, is everything OK?"

The mayor glanced at Jessica before saying, "False alarm, Officer. Sorry about that. But while you're here, I'd like to introduce you to someone. This is Yvonne's younger sister, Jessica. She may have some questions for the department. I'd appreciate it if you could help her with anything she needs."

The officer tipped his cap at Jessica. "My condolences, ma'am. I'll let the guys know to expect you and we'll do the best we can to accommodate you."

Jessica thanked him and he nodded. "Just doing my job, ma'am. If there's nothing else, I'll head back to the station."

The mayor dismissed him and once he left, there was an awkward silence. Jae and I were having a conversation with our eyes, like, *Should we say something? Do we leave the two of them alone? Do we interrogate Jessica to see if she might know anything?*

Finally, Mayor Reyes turned to us. "Thank you all for your time today. Jessica and I have a lot to catch up on, so I'll just contact Detective Park if I need anything. Jae and Lila, I'll see you at the soiree on Saturday?"

After we assured her that we'd be there, she said, "Good. I'll make sure to introduce you to that person of interest we were discussing, and I'll let you take it from there."

She walked us all to the door, but before I could leave, she pulled me aside. "Thank you again, Lila. I'm counting on you. We both are."

Mayor Reyes glanced back at Yvonne's sister, who was holding the framed photo of the mayor and Yvonne on their wedding day that I'd seen on the side table. She was far enough away that I couldn't see her expression, but her fingers were on the glass and her sadness and longing were almost palpable. I tore my eyes away from her private grief.

"I won't let you down."

Chapter Twenty-One

It was time for Mayor Gunderson's big soiree. This night was our best chance to talk to the councilman without rousing his suspicion. Zack had messaged me the other day saying he confirmed that Councilman Foster had been scheduled to be at the Corn Festival the day Yvonne died, so now we needed to find out if he'd actually gone and gotten in contact with Yvonne there.

I thought Adeena was ridiculous with her dreams of a sexy ballroom dance investigation, but she may have been onto something. When I first started dating my ex-fiancé, I used to love accompanying him to charity galas, drawn in by the glitz and glamour. I loved dressing up. I loved having an excuse to look cute while also networking with people in the Chicago hospitality industry. But the shine of those exciting new experiences quickly wore off after Sam and his family made it clear that I needed to step it up if I was going to be worthy of his family name. That's when those events became a source of anxiety instead of fun. Every conversation was riddled with land mines, and it became more and more difficult to ignore the whispers that I didn't belong, that Sam could do so much better.

When Mayor Reyes had informed me and Jae that we'd be going to the soiree as her guests, some of that old anxiety had come back. But unlike when I was with Sam, here in Shady Palms, I had my support system helping me get ready and I knew I was safe.

Elena styled my hair while Sana did my makeup. Adeena lent me her bangles and kept us laughing nonstop while Yuki dropped by with a hairclip her daughter, Naoko, had made for me. Bernadette lent me an old silk shawl from her pageant days that went perfectly with my dress. These were real friends, unlike all the people who had pretended to care about me but sided with Sam after I found out he was cheating on me.

And then, of course, there was Jae. When I walked down the stairs to meet him after the girls helped me get ready, I felt like Rachael Leigh Cook in *She's All That*. It wasn't like I'd had a major makeover or anything, but to be fair, in the movie all they did was remove her glasses and overalls and give her a cute dress. For me, that moment was about the confidence she felt and the way Freddie Prinze Jr. looked at her. Maybe that's what it was—the expression on Jae's face made me feel like the female love interest in a movie. Like he'd never seen anyone or anything so beautiful in his life. And as he smiled up at me, I felt my heart lurch. *Down, girl. Focus on the plan for the evening.*

Tita Rosie, Lola Flor, Detective Park, and the Calendar Crew were all there as well to see us off, and as usual, the Calendar Crew made a huge fuss.

"You should've gone with the yellow princess dress, but this isn't bad."

"You look wonderful! Money well spent, diba? No need to thank us."

"So sexy! Don't you think so, Dr. Jae?"

Jae held out his hand to help me down the last step, which was appreciated since even though I wore heels every day, I hadn't worn a pair this high in years. Also, I wouldn't normally wear shoes inside the house, but I wanted him to get the full effect of the outfit when he saw me. The heels were brand-new, so it's not like I was really breaking Asian Household Rule Number One.

"You look amazing, Lila." His eyes shone with admiration and a tinge of heat, which made the blood rush to my head. And there was something else there too, which I couldn't quite put my finger on . . .

"Picture time!" my aunt said.

"We really should get going—"

"Lila, pose for the picture!" Lola Flor ordered.

My godmothers arranged Jae and me in what I could only describe as cringeworthy prom poses, with my aunt directing Detective Park on the photos she wanted and Detective Park doing exactly what she wanted while holding back a laugh. By the time we were finally allowed to leave, I was STRESSED and the evening hadn't even started yet.

Pulling up in front of Mayor Gunderson's McMansion and turning over the car to a valet (valet parking in Shady Palms?) did not help my anxiety one bit. Which was why I literally jumped and screamed when someone grabbed me from behind and shouted, "Boo!"

"Xander, not cool, man." Jae held my hand tightly, as if he knew I was ready to make a run for it. "It's just Xander being a jerk, you're safe."

I turned around to see my friend trying to look guilty, but the grin he was fighting back didn't do him any favors.

I glared at him. "What're you doing here?"

His grin won out. "Hello to you too, Lila. I've been good, thanks for asking."

I laughed and swatted his arm. "Don't give me that. Why didn't you tell me you were going to be here? Actually, why didn't you tell me you were in town to begin with? I had to hear about it from the Calendar Crew."

"I wanted to surprise you. I stopped by Tita Rosie's Kitchen to say hi to your family and get some good food, and the aunties were all there getting lunch."

"Oh, I see where this is going."

"One thing led to another, and next thing I know, I'm picking up Bernadette and driving the whole squad to a restaurant in Shelbyville to gossip with some church ladies."

It was that time of year where a beautiful, sunny afternoon faded into a brisk, cold night, and the silk shawl Bernadette lent me wasn't enough for a Midwestern autumn evening. Xander must've noticed me shivering because he said we could finish the conversation inside and ran up the steps to open the door for me. I followed him and once inside I gave another shiver, this one in appreciation at the sudden warmth that enveloped me.

After showing our invitation to the staff at the door, I said, "Fine, you're off the hook for not contacting me, but how'd you end up here?"

"Mr. Cruz has been very generous during his time here in Shady Palms, investing in quite a few local businesses and getting some of his friends interested in doing the same," Mayor Gunderson said as he and his wife and Mayor Reyes walked up to join us, gazing at Xander with genuine affection. "When Mayor Reyes informed me he was in town and helping her get her in-laws situated, I had her extend an invitation to him."

"Didn't you arrive here a couple days ago?" Jae asked. "Where did you get a tux so quickly?"

"What else would I be wearing? It's after six. What am I, a farmer?" Xander paused for a moment, probably to see if anyone got that reference (pretty sure Jae was the only one who did), then added, "I have a pretty extensive wardrobe at my vacation house here. I'd planned on just picking up a few things and staying elsewhere, but I guess I hit it off with Mayor Reyes's in-laws over our initial calls. When I told them I'd also be in town, they asked if we could all share the house together. The place is meant to be a bed-and-breakfast, after all, though I usually hire someone to handle the breakfast part. Still, it's not like it'd be the first time I stuck around to cook and host."

"Thank you so much for agreeing to their request, Xander," Mayor Reyes said. "They're still a little stiff around me, but they warmed up to you immediately. I'm sure it was awkward sharing your home with strangers, but it means a lot to me. To all of us."

Xander smiled. "They're the ones doing me a favor! I hadn't planned on staying in Shady Palms for longer than a day or two, but now that I'm here till the end of the month, I'd much prefer the comfort of my home away from home rather than some hotel."

"The end of the month? Why so long?"

"I just need to get away from the city for a bit. I can do my work remotely, plus I promised Ronnie and Izzy I'd stop by the winery to talk strategy. Besides, I can't come all the way here and not stay for the closing festivities of the Corn Festival. Bernadette promised to show me around since she'll be off that day."

There it was, the real reason he was sticking around so long. It had been love at first sight for Bernadette (she'd never admit it, but we all knew), but considering they'd met because she was the nurse on duty the night his fiancée died, she'd never been able to let him know how she felt. However, it'd been almost a year since Xander had started coming to Shady Palms to relax, check out his investments, and spend time with my family and friends, whom he'd bonded with immediately. Bernadette had been resigned to being his friend, but things took a sexy turn after we all took a trip to his cabin on Lake Michigan over the summer. She still wouldn't tell me what happened, but ever since then, every one of his stops in Shady Palms has included several dates with Bernadette. Neither of them made it seem like something official, so I guess they were taking it slow. Good for them.

"Her birthday's coming up, just FYI," I said.

His eyes lit up. "We're gonna have to talk later. But for right now, I believe you had something you wanted to discuss with Mayor Gunderson."

Dang, he was good. I hadn't even briefed him on what I was trying to do, but he still knew there was an ulterior motive for me being here. It was too soon to jump into a murder discussion, but with Mayor Reyes here, there was another topic that I could naturally bring up.

"Recently, I overheard some of the PTA Squad talking about how they wished there were more opportunities for young people here in Shady Palms. They were worried that their kids would all leave after graduation and never come back. It's been happening more and more lately."

When I'd left town for university almost a decade ago, I was one of the few in my graduating class who'd done that. Most people went to community colleges in neighboring towns and stayed at home. But now, there were fewer and fewer jobs in Shady Palms and most kids saw no reason to come back after experiencing what else was out there. I was all for going out and finding your own path, but it was a shame that people felt like there was no choice, that they had to leave if they wanted better things. I wanted to help create something for those who were still in Shady Palms (willingly or not) because I'd come to see the potential the town had. I'd originally latched on to this idea as part of the investigation, but the more I heard about it and thought about it, the more I started to care about making this program a reality.

"Yes, yes, we all know that's one of our biggest problems," Mayor

Gunderson said. He looked upset that I'd dared bring up one of his town's failings, especially in front of our rival town's mayor. "What about it? I'm guessing you have some magic solution?"

"No magic, just a proposal. Mayor Reyes revamped the internship program for Shelbyville, providing on-the-job training for future government employees and other positions in town. Considering that internships generally require you to be enrolled in college, that's not helpful for the young people who choose not to go to a traditional school or need to enter the workforce immediately. I think we should study how Shelbyville runs its program and adapt it to meet Shady Palms's needs."

I'd practiced this speech with Sana, who in addition to teaching fitness classes also worked as a life coach for women of color entrepreneurs. Her previous life as a lawyer made her exceptionally good at crafting convincing pitches, presentations, proposals, and other business things that don't start with *P*.

Mayor Gunderson patted my arm. "It's sweet that you're thinking about the future of our town, but I don't know that it would work here. Besides, I wouldn't want it to seem like we're stealing Mayor Reyes's idea."

His words and gestures were so patronizing, I was speechless. Luckily, Mayor Reyes jumped in.

"I wouldn't look at it as stealing. It's an exchange of ideas between two town leaders. Besides, I think it's flattering and also affirming." She smiled at me. "I'd love nothing more than for this program I built my initial campaign around to inspire other towns in the same way."

Mayor Gunderson still looked unimpressed, and I wondered how thick I'd need to lay it on, when Xander came to the rescue again.

"Lila mentioned the proposal to me in passing and I thought it sounded like something my company would love to get involved in. With the winery and microbrewery here, plus with the increasing tourism, I might consider expanding to this area. I'd need a lot of young workers willing to learn on the job, though. I was hoping to set up a base in Shady Palms, but if Shelbyville already has the infrastructure for a project like this—"

"Whoa, let's not be too hasty now, Mr. Cruz! I didn't say no to Lila's proposal. I can't make snap decisions with the town's budget, that's all. I'm just being prudent, right? But if she'd like to submit an official proposal, I'd be happy to look it over and see if it's ready to put to a town vote."

I could practically see the mayor sweating as he walked back everything he'd just said to win Xander's (and his multimillion-dollar hospitality corporation's) approval. I mouthed "thank you" to Xander when the mayor had his back turned and he winked at me and continued working his charm on Mayor Gunderson. With Xander busy charming the mayor and Jae deep in conversation with Mrs. Gunderson, I looked around the room to see who I should chat up next.

Luckily, Mayor Reyes took the lead when she placed her hand on the small of my back and leaned close. "That's Councilman Foster by the bar. You wanted to talk to him, right? I'll make the introductions and then excuse myself. He's more likely to talk freely when I'm not around anyway."

We made our way across the room, stopping every few feet so the mayor could greet someone, sometimes with a hearty handshake, other times with a double-cheek air kiss. She always made sure to introduce me, and despite the political glad-handing, she managed to exude genuine warmth as she did this. Maybe because she not only seemed to remember the minute details of these people's lives ("Your youngest grandchild just had a recital, didn't they? How was it?" or "I heard your daughter just got into med school. Congratulations!"), but she actually took the time to introduce me to everyone and talk up the Brew-ha Cafe and my proposal for the job training program in Shady

Palms. Watching her, I could see why people offered up their babies to receive kisses from politicians (which always seemed kinda gross to me).

Speaking of kinda gross, I couldn't help but compare this experience to past ones at formal functions with my ex-fiancé, Sam. In the beginning, I'd been too nervous to converse with the other attendees even though I was dying to make connections with the high-end Chicago restaurant scene. I didn't want to embarrass myself or Sam, who'd grown up attending fancy events and was perfectly at home at society gatherings. So I forced myself to study and become more knowledgeable about the field (and all the gossip within it) so I could chat confidently with everyone. But the more outgoing I became, the less happy Sam was with me.

It took me years to realize that my role was supposed to be arm candy. To be seen and never heard. It got to the point where he wouldn't even introduce me when he came across people I didn't know. I was expected to just stand silently next to him while he conducted business and charmed everyone around him. I'd wondered why no one called him out on not introducing me at these parties until I overheard some women gossiping in the bathroom—they assumed I couldn't speak English since they'd never heard me talk in public and Sam encouraged that bit of misinformation.

I'd tried blocking all that from my memory since moving back to Shady Palms, but as I reflected on it, I realized why I'd freaked out so much at the beginning of the night about having to attend the soiree. These kinds of parties weren't just boring to me (which was what I'd told myself was the only problem for years), they were fairly traumatic. As I waited for Mayor Reyes to finish talking to her latest conversation partner, my eyes wandered the room and alit on Jae, who was still with the Gundersons. I got the sudden urge to talk to him, so I pulled out my phone and sent him a quick text.

Still haven't reached the target

Bored

I saw him receive my message, and he gestured to the Gundersons that he had to answer before replying:

Tell the mayor you're getting food.

Let me know if you need me to step in.

Ooh, that was a good idea. There was quite an impressive spread laid out next to the bar, so Councilman Foster would at least be in sight and I could stuff my face while I waited.

👍

Miss you. You still owe me a dance.

Grinning at Jae's last message, I tucked my phone back into my purse and told the mayor where I was going. She assured me she'd be along shortly, so I made my way to the long table laid out with food. Servers drifted around the room with trays of canapes and flutes of champagne, but the table held platters of finger foods that were more substantial than the tiny crostini and cheese-topped crackers that the servers offered. I piled my plate high with deviled eggs topped with caviar, pastry boats full of crab salad, tea sandwiches layered with butter and thin slices of cucumber, and warm dates stuffed with nuts and drizzled with honey. I'll say this for Mayor Gunderson: He knew how to cater an event. I even spotted a special table to the side marked

"Kosher/Halal" and was on my way to check it out when someone stopped me.

"Well, hello there. I don't think I've seen you at any of Mayor Gunderson's soirees," an unctuous voice beside me said. I turned around and came face-to-face (literally, the man was surprisingly short and standing ridiculously close to me) with Councilman Foster.

"Oh! Hello there," I said, taking a step back. "Yes, this is my first time at one of his parties."

"Rather stuffy for my taste, but the man knows how to turn out a decent spread." He held up his equally full plate. "I do like a woman with a good appetite. Could I get you a drink, Miss . . . ?"

I forced a smile. "Macapagal. Lila Macapagal. And I'd love a glass of Moscato or something bubbly."

I headed to the bar with him, and after he put in my order, he said, "You didn't have to follow me here. It's not like I'm going to put anything in your drink."

"Oh, I didn't think anything like that." Of course I did. I was a woman accepting a drink from a strange man. "I just figured there was no point in me standing around waiting for you. Also, you still haven't introduced yourself."

He smacked his forehead. "How silly of me! I don't know why I assumed you knew who I was. I'm Councilman Foster. Though I guess I'm technically not *your* councilman since I work in Shelbyville. You're from here, right?"

"How could you tell?"

"Oh, there's a certain . . . Shady Palms air about you. Besides, I'm sure I would've noticed a constituent as lovely as you," he added with a wink.

First of all, not everyone could pull off a wink. In fact, most people couldn't without looking super cringe. Instead of looking suave, which I'm sure was his intention, he looked more like Lucille Bluth from *Arrested Development*. Second, there was something incredibly condescending about the way he spoke about me and my town. Like, I'm sure me having a "Shady Palms air" wasn't an entirely flattering thing to him. And third, what a BS line that he would've noticed me. In a town of over thirty thousand people? Sure, buddy. I bet you say that to all the girls. But I had to interrogate him, and he'd actually sought me out, so I needed to roll with this and see what info I could pry out of him.

"So then you work for the Shelbyville government?"

"Sure do."

"Your poor mayor. How sad to lose your wife in such a tragic way."

He fixed an appropriately somber expression on his face. "Yes, so tragic."

"I can't believe I was there the day that woman was killed. I mean, I thought the Corn Festival was good, wholesome fun, and then a murder happens? What is this world coming to?" I shook my head, probably hamming it up a little too much, but he ate it up.

"I know exactly what you mean, my dear. We'd like to think of our sleepy little towns as safe places, but sadly that's not the case anymore. You know, the real problem is—"

"Were you at the Corn Festival that day?" I asked, cutting him off. I had zero interest in hearing what he thought the "real" problem was, but with a guy like him, I could easily guess.

He seemed disgruntled that I'd interrupted him while he was building up steam, but said, "Yes, I was there with my kids. They wanted to go into the corn maze, but I didn't have time for it and now I'm glad we didn't go in! What if we'd stumbled across that criminal?"

Success! He was there! But wait, if he brought his kids, I doubt he took the time to murder a woman in a corn maze.

"You brought your kids! How sweet. You mentioned not having

time though. Did you have to leave early?" I took a sip of my drink and tried not to look too eager for his answer. Ooh, this was good Moscato.

"I promised my ex I'd take the kids to the festival and stay with them all day, but I got called in for a work thing before we could get to the maze." He threw back the last of his whiskey and sighed. "She made a big fuss about having to pick them up, but it's not like I wanted to work on my day off."

"That sucks," I said, pretending to commiserate. "Especially when your boss got to play around all day. Did you see her there?"

"Yeah, well, all things considered, my day went better than hers, so I'm not going to complain too much. And no, I didn't see her at all. I did see her assistant though, that little brownnoser."

"Zack?"

"Yeah, that guy. I'm so used to them always being together that I thought it was weird seeing him alone. He's usually trailing after the mayor like a puppy hoping for a head scratch and some treats. But maybe he was running an errand, like grabbing her coffee or hitting up every booth to find her an after-dinner mint or something."

I laughed. "That's oddly specific."

"That man once drove to Dekalb to get her a particular type of off-brand grape drink mix because her stock was running low."

Dekalb was over an hour away from Shady Palms, so a two-plus-hour round-trip drive for some drink mix seemed pretty ridiculous and I said as much.

Councilman Foster rolled his eyes. "He would whittle her a year's supply of toothpicks if that's what she said she wanted."

"I didn't realize Mayor Reyes was such a demanding boss."

"Nah, she's actually decent if she thinks you're on her side. He did those things unprompted." He shook his head. "That kid is obsessed with her. I've tried to warn her about him, but she just waves it off. Says he's dedicated."

Considering how my whole group noted Zack's unusual loyalty to Mayor Reyes, the councilman's comments made me think over our interactions with Zack in a different light. I thought he'd spilled the beans about Yvonne's bribery because he was desperate to help the mayor. But what if he was trying to throw us off his track?

I wanted to ask the councilman if he remembered when he saw Zack at the Corn Festival, but Mayor Reyes popped up at that moment. "Councilman Foster! Always a pleasure."

"Mayor Reyes, I wasn't expecting to see you here tonight. You look lovely," Councilman Foster said, offering his cheek for an air kiss.

Mayor Reyes stuck out her hand for a firm handshake. "I would've loved to have skipped it, considering the circumstances, but this is an important time for Shelbyville–Shady Palms relations. Luckily, the Gundersons have been so kind and accommodating tonight. They shifted the original program a bit so that I could duck out after dinner without missing anything."

"Bill can be surprisingly thoughtful when he wants to be," Councilman Foster said with a smile.

"Bill?" I asked.

"Mayor Gunderson. The two of us go way back," he explained. "I've probably attended every one of his shindigs since he was first elected. Fascinating to see how he's grown."

I felt like a kid whose world is rocked when they find out their teachers have an actual first name and a life outside of school. It reminded me of the time I saw the local priest, Father Santiago, wearing a Hawaiian shirt and jeans at the grocery store. Like, who knew priests wore regular clothes and had to go grocery shopping like everyone else? Not ten-year-old Lila. I'd only ever heard people refer to our mayor by his title, so it somehow never occurred to me that there were people who called him by his first name. His own wife referred to him as Mayor Gunderson, at least in public (and I had ZERO interest in their private life).

Wanting to move on to a useful topic, I said, "Councilman Foster was telling me that he was at the opening day of the Corn Festival but had to cut it short because he had to go in to work. You have a very dedicated staff, Mayor Reyes."

"I didn't know that you went to the office that day, Carl." Mayor Reyes tilted her head. "Is there an issue I need to be aware of?"

"No, nothing like that. I just remembered some paperwork I forgot to sign off on and wanted to handle it ASAP. It gave me an excuse to not have to do the corn maze with my kids, so I didn't mind." Then, as if he remembered what happened in the corn maze that day and who he was talking to, he said, "Oh, and sorry again for your loss. Yvonne was a real firecracker."

Mayor Reyes's only response was a nod.

Councilman Foster looked back and forth between me and Mayor Reyes, clearly wanting to keep talking to me but not sure how to proceed through the awkwardness with his boss (was she technically the boss? She was at least the superior of the council members, right? I should've paid more attention in AP government). Finally, he excused himself, saying he saw a friend of his across the room.

"Save a dance for me, OK? I'm sure your boyfriend won't mind. See you later, Lila." With another terribly executed wink, he was gone.

"Sorry to chase him off when I'm sure you had more questions, but I cannot stand that man," Mayor Reyes said under her breath. "I always feel like I need a shower after talking to him to wash all the slime off. A stiff cocktail will have to do the trick instead. Care for a refill?"

"Yes, please."

I followed her over to the bar and ordered myself another glass of Moscato. It wasn't until I watched her order and toss back a dry martini that I realized she was definitely not doing as well as she'd like everyone to believe. I signaled for another drink for Mayor Reyes and waited until she had it in hand before prying.

"So, Yvonne's family is flying back tomorrow?"

The mayor nodded and took a healthy gulp of her drink.

"How did it go? I know it was your first time meeting them."

"Everyone was nice and polite and took care to say nothing of substance to me. Honestly, I was fully prepared for multiple screaming matches or a dramatic reveal at her funeral. But it was all very quiet and conservative. Pleasant." Mayor Reyes plucked the toothpick out of her glass and bit into one of the olives. Her lips puckered, but I couldn't tell if it was due to the brininess of the olive or the memory of her in-laws' visit. "Yvonne would've hated it."

I could sense there was more she wanted to say, so I took a sip of my wine and kept my eyes on her.

"The thing with Jessica . . . she was the one Yvonne was closest to before the family cut ties with Yvonne. She was the one I most wanted to meet. But she skipped out on her big sister's funeral and lied about not being in town in order to spy on me. Who does that?"

The mayor didn't seem like she could let her perfect mask drop, but in those words, in the flash that came and went in her eyes, I could feel the pain she refused to let anyone else see.

I put my hand on hers and squeezed. "I'm sorry. It all sounds complicated. I wish this wasn't the way you finally met Yvonne's family."

"Wishes. We had so many of them, Yvonne and I." The mayor stared down into her glass before looking up to meet my gaze for a moment. "You're a decent person, Lila. I appreciate everything you're doing. Truly."

Mayor Reyes tossed back the last of her drink and squared her shoulders. "Enough wallowing. It was never going to be a good night for me, but I got to enjoy good booze and some even better company.

Let's make the most of the evening. We wouldn't want Mayor Gunderson's lavish spending to go to waste, now would we?"

That drew a laugh out of me, and the mayor and I attacked the appetizers with energy.

The rest of the night was fairly entertaining, passing by in a haze of free drinks, delicious food, and inane chatter. I tried to pick up some clues here and there throughout the night, but halfway through dinner (as I feasted on the most perfectly cooked piece of lamb I'd had in my life) I decided I should try to, you know, enjoy myself. This was a rare fancy night out with Jae, and I'd picked up some interesting tidbits about Zack while also confirming that Councilman Foster was at the festival the day Yvonne died. I could take my amateur sleuth badge off for one night.

With Jae by my side and Xander being Xander, dinner was full of fun and good food and passed quickly. Even Mayor Gunderson's usual droning speech didn't annoy me as much as it usually did since I was doing a play-by-play in the Brew-ha group chat, and I had to fight not to laugh out loud at some of Adeena's comments. As promised, Mayor Reyes left after dinner, stating that she had to wake up early to drop off Yvonne's family at the airport, but her departure still took over half an hour because she insisted on stopping and saying goodbye to every acquaintance she passed.

I was tempted to leave as well, but Jae looked too good in his tux to not try and extend the evening. I was not a good dancer (that was Bernadette's area), but I really enjoyed it and hadn't gone dancing in years. Well, technically, Sana's Sangria Sundays often devolved into a drunken dance party, but there's a big difference between goofing around in your friend's living room and getting down on a proper dance floor.

"Jae, I believe I was promised a dance."

Jae held out his hand and I placed mine in his and he escorted me to the dance floor. They weren't playing the kind of music I was used to, but Jae led me through the steps with none of the awkwardness I'd expect from him in a situation like this.

"Where'd you learn to dance like this?"

He averted his eyes. "My mom loves ballroom dancing and she used to go with my dad every week. Now that he's sick and doesn't have the energy for it anymore, my brother and I take turns going dancing with her."

I lost the rhythm and tripped over my feet at the sudden, adorable confession. The expression on his face told me not to make a big deal out of it and ruin the moment, so I just tightened my grip on him and continued dancing the night away.

As we were preparing to leave, Xander popped up with one last surprise for us. "Hey, before you go, I've got someone who wants to talk to you!"

Councilman Foster ran his eyes over Jae before stepping forward and handing me a business card. "Mr. Cruz here told me about your interest in Shelbyville's job placement program. I worked on this with the mayor, so feel free to stop by if you have any questions. I'd be happy to discuss next steps with you. Perhaps over lunch?"

Ignoring the implication in that last question (and making a note to myself to never be alone in a room with him), I said, "Oh, that would be great! I'll be sure to stop by on Monday then."

After setting up an appointment time, I said goodbye to him and Xander and dragged an unusually quiet Jae out of there. We waited for the valet to bring out Jae's car in silence, but as soon as we got in and pulled away from the curb, Jae said, "I'm going with you."

"Jae—"

"You can't go alone, it's not safe."

I put my hand on his leg. "I won't go alone, but I don't think you should come along. That's a guy who lets his guard down around women, and I need him in a talking mood."

Jae kept his eyes on the road and didn't speak for so long, I was gearing up for an argument when he said, "Ask Beth to go with you."

Beth Thompson and Jae used to have a thing, and while I was over it and cool with Beth, it still took a few deep breaths before I could ask, "Why?" without sounding ridiculously jealous. Not jealous of their fling, but that, apparently, he trusted Beth enough to take his place on the recon mission to the councilman's office.

He must've noticed because he said, "She's one of the heads of the chamber of commerce, so it seems more legit to have her there. Plus, she's proficient in, like, three different martial arts. And she used to beat me at arm wrestling all the time."

"Dang, that's kind of hot."

I hadn't meant to let that slip, so I quickly added, "I mean, very cool. You're right, she's a good person to have watching my back. Thanks for the suggestion."

"You are very welcome." Jae finally glanced over at me. "I'm not ready for the night to end just yet. Do you have to go straight home?"

"No."

He grinned. "I was hoping you'd say that."

And so we spent the rest of the night together, preparing for the long week ahead.

Chapter Twenty-Two

The soiree was a wonderful diversion, but it was time to put what I'd learned into effect. After talking it over with the Brew-has, we decided that Elena would accompany me and Beth to Councilman Foster's office. I was surprised at how willing Beth was to come along considering how busy she was running the town's biggest company on top of her chamber of commerce duties, but then again, she'd been extremely receptive about the job placement program after I explained it to her. Plus, it's not like this was the first time she'd gotten involved in one of my investigations. Add free coffee and a box of her favorite Brew-ha Cafe pastries to the mix and she was ready to take on the councilman.

The three of us checked in with Felice at the reception desk and chatted with her for a few minutes. I was curious about the supposed work Councilman Foster had to do that cut his time at the Corn Festival short, and wondering how we could corroborate his alibi. Felice said she wasn't at city hall that day, but that she'd talk to the receptionist that comes in on the weekends. She also suggested having Detective Park request security footage, which I made a note to do. I doubted he or the police had bothered since the crime took place in Shady Palms and Yvonne didn't work at city hall, which meant they might've missed an important clue. If he'd gone to his office to handle some paperwork as he'd claimed during the soiree, surely the security cameras would attest as much.

We all thanked her and left her with her favorite drink and some pastries before heading to Councilman Foster's office on the second floor. The long, carpeted hallway was empty, but I could hear various conversations behind the closed doors. Not loud enough to hear what was being said, but enough to know that we weren't alone and that a closed door didn't necessarily mean you wouldn't be overheard. When we reached the door bearing a golden plaque with Councilman Foster's name on it, I met Elena's eyes and gave a brief nod. It was her job to record the conversation since Zack demanded concrete proof of the councilman's involvement, and since there was no way to search his computer, phone, or other records, this was the best we could do. She nodded back. It was time to set the plan into motion.

The door was slightly ajar, so I gave a quick knock and called out before we entered his office.

"Hey, Councilman Foster, it's Lila Macapagal and some members of the Shady Palms chamber of commerce. You said we could—"

I'd only made it a few steps into the room before I stopped so suddenly that both Elena and Beth bumped into me.

"Ow, Lila! What's your—"

"Elena, call 911. Right now. And don't step any further into the room, I don't want us messing up a crime scene. Beth, can you go down to the front desk and inform them of the . . . situation?"

As I delivered these orders as quickly and calmly as I possibly could, my eyes remained locked on Zack, who gaped back at me from his position behind Councilman Foster. The councilman couldn't partake in this staring contest because he was slumped across his bloody desk. From this distance, I couldn't tell if he was breathing or not, but somehow I just knew—he was dead.

After answering the fifty-millionth question the exact same way for the police officer from the Shelbyville Police Department, I couldn't help but wonder: Did I actually miss the fools from the Shady Palms PD? They were inefficient and unorganized and the sheriff was the worst, but at least they were predictable. I knew how to work with them, plus they knew me.

The cop interviewing me showed a spark of recognition when he heard my name, but if he did know who I was, he was thoroughly unimpressed. I understood that someone had just been killed, a local politician at that, but I wasn't the one found standing over the dead body. I didn't see why they had to keep trying to catch me in a lie.

Thankfully, help soon arrived in the form of Adeena and Amir. I'd texted them both while waiting for emergency services to arrive and let them know what was going on, and here they were an hour later, as promised. Amir put on his lawyerly voice: "Do you plan on charging any of these women for the crime? No? Then I'm taking them home. They've been through a traumatic experience and deserve some rest. You have their contact information if you need to talk to them again. In my presence, of course," and Elena, Beth, and I finally got to leave.

"I was going to have my own lawyer come get us, but Lila told me you were already on the way. Thanks for that, Amir," Beth said. "I did not miss this experience at all."

Beth was such a force of nature and regular part of my life that sometimes I forgot that we met because her husband was murdered and my cousin Bernadette was one of the prime suspects. Had it really only been a little over a year since then? It felt like I'd lived several lifetimes since I returned to Shady Palms.

Beth had driven us here, so we said our goodbyes in the parking lot and Elena and I rode back with Amir and Adeena. Elena followed Adeena to the backseat and clung to her, probably seeking comfort in her beloved to wash away the horrible sight in the councilman's office. Was this her first time seeing a dead body? Other than a funeral, it probably was. I didn't remember her being at the crime scenes the other times I'd stumbled across dead bodies. Matter of fact, I think Yvonne was probably the first time Adeena had seen a body as well. Shame reared its ugly head again as the full impact of everything that Adeena had experienced really sank in. I'd told myself more than once that seeing so many dead bodies hadn't hardened me, that I still felt sadness and disgust and horror every time it happened. And it was true, I did. But maybe a small part of me was getting used to it. And I hated that thought.

Something to bring up in my monthly therapy session, I supposed.

Amir drove the twenty-something minutes back to Shady Palms in silence, the soothing sounds of NPR (well, soothing to Amir, I'm sure) and the quiet whispers between the two in the back the only soundtrack to the ride. I figured he was busy thinking about his sister's case or whatever he'd been working on that he had to drop to come get us, so I just stared out the window, lost in my own thoughts.

When he pulled into the plaza that housed the Brew-ha Cafe, as well as Tita Rosie's Kitchen and Dr. Jae's Dental Clinic, he glanced at a message on his smart watch and finally spoke. "Detective Park will be here soon. He was already at the Shelbyville Police Department when you found Councilman Foster, but he was busy handling something on Mayor Reyes's behalf. Your aunt and grandmother are waiting for us."

I turned to look at my friends in the back. "Are you two up for this?

I know we should share this new information while it's fresh in our minds, but if you both need a minute or day or whatever, they'll understand. What you've both been through these last few weeks . . . it's a lot."

Understatement of the year, but I needed them to know that I got it. That I knew what they were going through. That they could rely on me.

Adeena and Elena held a conversation with their eyes before Adeena said, "I didn't do any of the cleanup when I closed the cafe. Elena and I will do that before we head over."

"Should I come too? It'll be faster with all of us."

But Adeena shook her head. "It's fine. It's not that much. Go visit with your auntie and grandmother. You haven't been there in a while."

Not wrong, but this reminder yet again of how I was not needed stung. I got out of the car without saying anything and headed into my family's restaurant, ignoring the CLOSED sign on the door.

Mondays were technically my aunt's and grandmother's day off and the only day the restaurant was closed (a recent development, since before they almost never took a day off), but they still came in to do inventory and any prep work that was needed for the week. I told Amir, who followed me in, to make himself comfortable and headed to the kitchen.

"Hi, Tita Rosie. Lola Flor. Need help with anything?" I asked as I washed my hands.

Lola Flor looked up from the pot she was stirring on the stove. "The latik is almost done. Get the bowl and strainer ready. And get the maja blanca out of the fridge."

I followed her orders, and as my grandmother strained the browned coconut curds, or latik, from the coconut oil, I cut the coconut and corn pudding into squares. I helped my grandmother sprinkle the coconut curds on top of the cut pudding and stuck the tray back in the fridge. The texture was best when it was cold, so it'd stay there until it was time for dessert.

Next, I cleaned up the vegetable peels from the ginataang gulay my aunt had simmering on the stove, while my aunt fried the vegetable lumpia she'd just finished rolling.

"Lila, can you taste the stew and let me know if it needs anything?"

I grabbed a clean spoon and helped myself to a large scoop. The simple yet hearty dish contained various vegetables simmered in a savory coconut milk sauce. Fried tofu replaced the usual shrimp or pork so that my friends could enjoy it, too. "Mmm, you've really nailed the vegetable broth, Tita. I think it's great. Just serve the patis and bagoong on the side and it'll be fine."

Adeena and Elena were vegetarians, but they occasionally indulged in seafood, so giving them the option to add fish sauce and fermented shrimp paste instead of cooking it into the dish was nice. My aunt and grandmother had the rest covered, so I set the table for seven with Amir's help. I was coming out of the kitchen with a steaming pot of rice when I almost crashed into Detective Park.

"Whoa there!" Luckily, he had excellent reflexes and managed to dodge out of the way while also steadying me so I didn't drop the rice. "Sorry about that. I should know better than to just barge into your kitchen. Need help?"

With Detective Park assisting, there were too many people in the kitchen, so I told Amir that I was going to check if Jae was free. I'd messaged Jae at the same time I'd texted Adeena and Amir, but he never answered. He didn't keep his phone on him while with his patients, so I didn't want to bother him. I'd just ask his receptionist, Millie, to send him over to the restaurant once he was free. It was still too early for him to close, but maybe he had time for a very late lunch.

"Lila! Always lovely to see you, dear," Millie said, looking up from her computer. "Is Jae expecting you? He's got back-to-back patients until closing time, but I can get him if it's an emergency."

"Important news, but it'll keep. I don't want to distract him from work. Just tell him I stopped by and to call me as soon as he can."

"Ah, about the councilman's murder and Zack's arrest?"

"Zack was arrested? Wait, how do you even know about the murder?"

"Felice told me, of course."

Of course. The receptionist was on duty when it all went down and was the one who directed the EMTs and police when they all arrived. Obviously she'd know about this. But Zack was taken in for questioning at the same time I was, and I hadn't heard anything about an arrest. Not that the Shelbyville PD would tell me, I guess.

I glanced at the clock on the wall. I wanted to pump her for more information, but Detective Park had just arrived anyway. If anyone would know about Zack getting arrested, it'd be him.

"I need to head back to the restaurant, but I might have more questions for you later. Is that OK?"

Forget OK, Millie looked delighted. "I'd love that! Felice and I have been wondering when you'd finally understand what a valuable resource I am. Happy to chat whenever is good for you."

"I know how valuable you are even if you don't help me with any of my investigations, Millie. See you later."

By the time I made it back to my aunt's restaurant, Adeena and Elena had arrived and everyone was standing around waiting for me.

"Sorry! I went to check on Jae and ended up talking to Millie longer than I thought. Jae can't make it, but I'll fill him in later." I waited until my grandmother sat down before seating myself. "Detective Park, what's this I hear about Zack getting arrested?"

"Didn't even give me time to fill my plate, just straight to the point, huh?" Detective Park said. "Not going to bother asking who told you since you were just with Millie. Anyway, the reason I wanted us all to meet is because earlier today, Mayor Reyes received an anonymous letter accusing Zack of murdering Yvonne."

"Anonymous letter?" I asked. "That sounds rather convenient. What did the mayor think about it?"

"She wanted to brush it off as a prank, but even she admitted that the argument in the letter was rather compelling. She called me in to ask what she should do about it, and while I was there, she received news of the councilman's death. After that, I headed to Shelbyville PD to talk to them about Zack since there will be jurisdiction issues if Zack is charged with Yvonne's death in Shady Palms and the councilman's in Shelbyville. Just got back from reporting what I learned to Detective Nowak."

"Don't you find the timing a little convenient?" I asked.

Elena snorted. "Good. Let things be convenient for us for once. All I'm hearing is that Adeena is cleared of suspicion. Am I right, Detective?"

"It's too early to say," Detective Park cautioned. "But based on the information I gathered from the detective in Shelbyville as well as Detective Nowak here in Shady Palms, Adeena isn't considered the main suspect anymore. I believe cases are being made against Zack now."

Adeena was safe. Adeena was free. It was everything we had been working toward these last few weeks. So why did things still feel so off? So wrong?

Because Zack didn't kill Yvonne, a voice inside me whispered.

How could you possibly know that? I demanded. *You don't know him. You've already had to chastise yourself for getting too close to suspects. Don't fool yourself into thinking he's innocent just because you weren't the one to catch him.*

That last thought brought me back to myself. Was that what this was? Was I really so self-centered that the reason everything felt weird about the situation was because I hadn't been the one to wrap things up nice and neat? What a sickening realization. I had to be better than that. I had to be.

I chanted those words in my head over and over as I laughed and chatted along with everyone over the meal. I did not allow myself to think that we were celebrating while a possibly innocent man sat in jail.

I did not.

Chapter Twenty-Three

And so our lives went back to normal. Or what passed for normal here in Shady Palms.

Did I think that Zack killed Councilman Foster? Maybe. If he thought the councilman was a proper threat to Mayor Reyes, who knows the lengths he would go to protect her. But did I think he killed Yvonne? No. Again, his focus was on the mayor and her reputation. Considering that Mayor Reyes and Yvonne were getting divorced and all their drama was already being handled, there was no reason for him to do something that would only hurt his beloved employer.

However, there was more than enough evidence against him and, now that I thought about it, the divorce wasn't finalized yet. Even with it, there was no promise that Yvonne wouldn't become an issue again later on. Maybe in his paranoia, Zack sought a faster, more final solution to what he saw as the Yvonne problem.

Anyway, my goal was to clear Adeena's name. With her safe, there was no need to continue putting myself in danger's way. It was up to the two towns' police and legal departments to see justice served. The last weekend of the Corn Festival loomed near and the Brew-has and I threw ourselves into preparing for it, hoping to go out with a bang.

"Lila, can you stop by Gladys's later? I put in a special order for this weekend and she just messaged me to say it's ready," Elena said.

Things between the two of us were still slightly awkward, but I think we both wanted to put the events of the past month behind us and were making an effort to reclaim the ease of our early friendship.

"Sure. I just finished prepping the cookie dough for the weekend anyway, so I've got some free time. Adeena, you need me to stop anywhere while I'm out?"

"If you're going to be in Shelbyville anyway, can you drop this at Quinn's?" Adeena held up a tote bag filled with skeins of yarn, knitting needles, and several sheets of paper. "When we were at her shop, I told her I also knit, and she said she wanted to give knitting a try. I put together a starter kit for her but haven't had a chance to drop it off. She's still kind of weird around me, so it might be better if you do it."

"Oh, perfect. I need to take Longganisa out for a walk anyway, so I might as well bring her with me so she can see Cleo."

After adjusting Longganisa's sweater (another Adeena creation, this one green and covered with corn cobs) and clipping on her leash, I grabbed the bag of dog treats Elena prepared as well as the tote bag for Quinn and made the drive to the Olive Oil Emporium. I put Longganisa in her carrying sling and clipped it to her collar before entering the store.

"Lila! It's so good to see you, honey. Are you here to pick up Elena's order?" Gladys stood in front of the shop greeting customers as they came in, and she made her way over as soon as she saw me. "Well, hello there. Who do we have here?"

"This is my dog, Longganisa. We're here to pick up Elena's order and then we're going to pay Quinn a visit."

"I like that Elena, she drives a hard bargain. Did you know she managed to haggle down the wholesale price of this olive oil in exchange for a discount on her uncle's honey?"

I smiled. "No, but that definitely sounds like an Elena thing to do. She did mention wanting to use the oil for soap, hair masks, and other moisturizers, so it makes sense that she'd want it in bulk."

"Tell her to send me some samples once she's done. I'd love to carry her products in my shop."

"Will do. In exchange, you should make time to stop by the cafe. Adeena and I would be happy to let you try the drinks and desserts we came up with using your products."

One of Gladys's employees called for her and Gladys held up a hand in acknowledgment. "I've got to go, but let me grab Elena's order for you." Once she returned, she said, "I'll make sure to stop by once the Corn Festival is over and things have settled down a bit. Oh, and tell Quinn to stop ignoring my messages if she knows what's good for her."

"She's not answering you?"

"She's been acting strange since Yvonne's funeral, and—"

"Oh, I forgot her funeral had already passed! I would've come to pay my respects."

"It wasn't open to the public. Judy wanted a quiet affair with just me, Quinn, and Yvonne's family. Yvonne would've wanted a more boisterous atmosphere, with drinking and salacious stories, but I think Judy was trying to be respectful to her in-laws. They seemed rather conservative and private, and she probably didn't want to make them uncomfortable by subjecting them to the nosiness of the towns-people."

Gladys's employee called for her yet again, and I didn't want to hold her up any longer than I already had, so I assured her I'd pass on her message to Quinn before saying my thanks and exiting the store.

"I wonder what's up with Quinn, Longganisa," I asked my dog as I made my way to the Blue Violet Boutique. It was such a short walk I didn't bother letting her out of her sling and was soon standing in front of the shop's locked door with a big CLOSED sign in front.

I checked the store sign listing the operating hours, and sure enough, it had been closed earlier for private shopping hours but was supposed to be open at this time. Maybe Quinn had an emergency? I called her, but it rang a few times before going to voicemail. I sent her a text and waited for a response, but after a few minutes passed and it hadn't even been read, I decided to head back to the cafe. I didn't need to see her for any urgent reason, and this way Adeena could give her the knitting kit in person in case she needed to demonstrate anything.

Longganisa let out a whimper and I remembered that I hadn't given her an afternoon walk yet.

"I'm sorry, baby, I didn't mean to forget you," I crooned as I unclipped her from her sling and set her on the sidewalk. I'd just attached her leash when I heard someone call out to me.

"Lila? What are you doing here?"

I turned around and saw Quinn pulling Cleo out from her spot on the floor of the passenger side of her car.

"Hey! Adeena wanted me to drop off the knitting kit she promised you, but I didn't know you were closed today."

"Sorry about that. It was time for Cleo's annual checkup and there weren't many available slots, so I had to close early."

"How's she doing?" I asked, rubbing Cleo's graying head.

"Getting on in age, but healthy enough according to the vet. Were you about to go on a walk?"

"Yeah, I haven't had time to walk Longganisa yet. Would you like to join us? We'd love the company."

Quinn hesitated long enough for me to think she was going to turn down my offer, but then Longganisa barked and put her front paws on Quinn's leg as if to ask permission to play with Cleo. Quinn smiled and set Cleo on the ground, and the two dogs started sniffing each other immediately.

After grabbing Cleo's leash from the backseat of her car and attaching it to Cleo's collar, Quinn said, "There's a dog park not too far from here. Why don't we check it out?"

We spent the fifteen minutes it took to reach the dog park chatting about nothing in particular when Quinn suddenly drew up short.

"What's wrong?" I asked, looking around to see what had caused that reaction.

"Sorry, I just remembered I forgot something back at the store. I need to—"

"Quinn!"

I turned toward the voice and saw Jessica, Yvonne's younger sister, crossing the street to reach us.

"I thought that was you! Why haven't you returned any of my calls?" Jessica glanced at me and I saw the recognition in her eyes. "Oh! You were at Judy's house that one time."

I switched Longganisa's leash to my left hand and held out my right. "Hi, I'm Lila. I didn't get a chance to introduce myself last time. How are your accommodations? I hope Xander is being a good host."

The rest of Yvonne's family had flown home the day after the soiree, but Xander told me Jessica was staying at his place for another few days. After getting off on the wrong foot with Mayor Reyes, it seemed Jessica wanted a chance to finally get to know her sister-in-law.

Jessica lit up. "Oh, he's been wonderful! You must be the friend who called in the favor. Thank you so much for that."

"Don't mention it. I'm just sorry we had to meet like this. We should—"

"Hey, sorry to interrupt, but I really need to get going," Quinn said. "I forgot I had to do something at the boutique."

She tried to walk away but Jessica grabbed her arm. "Quinn, wait! Why won't you talk to me? I know it's been a long time, but we just want to help."

"I appreciate that, but I'm fine."

"But it was wrong of Yvonne to just leave you in the lurch like that! Whatever happened, we're still family—"

"Jessica, please. I can't right now. I have to go."

After emphasizing that last word, Quinn turned on her heel and walked away as quickly as Cleo's little legs would let her. I was torn between chasing after her and asking Jessica what was going on. Probably best for me to get the full story before bugging Quinn in case it was better to leave her alone.

"Um, sorry if it's not my business, but what was that all about?"

Jessica sighed. "Yvonne had planned to move back to California to work for my family's business once the divorce was finalized."

I stilled. "Did Quinn know?"

"Not until a few weeks ago. Yvonne let it slip during our last phone call that she hadn't told Quinn she was leaving. I told her she was being a crappy friend and that they needed to have a proper discussion considering they were business partners."

Interesting timing. As I turned over that new piece of information in my head, Longganisa pulled on her leash, causing the tote bag I was still wearing to slip off my shoulder.

"Oops, I forgot to give this to Quinn. Hopefully I can catch up to her," I said, adjusting the bag.

"When you talk to her, please let her know that there's a position waiting for her at my family's company. She doesn't have to be alone out here."

I promised Jessica that I'd pass on the message before jogging after Quinn in the hopes that Cleo's slow pace would allow me and Longganisa to catch up with them.

Luckily, we managed to reach them a few stores down from the boutique.

"Quinn, wait!"

"I don't want to talk about it, Lila." Quinn tried to speed away from me, but Cleo couldn't keep up so Quinn scooped her up and looked like she was going to make a run for it.

"I'm sorry, you don't have to talk about it if you don't want. I just wanted to make sure you were OK. Gladys asked me to check on you and I wouldn't feel right reporting back to her about this. You know how she worries about you."

"I wish everybody would mind their damn business. I'm fine!"

I reared back as she yelled those last two words. "Right. Guess I should get going then . . ."

I tugged on Longganisa's leash to lead her back to my car, but she stubbornly refused to move. "Are you seriously going to make me carry you?"

I rolled my eyes and moved to pick her up but Quinn stopped me. "Wait, Lila. I'm sorry. I shouldn't have snapped at you like that."

"I shouldn't have butt in to your business when you clearly didn't want to talk about it. So it's fine."

"Why don't you and Longganisa come upstairs for a minute? Gladys gave me a pound cake and there's no way I'll finish it on my own."

"I'd love that. Elena also packed treats for the dogs, so Cleo and Longganisa can have a snack, too."

We went up to Quinn's apartment above the boutique and I made myself comfortable on the couch after giving the dogs their treats and washing my hands. While Quinn prepared the pound cake and coffee, I texted the Brew-has to let them know I'd be late.

> Btw super awkward right now. Might need an
> emergency

Elena messaged back, Call you in 10?

I sent a thumbs-up emoji and set my phone facedown as Quinn came back into the room with a tray holding filled plates and mugs. I moved the couch cushions to make space for her before taking the dishes she offered me. I waited until she was settled before shoving a large chunk of pound cake in my mouth.

"Mmm, this is so good! Simple, but so moist and flavorful. And the texture is great."

I'd planned on using Gladys's Meyer lemon olive oil to make a pound cake for the cafe, but I didn't think my version would come close to hers.

"Her secret ingredient is cornmeal." Quinn took a sip of coffee before starting on her cake.

I waited for her to bring up the earlier scene with Yvonne's sister, but when she seemed content to just eat cake in silence, I knew I had to say something.

Ignoring the weird vibes Quinn was giving off, I said, "Um, thanks for inviting me in. I know you don't want to talk about it, but Jessica wanted me to tell you—"

Quinn cut me off. "I'm not going back to California with them, so you can just stop right there. At least here, I have the boutique. There's nothing for me out there."

"It seems like Yvonne's family wants you to work for them."

"And I'll tell you what I told them. I do not want or need that position, so they should give it to someone who deserves it. I certainly don't."

"Why not?" Something about the way she said that last part stood out to me. "Quinn, why don't you think you deserve it?"

"I just don't. Now let it go."

"But—"

My phone rang, making both me and Quinn jump. Probably Elena checking if she needed to invent a fake emergency so I could leave. I reached for my phone, but Quinn grabbed my wrist, stopping me.

"Quinn?" I stared at her and for the split second she stared back, I saw panic. Panic and something else. Something else that made my brain scream, *GET OUT OF THERE!*

"Oh! Sorry. I don't know why I did that. I think I'm just a little on edge," she said, forcing a laugh as she let go of me. The phone stopped ringing. "Sorry to make you miss your call. Why don't you—"

My phone rang again, cutting her off.

"Sorry, I need to answer this," I said, keeping an eye on Quinn. "If they called twice in a row, it might be an emergency."

"Hey, are you OK?" Elena asked as soon as I answered the phone.

I gave a little laugh. "Oh sorry, I forgot to tell you. Quinn invited me up to her apartment above the boutique. We're just having cake and chatting."

"So, you are OK? You don't need us to do anything?"

I definitely did because the voice in my brain was shouting to not trust Quinn loud and clear. But how to say that without tipping her off? My eyes landed on the tote bag Adeena gave me.

"Oh, thanks for reminding me! I forgot to give her the knitting kit.

Tell Adeena she better have more of that yarn for my next outfit. You know how much I love bright colors."

There was silence on the other end and I prayed for Elena to understand. Even with our earlier arguments, surely she knew me well enough to get that this was code?

"No problem. Oh, and Detective Park and Jae wanted to know if you were free for dinner. I'll let them know where you're at."

"Got it. Thanks."

I hung up and turned my attention back to Quinn. "Sorry about that."

"Is everything OK at the cafe?"

"Yeah, but I promised them I'd be back in time for closing, so I should head out once I'm done with my cake. Sorry to eat and run."

I wanted to bolt out the door right then with the suspicious way she was looking at me, but I thought it'd be too obvious if I did so. I forced myself to eat at a steady pace and keep up the conversation as if nothing was wrong.

Once I cleaned my plate, I set it on the coffee table and stood up. "Thanks for that. And please tell Gladys that I need the recipe. I'll see you—"

"Lila. Sit down."

"But I really should—"

Quinn grabbed Longganisa's leash. "Sit. Down."

"Wait, what are you doing?"

Quinn's suspicious behavior and my panic came on so suddenly, I didn't know how to react. My brain filled with endless questions like: *What's going on? Why is she doing this?* And most importantly, *How do I make sure that Longganisa and I get out of here safely?*

It wasn't until I saw Quinn bend down toward my dog that I snapped out of it. "I'm sitting, I'm sitting! Please don't hurt her."

Quinn picked up Longganisa and Cleo and put them in what I

assumed was her bedroom and shut the door. "I won't hurt her. But you and I need to have a talk."

"What about?"

I glanced at the time on my phone screen. It'd only been fifteen minutes since my call with Elena and it would take about half an hour for anyone to arrive if they were driving from Shady Palms. Twenty-five minutes, minimum, and that's if Elena was able to reach Detective Park and Jae as soon as we hung up. I could stall for another fifteen, twenty minutes, right? Not like I had a choice.

"Ah ah, none of that." Quinn must've thought I was looking at my phone because I wanted to call for help because she grabbed it and stuck it in her bag. "I've changed my mind. No talking. Just sit there quietly while I figure out how I want to handle this."

Yeah, sure, I'll let you think about how you'll dispose of my body, no worries. It was risky, but the only way I could distract her long enough for help to arrive would be to provoke her. I wished I had run when I had the chance, but there was no way I was leaving Longganisa behind. Time to poke the bear.

"She was your best friend. How could you do it?"

"I told you to be quiet."

"Whatever her faults, Yvonne didn't deserve it."

"Don't talk about things you know nothing about."

"I know that she planned on moving back to California once her divorce was finalized. And I know the only reason she told you was because her sister guilted her into it."

"Jessica told you."

I saw no reason to deny it, so I just nodded.

"She doesn't know the full story, though. She doesn't know how deep the betrayal goes."

"Tell me."

She looked away.

"Quinn, what happened that day?"

"You would never understand. You have everything. A loving family. A thriving business. A best friend who supports you, who would never choose their lover over you."

"Yvonne chose Mayor Reyes over you?"

"All the time. *Every* time. We weren't supposed to settle down in Shelbyville, you know. We were supposed to move on to Chicago or New York. But she convinced me to stay since Judy had the money to invest in our boutique. I wanted to start selling my own designs right away, but Judy said that was too expensive and risky for an unknown designer. And Yvonne agreed with her. So our boutique sourced clothes from other designers and I had to fight and claw to get the money to start producing my own designs for the store since they wouldn't back me. But the last straw was when I found out she'd been stealing money from the store to bribe that councilman. We're bankrupt, did you know that?"

"Because of Yvonne?"

"Because of Yvonne. Everything I worked for. The last twenty-something years of my life. All gone. Because Yvonne always put Judy's needs above mine. She didn't stop to think how her actions would impact the business we built together—how it would affect *me*. Even at the very end, all she worried about was how this news would negatively impact Judy's image in the community if it got out."

There was so much to unpack about all of this, so much to wonder about the choices both Yvonne and Quinn made, but my brain couldn't even begin to sift through the ashes of their broken friendship. So I just asked, "Did you hate her?"

She dropped her head into her hands. "I loved her. She was all I had in this world, you know? I needed her." Quinn raised her eyes to meet mine and the despair in them haunted me. "But she never needed me. She could leave me behind so easily."

I'd be lying if I said I didn't understand her pain and fears even a little. "She was just going to move back to your hometown and have you deal with the fallout?"

"She said I could move back too. That she'd get me a job at her family's company. Some boring desk job at a shipping company in my terrible hometown near my shitty family. I'd rather die."

I gentled my voice. This was it, I could sense it. "But it was Yvonne who died. How did it happen? Please, help me understand."

Was I stalling for time, hoping someone would save me before things got ugly? Of course. But I did genuinely want to understand. How a friendship could get so twisted. How jealousy could drive you to kill the person you loved and who knew you best in the world. And how I could avoid making those kinds of mistakes with Adeena.

(Not the murder part, obviously. It would never come to that. But everything else . . .)

I think Quinn sensed it. She'd seen me and Adeena and Elena together. She knew what it was like to be the third wheel, even if the other parties involved absolutely did not think of you that way. Or at least, tried not to treat you that way. She knew that when I said, "I want to understand," that I wasn't judging her. That I really meant it. So she kept on talking.

"I was getting ready to meet Judy and Yvonne at the Corn Festival when Councilman Foster called and told me to meet him at the boutique. Said it was urgent. He was the one who let me know what Yvonne had been doing, showed me the ledgers saying we were bankrupt. He was also the one who told me they were getting a divorce. My own best friend hadn't told me. And he said that it was my job to convince Yvonne to continue the payments or else. He didn't say what 'or else' meant, but it didn't matter. The threat was there and very real."

I was literally at the edge of my seat, because of the story and also because I was waiting for the right moment to run. She was between me and the door to where she'd shut Longganisa, but maybe if I had the element of surprise . . .

"After, I met Yvonne to do the corn maze as planned. I'd wanted to wait until we were in private to discuss the things the councilman brought up, but it's like all the accusations burst out of me as soon as we were alone."

"How did she react?"

"She admitted to everything. And apologized for nothing."

My jaw dropped. "She didn't even apologize? That seems like the least she could do."

Quinn scoffed. "Yvonne had never apologized for anything in her life, and she wasn't going to start with me. She just did what she usually did to smooth things over—offered me money. She said the boutique was sunk but she made sure her parents had a cushy job waiting for me. As if that would make everything OK.

"You know when people get really angry and they say they saw red? I always thought people were exaggerating or being poetic, but no. At that moment, my vision went blurry and it was like everything went red. I don't remember too much, but I must've seemed enraged because Yvonne looked terrified. I thought she wasn't afraid of anything. I saw her get in a fistfight with a drunk guy twice her size who'd grabbed her butt at a bar. She didn't hesitate for a second, just started swinging. But that day . . . she kept backing away from me. Telling me to stay away. I guess I kept walking toward her? She pulled out her knife and warned me to get away from her, and that was just . . . I just . . ."

"You snapped."

She nodded. "After everything we'd been through together, after everything we were to each other, she not only betrayed me, but she thought so little of me that she threatened me with a knife."

"Did you fight over the knife? There must've been a struggle."

"I don't know what came over me, but I tackled her to the ground and she dropped the knife from the impact. She tried to scramble away, but I grabbed the knife and I . . ."

She didn't describe what she did next, but she didn't need to. I'd seen the aftermath of her actions. The image of Yvonne lying there in the maze flashed in my head and I thought I was going to be sick. But there was still so much more I needed to know and I had no exit plan just yet. So I kept on talking.

"But what about Councilman Foster? You didn't mean to kill Yvonne. Not really. It was a heat of the moment thing, right? I don't understand what the councilman had to do with anything though."

"He knew it was me. Maybe because Yvonne happened to die right after our talk, I don't know, he didn't say. He just said that it was my fault he could no longer squeeze Yvonne for money, but if I helped him set up Zack to take the fall for her murder, he'd keep quiet about what I did and help pull my store out of bankruptcy."

"That sounds like a pretty sweet offer, actually. I mean, you were already trying to pin the murder on Zack. All you had to do was go along with his plan and you would've gotten everything you wanted."

She shook her head. "You clearly don't know Councilman Foster. Sure, on the surface I'd be getting what I wanted. But then he'd have a secret to hold over me forever, with no proof on my side that he was involved. And if he was willing to help me frame Zack simply because he wanted Judy's right-hand man out of the way, what would he try to do to me? You can't trust a man like that. I'd made the mistake of trusting Yvonne and look where that got me. No, it was better to just eliminate the threat when I had the chance. The fact that Zack stumbled across the scene made everything that much more perfect."

Quinn said this last part all matter-of-fact, like of course I would agree with her, wasn't it all so logical? But it gave me chills.

"And Adeena? Why frame her?"

She shook her head. "That was just a matter of convenience. Nobody else had seen me with Yvonne at the festival and I was hoping to make a quick getaway, but I was only in the next aisle over when your friend stumbled across Yvonne. She made such a commotion, I was worried everyone would catch me there. But then she passed out, and it was just a matter of getting rid of the murder weapon and disappearing through the wall beside them." She paused for a moment before adding, "I am sorry I got her mixed up in this, though. She had nothing to do with it."

She studied me for a moment. "I'm sorry about this, too. You know I don't want to do this, right?"

I didn't know what "this" meant, but I knew it couldn't be anything good. I took a deep breath and tried to project an outward calm I sure as heck didn't feel.

"Then don't. Just let me and Longganisa leave and we can pretend this never happened. Adeena's name is cleared. I have no reason to shake things up now."

"Too many loose ends, I can't risk it." Quinn reached into her purse and pulled out a knife, just like the one that had killed Yvonne. She must've noticed me staring at it because she said, "Yvonne gave me this. Said there were a lot of creeps out there and I needed to be careful. The irony, I know. But don't worry, I won't stab you. That would be way too hard to cover up."

"What are you going to do?" I asked, keeping my eyes on the knife as she flicked it to extend the blade.

"You are going to take a tragic fall down the stairs after getting tangled up in your dog's leash."

"But Longganisa might get hurt if she falls with me."

"Don't worry, you'll be alone when you go down. I'll let her out after I'm sure you're no longer a threat."

I tried to gauge how much time had passed since my call with

Elena. Could I count on Detective Park or Jae to suddenly arrive and save the day, or did I need to take matters into my own hands? Either way, I needed to continue to stall Quinn and her plans.

"Can you let her out now? I just, I want to say goodbye to her. Please."

Quinn's eyes softened at my request, but she still kept her knife pointed at me. "Fine. But if you try anything, I will stab you and make it look like self-defense. Now stay seated."

Quinn backed slowly toward the room with the dogs and opened it to let them out. Longganisa bounded over to me and I scooped her up and held her close. If this really was it, I needed to let her know how much I loved her.

"I'm sorry, baby. But Jae will take good care of you." I rubbed my face against hers and let her give me a kiss before setting her down on the couch next to me. She moved to sit on one of the couch cushions, knocking over Adeena's tote bag in the process. My attention snapped over to the spilled contents and in that moment, I knew what to do.

"OK, time's up. Let's go—"

Faster than I've ever moved in my life, I snatched one of the cushions and threw it at Quinn, which distracted her long enough for me to grab one of the knitting needles from the tote bag and jab it into the hand holding the knife.

She screamed and dropped the knife, which skittered under the couch. I grabbed Longganisa and ran for the door, but she'd recovered enough to reach for Longganisa's leash with her uninjured hand. Before she could do anything, Cleo came barreling out of the room, barking her head off and snapping at her owner. Was she trying to protect Longganisa?

"Cleo, what are you—?"

I took advantage of the distraction and bolted toward the door with Longganisa in my arms. I swung it open and nearly crashed into

Detective Park, who was coming up the stairs followed by Jae and a couple of Shelbyville police officers. I backed into Quinn's apartment to let everyone in and collapsed into Jae's arms, finally allowing myself to cry.

It was over.

Chapter Twenty-Four

"You know what, Ronnie? You were so preoccupied with whether or not you could that you didn't stop to think if you should."

Jae stared down at the glass of sweet corn wine my cousin had just handed him.

"Bro, you can quote *Jurassic Park* all you like, but you've still gotta taste it. I promise you, it's good."

"You've pranked me one too many times for me to be cool with this."

Jae continued to look dubiously at the liquid, so Ronnie's girl-friend, Izzy, said, "You know I wouldn't let him serve anything to guests that wasn't legit. I think you'll be very pleasantly surprised."

"Izzy I trust. OK, here goes . . ." Jae took a small sip and his eyes widened. "Whoa, that's so weird! You can definitely taste the corn, but it's a sweet, mellow flavor. How did you do that?"

Ronnie grinned at him. "A lot of trial and error and internet searches. Not bad, huh? It's not worth the effort to make year-round, but I think making it a seasonal wine only available for the festival makes it that much more of a hot commodity."

While my boyfriend and cousin discussed the merits of sweet corn wine, I sipped a nice cider while relaxing with Adeena and Elena. It was the last day of the Corn Festival and the Brew-ha Cafe booth had sold out early enough for us to spend the rest of the day hanging out in Shady Palms Winery's beer garden. After Jae and Detective Park had come to my rescue at Quinn's apartment, Quinn was arrested for Yvonne's and Councilman Foster's murders. Shady Palms and Shelbyville were still fighting over jurisdiction issues, but that was most definitely not my problem. I was happy to go back to running my cafe with my besties, where my biggest concern was what new dessert to experiment with next.

The Brew-has and I were finally on the same page again—after my latest near-death experience, I sat down with Adeena and Elena and poured out all the hurt and toxic thoughts I'd bottled up for the past month. And in return for my honesty, Adeena and Elena shared their feelings on everything that had happened and all the ugliness they'd been hiding not just from me but each other as well. No joking around, no sarcasm to mask the hurt. Just real talk and a lot of tears. I guess my therapist was right and I should actually try to communicate with the people I care about more often.

How annoying. But how freeing to know that it actually works.

"Excuse me, is this seat taken?"

We looked up to see a friendly and familiar face.

"Gladys! And Cleo, too. How lovely to see you both. I wish I'd known you were coming; we would've saved you something from our booth," I said, scooching over to make room for her at our table.

Once the truth had come out, there was a discussion on who would take custody of Cleo. At first, the police tried to get Mayor Reyes to take her in, but she refused.

"I'm sorry. I know it's not Cleo's fault. And I know how much Yvonne loved her. But I can't look at her and not remember what Quinn did to my wife. It's just too hard right now," she had said.

So Gladys had stepped in.

"How's Cleo acclimating to her new home?" Adeena asked, reaching down to give Cleopatra Louise head scratches.

"She's a trouper, that's for sure," Gladys said, smiling down at the dog. "I must say, it's nice to have the company, what with my husband gone and my kids living their own lives."

"Do you think she misses Quinn?" Elena asked. "They seemed so attached when they visited us at the cafe."

Gladys sighed. "I'm sure she does. For that matter, I miss Quinn. Not who she'd become, of course. But she and Yvonne were part of my family. It's hard losing both of them like this. Cleo is a nice consolation, though."

The four of us sat in silence for a moment, to acknowledge what Gladys had just shared. Then she changed the subject and we spent the next hour chatting, drinking, and snacking as the sun set over the Corn Festival.

When it was time to leave so the Shady Palms Winery employees could clean up, the Brew-has all walked Gladys to her car.

"I'll make sure to come back soon to check out your lovely cafe. Now you be good to each other, OK? Make sure to take care of one another."

I glanced over at Adeena and Elena, my beautiful best friends who'd helped me through so much, and smiled.

"Don't worry, Gladys. We will."

Acknowledgments

Five books into a series that I'm still amazed I get to write, I'm running out of funny, eloquent (OK, I've never been eloquent) things to say in this section. However, my love and gratitude for the people who continue to support me in so many different ways grow stronger and stronger the further I go down this ridiculous (at times, treacherous) road we call publishing.

As always, huge thanks to the team that makes this all possible: my wonderful agent, Jill Marsal; my editors, Angela Kim and Michelle Vega; and the rest of my Berkley team—senior publicist Tara O'Connor, marketing manager Anika Bates, production editors Lindsey Tulloch and Jennifer Lynes, copy editor LeeAnn Pemberton, and managing editorial team Christine Legon, Heather Haase, Sammy Rice, Emma Tamayo, and Brittney West, as well as Vi-An Nguyen for continuing to give me the best covers ever. I'd also like to thank Ann-Marie Nieves and the rest of the Get Red PR crew for all their amazing help.

Shout-out to the Berkletes who've been there with me since the beginning of this pub journey (you beautiful Jaded Old Hags <3), as well as to the new crew—you've made these last few years not just bearable but unbelievably fun. I don't know how I'd make it through publishing without you all.

Thanks to my writing groups, such as Sisters in Crime, Crime Writers of Color, Banyan: Asian American Writers Collective, my Chicagoland kidlit writer peeps, and many more. Special shout-out to the Cold Turkey writing app and Isabel Cañas for introducing it to me. I have no idea how I ever drafted without it. And I will always have to thank Lori Rader-Day and Kellye Garrett for their guidance and encouragement from long before I ever dared to call myself a writer.

Much love to my IRL besties, who keep me grounded and remind me there's a world outside of writing: the Winners Circle (Kim, Jumi, Linna, and Robbie), Amber and Aria (and Matt), and Ivan aka Snookums. And to my DnD group, Ye Olden Girls, for all the support and laughter you've brought me these last few years. I still say it was right to boop that dinosaur on the nose; I don't care that it nearly killed our party.

Huge thanks to my family, who have always supported me, make an amazing street team, and continue to be the best guinea pigs aka recipe testers. And of course, to James and our precious doggos, Gumiho and Max Power. All of you annoy me so much and I'm sure the feeling is mutual. Love love!

And finally, to my readers. You are all the best and I appreciate the many ways you support me, but need to especially recognize my Ko-fi Pamilya tier members: Sarah Best, Matthew Galloway, the Bradfield Ohana, Maria Remedios Boyd, Christine K. Asuncion, Faye Bernoulli Silag, Willard L. Hayes, Eliose Celine Labampa, Krystina Madriaga McHale, Jason and Maria Reyes Doktor, Katie Davidson, Tim and Kristen Sorbera, Kasey B. Boucher, Sam Bertocchi, and Sarah Rogers, you all mean the world to me. Maraming salamat!

Recipes

Tita Rosie's Ginataang Gulay

Ginataan refers to any Filipino dish cooked in coconut milk, and while it might seem like a cooking method for desserts, there are many savory preparations as well. Roasting is not typical in Filipino cooking (who wants to turn on the oven in that kind of heat?), but it's a great way to bring out the sweetness of the veggies and add a ton of flavor without resorting to animal products or lots of butter or oil. This is a dish that Tita Rosie developed for the Park brothers' father, who doesn't think vegetarian dishes can be tasty and satisfying. As written, it's a pescatarian dish, but you can, of course, make this completely vegetarian by leaving out the fish sauce and shrimp paste. You'll want to find a way to replace those flavors, though, without resorting to tons of salt. I haven't tried it yet, but I've heard mushroom powder and vegan Japanese dashi powder can help replace that lost umami.

Recipe inspired by Yana Gilbuena-Babu's Ginataang Manok
with Gulay (with her permission)

YIELD: 2–4 SERVINGS

Ingredients:

4 ounces dried shiitake mushrooms

1 medium-size sweet potato, cubed

1 to 2 cups cauliflower florets

Olive or coconut oil, for drizzling

Salt and pepper, to taste

1 teaspoon coriander seeds

1 head of garlic, crushed, peeled, and diced*

1 medium shallot, finely chopped

1 tablespoon lemongrass, pounded and finely chopped*

1 thumb-size piece of ginger, peeled and finely chopped*

1 (15-ounce) can coconut milk (light or full-fat)

2 cups vegetable stock

1 (14-ounce) container extra-firm tofu, drained and cubed

3 Thai chiles, finely chopped (optional)

3 tablespoons fish sauce (read notes in heading)

*1 tablespoon bagoong (fermented shrimp paste; read
    notes in heading)*

1 teaspoon calamansi or lime juice

**When I'm in a rush, I'll often use lemongrass paste and ginger paste
(which come in tubes in the refrigerated section), and they work great. I
don't love using garlic paste/preminced garlic as much as the other prepared options, but if that's all you have the energy for, go for it. You're the
one cooking and eating it, not me.*

DIRECTIONS:

1. Preheat the oven to 425°F.

2. In a small bowl, add the dried shiitake and 1 to 2 cups of warm water. Set the bowl aside for the mushrooms to reconstitute while the veggies roast.

3. In a medium mixing bowl, drizzle the sweet potato and cauliflower pieces with olive or coconut oil and a few grinds of salt and pepper, and toss to season evenly.

4. Spread the vegetables onto a baking sheet and roast for 20 minutes. Pierce the cauliflower and sweet potato with a fork or knife. If they are tender, transfer to a plate and set aside; if not, give them 5 minutes more, making sure to flip and stir so they cook evenly.

5. Once the vegetables are done roasting, strain the shiitake, making sure to reserve the water. Thinly slice the mushrooms.

6. In a pan over medium-high heat, warm a drizzle of olive or coconut oil and add the coriander, garlic, shallot, lemongrass, and ginger. Sauté until the mixture starts browning and is very fragrant.

7. Add the coconut milk, vegetable stock, and 1 cup of the reserved mushroom water. Bring to a boil, then lower the heat and simmer, uncovered, for 10 to 15 minutes, or until the sauce reaches your desired thickness.

8. Add the veggies, mushrooms, tofu, and Thai chiles, if using. Stir everything together and simmer for another 5 to 10 minutes to allow the flavors to meld.

9. Add the fish sauce, bagoong, and the calamansi or lime juice. Taste and adjust flavors accordingly (if it's too salty, add more water or coconut milk, for example).

10. Turn the heat off and cover. Let sit for a few minutes to let the flavors develop.

11. Serve with lots of rice and more fish sauce and/or bagoong on the side. Garnish with scallions and fried garlic, if desired. Enjoy!

Lola Flor's Ginataang Mais

Sweet, simple, and satisfying, just like all of Lola Flor's desserts. Ginataang mais is a sweet rice porridge made of glutinous rice and corn cooked in coconut milk. Typically served for breakfast or meryenda, you can enjoy this dish hot, warm, or even cold, like a rice pudding. The recipe as written below is plenty sweet, but if it's not enough to satisfy your raging sweet tooth, you can serve it with additional sugar or even condensed milk on the side.

YIELD: ROUGHLY 4 LARGE SERVINGS OR 8 SMALL ONES

Ingredients:

½ cup glutinous rice (sometimes called "sweet rice" or
    "sticky rice")
2 (14-ounce) cans coconut milk (light or full-fat)
Pinch of salt

1½ to 2 cups fresh or frozen corn OR 1 (12-ounce) can
   whole corn kernels, drained
½ cup granulated sugar

DIRECTIONS:

1. Put the rice, coconut milk, and salt in a medium pot and bring to a boil.

2. Lower the heat and simmer the mixture for 10 to 15 minutes, stirring often so the rice doesn't stick together or to the bottom of the pot.

3. Add the corn and sugar, stirring everything together, and simmer for another 5 to 10 minutes until the rice is cooked to your desired softness and the coconut milk has reached your desired thickness. Don't forget to stir occasionally!

4. Let cool slightly and serve. The coconut milk will thicken as it cools. If the mixture gets too thick, add some water, milk, or coconut milk, and reheat slowly. Enjoy!

Lila's Ginataang Mais Butter Mochi

The dense, chewy texture of the butter mochi paired with the unique flavor combination of corn and coconut is surprisingly delicious and so easy to throw together. Not only is it gluten-free, it receives the highest honor an Asian person can give a dessert: "It's not too sweet!"

YIELD: ONE 8 X 8-INCH BAKING PAN

Ingredients:

*1 (15-ounce) can whole corn kernels OR the kernels from
    2 to 3 fresh ears of corn*

1 (13.5-ounce) can full-fat coconut milk

2 eggs

4 ounces (½ stick) butter, melted

1 cup glutinous rice flour

¼ cup freeze-dried corn powder

1¼ cups granulated sugar

1 teaspoon baking powder

½ teaspoon salt

2 teaspoons vanilla extract

2 tablespoons shredded coconut (optional)

DIRECTIONS:

1. Preheat the oven to 350°F. Grease an 8 x 8-inch baking pan.

2. Put all the ingredients except the shredded coconut in a large blender and puree until smooth.

3. Pour the batter into the prepared pan and bake for 50 to 60 minutes until a thin knife inserted in the middle comes out clean.

4. If you're using the shredded coconut, sprinkle evenly on top of the batter halfway through the bake time.

5. Let cool and enjoy!

Ms. Torres's (Elena's Mom) Atole de Elote

Mexican atole is a simple milk-based drink thickened with masa harina (the same type of corn flour you use to make tortillas) and sweetened with piloncillo* and cinnamon. This version is the special one that Ms. Torres whips up for her restaurant, El Gato Negro, during the Shady Palms Corn Festival, and she was generous enough to allow the Brew-ha Cafe to use her recipe as well. It contains pureed corn, which adds a subtle but delicious flavor to this classic Mexican drink.

YIELD: ABOUT 3 CUPS

Ingredients:

1 cup water

1 cinnamon stick

¼ to ½ cup piloncillo OR brown sugar**

1 (15-ounce) can of whole corn kernels, drained, OR 2 cups fresh or frozen corn

½ teaspoon vanilla extract

2 cups milk of choice

2 tablespoons cornstarch or masa harina

---

*Piloncillo is a type of raw sugar common in Latin America and is also known as panela. It's similar to, but not exactly the same as, jaggery, panutsa, gula melaka, etc., which are all types of raw sugar, but are processed in different ways and/or come from different sources.

**Many versions I've had are quite sweet, but I personally prefer my atole lightly sweet and heavy on the cinnamon. I suggest starting with the lower amount of piloncillo or brown sugar and tasting before adjusting to your desired sweetness.

DIRECTIONS:

1. In a medium pot, bring the water and cinnamon stick to a boil, then lower the heat and let simmer for about 5 minutes until the water is well-infused with the cinnamon.

2. Add the piloncillo/brown sugar and stir until it dissolves.

3. Blend the corn, vanilla extract, and 1 cup of milk in a high-powered blender until completely smooth, then add to the pot. If your blender isn't very strong, you might want to strain the mixture so that it's smooth.

4. Simmer the mixture for about 5 minutes, whisking frequently to make sure it doesn't stick to the bottom and burn.

5. Mix the remaining cup of milk with the cornstarch/masa harina until fully combined to make a slurry, and add to the pot.

6. Simmer the atole for 5 to 10 minutes, whisking often, until the mixture coats the back of a spoon and has reached your preferred thickness (some people like it thin, some prefer it almost pudding-like).

7. Discard the cinnamon stick and pour into heatproof cups. Dust with cinnamon, if desired. Enjoy!

Keep reading for a special preview of

Death and Dinuguan

the next Tita Rosie's Kitchen Mystery
from Mia P. Manansala

Chapter One

"This might be the most delicious thing I've ever eaten."

Adeena Awan, my best friend and business partner, stared down at the pistachio rose white chocolate bar she'd just bitten into. The creamy white chocolate bar was studded with whole pistachios, dried rose petals, and flecks of cardamom, creating a feast for the eyes as well as the tongue. She glanced at Elena Torres, her girlfriend and my other partner at the Brew-ha Cafe, who was sampling the Mexican Hot Chocolate bar. The bittersweet chocolate was flavored with cinnamon and chiles, as well as cacao nibs for texture and vanilla bean for richness.

Elena's eyes were closed to fully experience the complex flavors, so she didn't see her girlfriend move to swipe the chocolate bar out of her hand. "Hey! You could've just asked, you know. I would've been happy to share."

Adeena broke off a large piece before handing back the chocolate with a grin. "I know, but it's so much more delicious when I steal it from you."

The two of them bantered back and forth while our guests chuckled over their drinks.

"I'm sorry you have to deal with our ridiculousness so early in the morning," I said to the two chocolatiers, who sat watching us in amusement while they sipped their spiced mocha and white chocolate chai. "I appreciate you developing these specialty chocolates for us when you already have so much on your plates."

"No worries. After these last few weeks, I'd be disappointed if you didn't help us start our day with some fun and banter. Plus, these drinks are amazing, so no complaints from me. What do you think of the ube truffles?"

Hana Lee was not only the newest arrival to my hometown of Shady Palms, Illinois (two hours outside of Chicago), she was also my boyfriend's cousin. I'd been wanting to meet her for a while since I knew she was a big-sister figure to my boyfriend, but she'd always been too busy. However, her husband's sudden passing gave her a need for a fresh start, so she moved to Shady Palms at the end of last year to work at Choco Noir, the new chocolate shop that her friend Blake Langrehr had just opened in town. Choco Noir offered the most amazing confections, from Blake's simple, good-quality bean-to-bar chocolates to Hana's inventive creations. With Valentine's Day just a month away, the two of them were hard at work prepping for the big day and were also kind enough to collaborate with my business to create chocolates for us to sell as a cross-promotion for the new shop.

The pistachio rose bar was meant to represent Adeena's Pakistani background while the Mexican hot chocolate bar was for Elena's Mexican heritage (shocker). I wanted something simple and decadent for my Filipino chocolate representation, so Hana created white chocolate and milk chocolate versions of ube truffles. The subtle earthy vanilla tones of the purple yam paired well with both types of chocolate, and the beautiful violet color drew your eyes to the small spheres. Everything Hana and Blake presented to us was an absolute winner, and my partners and I quickly signed off on the collaboration.

"I'm sorry my cousin couldn't make it to this meeting. Now that they've got the event space fixed up, he and Izzy have been spending all their time getting ready for the big Valentine's Day event they're hosting," I said. "It's their first time doing it, so they want everything to be perfect."

My cousin Ronnie and his girlfriend, Izzy, ran the Shady Palms Winery and were also supposed to be part of this collaboration. Chocolates and wine, what could be a more perfect pairing for Valentine's Day? Throw in my desserts, Adeena's coffees, and Elena's teas, and that was my idea of a perfect party.

"We were able to secure a meeting at the event space later today while the florist is there. It makes more sense for us all to meet there anyway to make sure our contributions all vibe together," Blake said. "From what I heard, the florist has a genius touch, so I'm looking forward to meeting her."

"You won't be disappointed," Elena said, puffing with pride.

The florist for the big event was one of Elena's fifty million cousins, and she was right to be proud of her. Rita had taken over the old flower shop after the owner retired last year and quickly made a name for herself with her beautiful blooms, inventive bouquets, and extensive plant knowledge. It helped that much of what she sold was grown in Elena's mom's greenhouse since Shady Palms citizens loved supporting local businesses. Which wasn't all that hard, honestly, considering how few chains made their way here, and those that did often didn't last long. I wasn't sure if it was by design or just bad luck for Big Business, but Shady Palms kept its unique small-town charm by investing in its local entrepreneurs. Made for a thriving, though rather contentious, chamber of commerce.

Especially lately, considering the number of burglaries that had hit several Shady Palms shops this past month. All the businesses affected were woman-owned, but so far, the police weren't sure if women entrepreneurs were purposely being targeted, or if it just skewed that way since most of the successful businesses in town happened to be run by women. A fact that quite a few misogynistic members of the chamber of commerce had been grumbling about for a while.

"Adeena, this white chocolate chai is amazing," Blake said. "Do you think the drink mixes will be ready in time to launch for the event?"

Adeena was the cafe's barista and mixologist, and Blake had been after her to create packaged mixes for the chocolate-based drinks we offered. She wanted to sell the mixes as well as some prepared drinks at Choco Noir as more cross-promotion. Something about synergy. I didn't really get it when she was making her pitch, but Elena, our strongest salesperson and marketer, latched on to the idea.

In response, Adeena got up and plucked a few bags from the counter. "Test it out later and let me know what you think. I wrote the instructions on the bag, but I don't know if I'm one hundred percent happy with the chocolate-to-spice ratio. Of course, what type of liquid you use also changes the flavor, so I can't account for all the variables."

"I'll keep that in mind." Blake's phone alarm went off, signaling the end of our meeting. "The security system people will be at the shop soon, so we need to head out."

"Did you go with the company that Detective Park suggested?" I asked.

Private detective Jonathan Park was not only my boyfriend's

much older brother, but he was also dating my aunt, Tita Rosie. He used to be a detective with the Shady Palms Police Department, but for various reasons had left the force and opened his own private investigation agency. He had quite a few connections in the security world as well, and with the rash of burglaries lately, he'd advised us all to upgrade our security systems. I hadn't been sure it was worth the expense (we were a cafe; it's not like we were making the big bucks anyway. And what were they going to steal? Our artisanal flavored syrups?), but when my boyfriend, Jae, pointed out that our espresso machine cost almost ten thousand dollars, Adeena had screamed and run to hug it.

"No one's taking Mr. Peppy! Lila, quit being cheap and get that security system installed."

That was all the push I needed, and we'd quickly contracted Detective Park's friends at Safe & Secure Solutions to update our system.

"My cousin promised that his buddy's company was the best one in the area, so we went with them. They're a bit pricey, but hey, we're a new business and the last thing we need to deal with is a smash-and-grab. Besides, better safe than sorry, right?" Hana said, gathering her notes from our tasting.

"It's a cliché, but it's a cliché for a reason. Definitely better safe than sorry," I said.

Especially in this town.

Chapter Two

"Ronnie, when you told me to close the cafe early for an urgent meeting, this isn't exactly what I had in mind."

About two hours before closing time, I'd gotten a call from my cousin saying he needed me, Adeena, and Elena to come over to the Shady Palms Winery event space ASAP. Considering how ridiculous my life has been the past couple of years, I thought we'd get there and find him standing over a dead body. Instead, the three of us rushed into the event space only to see Ronnie, Izzy, Hana, Blake, and Rita standing around drinking wine and nibbling on chocolates.

My cousin's girlfriend and business partner, Isabel "Izzy" Ramos-Garcia, held up a bottle of wine. "Don't be too mad at him, there really is an emergency. We're just testing this new chocolate wine to try and make the best of a crappy situation."

While she poured each of us a glass, Elena made her way over to her cousin. "You OK, prima?"

Rita sat hunched over next to the tasting table, staring into her half-full glass. At her cousin's voice, Rita set down her drink and jumped up to wrap her arms around Elena. "I'm so glad you're here!"

Elena squeezed her cousin in a tight hug and then stepped back, her hands on Rita's shoulders. "You're shaking. What happened?"

"Someone broke into Mundo Floral last night."

Adeena gasped and started to say something, but Elena waved her hand to get Rita to continue.

"I went in this morning to open up and there was a huge mess. All my cash is gone and the place was ransacked, like they were looking for more valuable stuff. I doubt that they found anything, but the police want me to do an inventory to see if anything else was taken."

"Was there any physical damage to the shop? Broken windows, torn-up plants, anything like that?" I asked.

My aunt's restaurant and my godmothers' laundromat had been the victims of vandals, not burglars, but the memories of both events were traumatic enough that I worried about the state of Rita's shop and was already mentally creating a checklist of what needed to be done.

Rita shook her head. "Some of the plants were knocked over and one of the vases was broken, but it looked more like an accident that happened when the burglar was looking for something and not deliberate damage."

"Well, that's something at least," Elena muttered. "You said the police wanted you to log the inventory? So you already filed a police report?"

Rita nodded. "I called them as soon as I saw the shop was messed up and waited outside since I wasn't sure if the burglar was still there or not. They had me do the report and take pictures for insurance. I don't know what else I need to do after that."

"I'll put you in touch with my brother," Adeena said. "He can advise you since he's had a lot of experience with that lately."

Rita thanked her before taking a deep gulp of her wine and sighing. "I haven't told the rest of the family yet, but I don't know how much longer I can put it off."

"What? Why no—" Elena cut herself off. "Wait, never mind, I get it. Want me to put it in the cousins group chat and have my mom handle all the tíos and tías?"

Rita let out a deep sigh and her shoulders sagged as Elena took the metaphorical weight off of them. "I'll tell my parents 'cause I'll never hear the end of it if they have to find out from Tía Carmen. But I'll leave the rest to you. Thanks, prima."

Elena once told me that her mom was the second-oldest of seven kids, and all of the siblings had children, most of them multiple children (Elena and one other cousin were the odd ones out as only children), so family gatherings and gossip could often be . . . a lot. Wonderful when you needed help since everyone was all too willing to jump in and do their part (like when Elena's mom took over her younger brother's restaurant due to some unpleasantness) but also overwhelming because they did not know how to let things go or leave you alone. Like me and Adeena, Elena was both blessed and cursed with a family that loved hard and didn't know how to mind their own business.

Once the two of them had delivered the news and dealt with their family's responses, I made a suggestion. "Why don't you all come over to my aunt's restaurant for dinner? Detective Park will be there, since he's always there, and we can invite Amir, too. That way you can ask questions about next steps and also talk to Detective Park about that security company his friend owns."

"Oh, that's perfect. I wanted to stop by El Gato Negro and drown my sorrows in tamales, but I didn't want to have to deal with my family just yet," Rita said.

"Can't top good food and free legal advice," Adeena said. "I'll call my brother. Elena, you ride with Rita since she shouldn't be alone right now. We'll meet you there."

"Wish we could join you, but we have to talk to our contractor about some issues we're having," Ronnie said. "Tell my mom and Lola Flor that I said hi and that we'll be over for lunch tomorrow. Rita, let us know if there's anything we can do to help."

"Hana, Blake, are you two free?" I asked. "No worries if you're busy, I just want to give my aunt a heads-up on how many people to expect."

"I don't want to intrude," Blake said, glancing over at Rita. "It's a sensitive time right now and—"

"No, please, join us. I wouldn't want you to miss out on a good meal on my account," Rita said, managing a weak smile. "I'd appreciate having more people around, actually."

Blake returned her smile. "Then count us in."

Plans made, we headed over to Tita Rosie's Kitchen.

I'm sorry to hear that, Rita. You've got great timing though. Ben runs Safe & Secure Solutions, and he's one of the best guys I've ever worked with," Detective Park said, clapping his hand on the shoulder of the man next to him.

Ben Smith was a tall white man in his early fifties with tan, weathered skin, hands that felt like sandpaper when you shook them, and possibly the kindest eyes I've ever seen. Rather than the head of a security company, he fit the image of a friendly gardener who offered you clippings from his plants and a basket with way too many zucchinis in the summer. When he'd visited the Brew-ha Cafe to inspect the place after we told him we were interested in a security update, his calm presence immediately put the three of us at ease and we knew our cafe was in good hands.

"Appreciate you putting in a good word for me, Jonathan. We've been busier than ever thanks to you talking us up," Ben said, gesturing to the two employees who were with him. "Hector's been with the company since the very beginning, but poor Vinny here's been thrown in the deep end with all the work we've been getting."

Vinny, who was the younger of the two employees, nodded, quickly chewing and swallowing the huge spoonful of rice he'd shoved in his mouth. "I'm not complaining. Between word of mouth and all these burglaries lately, business has been great!"

Ben frowned. "Don't talk like that. It makes it seem like you're happy about the burglaries."

Vinny flushed. "I didn't mean it like that, boss. I was just happy that people are starting to see our value."

Hector, who looked like he was around Detective Park's age, said, "It would be nice to live in a world where our services aren't needed, but as long as they are, we'll be here to provide them."

Ben smiled and nodded. "That's right. Now, Rita, if you're worried about the cost, we could always . . ." And the two of them started talking about flex plans that would fit Rita's needs.

With those two occupied, I turned my attention to Vinny, who was refilling his plate. "You're really enjoying that dinuguan, huh? Have you ever tried it before?"

He shook his head. "Your aunt called it 'chocolate meat,' so I thought it would be similar to mole, but it's not. I can't really describe the taste, but there's something familiar about it. It's really good, even if the texture is a little . . . different."

Hana agreed. "There's definitely something familiar about it, but I can't put my finger on it. Maybe a Korean dish my mom used to make?"

I laughed. "'Chocolate meat' is a euphemism some older Filipinos use since Westerners can be kind of squeamish about our food. If it reminds you of a Korean dish, you're probably thinking of soondae."

"Blood sausage?"

I nodded.

Understanding dawned in Hana's eyes. "Oh, now I get it. The stew is thickened with pig's blood, isn't it? There's a Korean soup that has cakes of blood in it, so that also reminds me of this."

Vinny set his spoon down. "OK, I'm trying to not be judgmental, but I mean, blood? Something about eating it makes me feel a little . . . you know?"

He glanced down at his plate, and the expression on his face made me think he was debating if he should continue eating it to be polite or push it away.

Hector didn't seem to have that problem considering the way he steadily plowed through the giant mound of food on his plate. "I get what you're saying, but isn't morcilla one of your favorite foods? How is blood sausage any different from this?"

"Because no one really thinks about what's in a sausage, right? It's like, better off not knowing. But in a stew . . ." He eyed the dish for a moment before picking up his utensils again. "You know what? It tastes good and that's all that matters. Just ignore me. I'm gonna keep quiet and eat before I offend anyone."

Tita Rosie, who wasn't eating with us since the restaurant was still open but had just come to check on our table, smiled at him. "I appreciate you being open-minded about my food. I'm sorry if it seemed like I was hiding something from you, but 'chocolate meat' is such a common way to refer to dinuguan, I didn't really think about it."

The young security guy grinned at my aunt. "Don't worry about it. Every time Jonathan brings us here, he introduces us to something new and delicious. As long as you're the one cooking, you'll hear no complaints from me."

That brought a huge smile to my aunt's face, and I decided Vinny was a decent guy if he could make Tita Rosie react like that. She thanked him for the compliment and left to check on her other customers.

Blake, who didn't eat pork, had passed on the dinuguan and was slurping down a large bowl of shrimp sinigang along with Adeena and Elena, who were (mostly) vegetarians. She was in conversation with Amir, Adeena's older brother and a local lawyer, who was chowing down on his favorite chicken adobo.

"Have you figured out what to get Sana for Valentine's Day yet?" Blake asked.

Sana Williams was Amir's girlfriend and the owner of the town's fitness studio, and she also did business coaching for women of color entrepreneurs on the side. I'd introduced Hana and Blake to Sana back when they first moved to Shady Palms, and they'd quickly become part of our group. Blake was worried she didn't belong as one of Sana's clients since she was white, but Sana said that since her business partner was Korean, it was important that she understood some of the difficulties that Choco Noir would face. Not just as a woman-owned business, which Blake was used to, but the unique challenges that many women business owners deal with based solely on their skin color or ethnic background.

Amir shook his head. "I forgot about Valentine's Day last year, and even though she said she doesn't care since it's just a manufactured holiday, I still feel bad. I want to do something nice for her this year. Something special, but not over the top. That's not really her style."

"She's elegant, but not fancy, if that makes sense," Blake mused. "I think something one-of-a-kind, but not expensive or flashy, would suit her best."

Amir smiled. "Exactly. But what would that be? Custom jewelry? A nice art piece for the house?"

"We're all meeting up tomorrow for Sana's Sangria Sundays, so we could do a little detective work for you," I said. "See if there's anything she really wants."

"That would be great," Amir said, the relief evident on his face.

"And hey, if worse comes to worst, you can't go wrong with chocolate." Blake winked at him, and we laughed.

As dinner drew to a close, talk turned back to the burglaries that had been plaguing the town lately.

"Happy to be working with you, Rita, but I'm so sorry about your shop," Vinny said. "The paper said only established businesses have been hit so far. I thought you'd be safe since you just opened."

Rita mustered a smile. "Maybe since I took over an older store, the burglar added me to their list. I'm just glad they didn't take much. Did you hear about the photography studio last week? I heard the owner lost thousands of dollars' worth of equipment. I feel so bad for her."

Detective Park frowned. "With a haul that big, you'd think the SPPD would be closer to finding who's behind all this. There's no way they can offload that much equipment without raising some kind of notice."

Ben laughed without humor. "I bet you said that to them and they told you to mind your business again."

"As always."

Detective Park had left the SPPD for many reasons, but his sense of justice was as strong as ever. That was why he opened his own detective agency. He wasn't trying to show up the department. In fact, he was constantly offering his assistance. But whether it was the sheriff's incompetence, the new detective's pride, or lingering resentment from his former colleagues (or all of the above), they never took him up on it.

Ben clapped him on the shoulder. "Hey, just means more business for us. Too bad the people of Shady Palms have to suffer for their egos.

Anyway, let's just count ourselves lucky that nobody's gotten hurt and there hasn't been permanent damage."

"That's true. Even with the big losses at the photo studio, I heard that insurance is covering most of it. Everyone affected should be back on their feet soon," Hector said as Tita Rosie arrived to box up the leftovers.

"Thank heavens for small blessings, ah?"

I loved my aunt's optimism, but it felt like we were setting the bar kind of low to be thankful about something like that. Then again, considering the alternative, I'd take what I could get.

Small blessings indeed.

Photo by Jamilla Yip Photography

Mia P. Manansala is an award-winning writer and book coach from Chicago who loves books, baking, and badass women. She uses humor (and murder) to explore aspects of the Filipino diaspora, queerness, and her millennial love for pop culture. A lover of all things geeky, Mia spends her days procrastibaking, playing RPGs and otome games, reading cozy mysteries and diverse romance, and cuddling her dogs, Gumiho and Max Power.

VISIT MIA P. MANANSALA ONLINE

MiaPManansala.com

⬤ MPMtheWriter

✕ MPMtheWriter

⬤ MPMtheWriter

Ready to find
your next great read?

Let us help.

Visit prh.com/nextread